"Patrick McCabe is an outstanding writer . . . American readers should pay close attention to this man."
—Thomas McGuane

RESOUNDING PRAISE FOR
PATRICK McCABE
AND *THE DEAD SCHOOL*

"Narrated in an ironic, macabre and irreverently colloquial voice . . . The author's unfaltering mastery lies in his ability to employ the colloquial dialect of modern Ireland as an artful

Please turn the page for more extraordinary acclaim. . . .

"The richness of McCabe's voice, his driving, highly tuned duplication of Irish speech, his quirky humor, the denseness of atmosphere and hypnotizing lack of space permeates the novel and so skillfully parallels the mood of its principals."
—*Los Angeles Times*

"Patrick McCabe has the brilliant ability to get inside people's heads. . . . One can well understand why McCabe is being compared to such literary legends as James Joyce."
—*Detroit Free Press*

"A savagely acerbic riff on the decay of modern life and the modern Irish . . . McCabe [is] as skilled and significant a novelist as Ireland has produced in decades."
—*Kirkus Reviews*

"A more complex and ambitious work than McCabe's award-winning novel *The Butcher Boy*."
—*Library Journal*

By Patrick McCabe

The
Dead
School

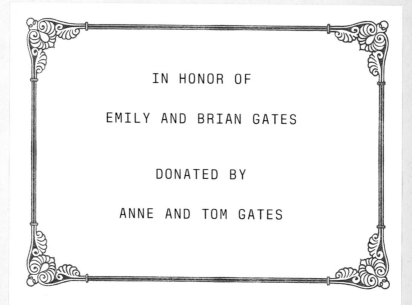

IN HONOR OF

EMILY AND BRIAN GATES

DONATED BY

ANNE AND TOM GATES

A Delta Book
Published by
Dell Publishing
a division of
Bantam Doubleday Dell Publishing Group, Inc.
1540 Broadway
New York, New York 10036

ISBN: 0-385-31423-X

Reprinted by arrangement with The Dial Press

Manufactured in the United States of America

June 1996

10 9 8 7 6 5 4 3 2 1

BVG

The author would like to express his thanks to the Authors' Foundation for their grant. Thanks also, to the Polish artist Tadeusz Kantor for inspiration.

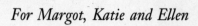

For Margot, Katie and Ellen

Hello There

Boys and girls and I hope you are all well. The story I have for you this morning is all about two teachers and the things they got up to in the days gone by. It begins in the year of Our Lord 1956 in a maternity hospital in Ireland when a wee fat chubby lad by the name of Malachy fell out of Cissie who was married to Packie Dudgeon the biggest bollocks in the town. At first he was a happy-go-lucky little fellow who liked nothing better than to ride around on the scooter his father had made for him, shouting "Hello there!" and "Not a bad day now!" to all his neighbours but it wasn't long before he quit that carry-on. As Alec and the lads who worked the trawlers said one day "Would you look at Dudgeon, the auld stupid walk of him. It wouldn't take long to fix that. A good root up the hole and we'd soon see how much he'd walk." Of course there were times when Malachy felt like shouting back something like "Ah shut your mouths" or "What business is it of yours anyway?" maybe. But like everybody else he knew that wouldn't be a good idea. It wouldn't be a good idea at all. So anytime they said anything to him he just nodded his head. If they had said "Jesus Christ was a murdering bastard, wasn't he?" he would have replied "That's right." He didn't want to. Of course he didn't. But that was the way it was.

Unless, that is, your name happened to be Raphael Bell or should I say *Mister* Raphael Bell, God's gift to Irish education, who not only would have known exactly what to do with foul-mouthed young curs who would come out with the like of that but would have been on them in a flash and thought nothing of beating them senseless, giving it to them each and every one of them until they went down on their knees and begged for mercy. Oh yes, he'd have sorted them out all right, the dirty, ill-bred pups, for that's all they were, and when he was finished with them, it would be a long time before they'd ever call Our Lord names again, or anybody else for that matter! And when his work was done, he'd compose himself once more, and then, with a twirl of his umbrella, stride off into the evening sunset—The Master!—the one and only Raphael Bell, pedagogue par excellence, sum-teacher, spelling corrector, guardian of peace and of morals, his hairless dome shining as off he went, proud as punch, another good day's work behind him, and what a happy day it would have been if only Malachy Dudgeon could have been like him. If only he hadn't been old Skittery Doodle Half-Wit Bollocks afraid of his own shadow, running around the town thinking about love being in the grave and all that stupid old rubbish that used to come into his head—how different my little tale might have been then, boys and girls! How different it all might have been then!

Love In The Grave

But no, he had to be just stupid old Malachy Bubblehead didn't he, flashing his big bright eyes and driving his poor old ma daft with all his questions. "Questions, questions, questions—that's all I ever hear out of you, Malachy Dudgeon," Cissie would say. "Do you know what it is—you have me astray in the head! Astray in the head you have me you little rascal, and that's a fact!" Whenever she said that she always threw her eyes up to heaven as if she didn't know what she was going to do about it at all at all but Malachy knew well she didn't mean it. She was only codding. Or "acting the jinnet" as his da called it. "Man dear but your mother's an awful woman for acting the jinnet," he'd say. "I never seen the like of her in all my born days, our Malachy." Malachy liked the way he ran his fingers through his curly red hair and smiled when he said it, sort of like he was proud that she was his wife and nobody else's. One night after he came home from The Marine Hotel with a few bottles of Guinness, he said to Malachy "I'll never forget the day I walked up the aisle with your mother. She was the most beautiful girl in this town, our Malachy." Sometimes he would go on repeating it to himself under his breath—"the most beautiful girl in the town." Every night before he went to sleep, young Malachy would smile to himself as he thought of those days long before he was born, with his ma and da coming striding up the aisle as proud as punch and everybody throwing flowers and confetti and saying happily "Don't they look terrific?" and "God—isn't she a picture?" instead of "I wonder is Jemmy Brady going to give her a rub of the relic tonight?"

Which was all Malachy seemed to hear these days. Particularly from Alec and Company. If there was one man in the town they liked talking about, it was Jemmy the cowman. "Jemmy Brady," they'd say, "Bloody Jemmy Brady! What a cunt!"

Hardly a day went past but Malachy would hear someone shouting "Hey! Dudgeon! Where the hell do you think you're going? Get over here till we talk to you!" They would never start on about Jemmy straightaway of course. They liked to leave that part till last because, as Alec said, it was "more crack." Which was why they went on about the masters above in the school and how he was getting along and all the rest of it. "So—tell us then," they said, "how are you getting on up there?" "Fine thank you," Malachy would say, and whenever they heard that, they thought it was just about the best thing since sliced bread. "Fine thank you!" they repeated, "Fuckingwell fine thank you!"

Then they went into fits of laughter. "Sweet mother of Christ," said Alec with the tears nearly rolling down his face. Then came the bit about Jemmy and all the carry-on that had been going on lately out at the boatshed. "Do you know what I'm going to tell you?" said one of them as he lit a cigarette. "I was coming past the shed this morning and I went over to take a look in and what did I see only the bould Jemmy standing there. Standing there I swear to Christ, naked as the day he was born and him with the baldy lad in his fist. I mean—would you credit that? Would you credit that now, boys? Would you, Alec?"

Alec scratched his head and said that he would not. Then he said "Oh now, you have to hand it to him all the same. You have to hand it to the cowman. He's some operator now, the same boy. When it comes to the women he knows what's what. Jemmy's the boy knows what the girls want, eh, boys? Indeed and he does surely! He has what they want and he's ready to give it to them!"

Jemmy was well known about the place. He drove cattle all over Ireland. Cork, Tipperary, Dublin—you name it, Jemmy drove cattle there. "Good man, Jemmy," you'd hear the people shouting. "There you are now, Jemmy! How's she cutting?" As Alec and the lads said—he was like a stray ass. Everybody knew him.

To tell you the truth, for the first while Malachy hadn't a bull's notion what they were on about. Sure he was far too young to be bothered about the like of that. All he knew about in those days was strolling about the town with his mother and going down the harbour and staring off out at the yacht sails bobbing away as she squeezed his hand and said things like "Do you know what it is, our Malachy, there's times I think this is one of the best wee towns in the world" and "There's nothing I like better than coming down here to have a look at the boats, yourself and myself." That was all he knew about in them days. He didn't know anything about things going wrong and love dying and going away and never coming back again and all that stuff. I mean—how would he? Even if you had told him, it would have been ridiculous. But it wasn't ridiculous of course, as he was soon to find out. It wasn't ridiculous at all. It was expecting love to stay that was ridiculous.

After all, you couldn't expect to have happy hand-squeezes and warm toast feelings and fun and games and laughs all your life. These had to come to an end sometime. Of course they had. And once Malachy began to realise that, he soon started to see what he ought to I suppose, realistically speaking, have seen long ago—that his father knew all about it. Anything there was to know—he knew all right. You could tell by the way he stared into space when he thought you weren't looking. And by the little bit of a tear you could see just there in the corner of his eye. It wasn't that much of a tear. Which was just as well—I mean—you didn't want him to start bawling about it in public! But it did the trick all right. You could see enough to know. Just enough to let you know what was going on.

One night after it had begun to dawn on him at last the way things really were, Malachy lay on his bed thinking back on that long-ago happy day with them coming proudly up the aisle, saying I love you and marry me and all that. He was sad thinking it. Of course he was. I mean, there would have been something wrong with him if he wasn't. But he was getting sensible enough now to know that if someone didn't love someone else, well there wasn't really an awful lot you could do about it. His father's face told him that. If you needed convincing, all you had to do was take one look at his face when he thought you weren't looking. You'd know then all right. Especially with that old shining eye of his.

Cissie hadn't set out to hurt his father. He knew that she wasn't going to do that. Not after having walked up the aisle with him and told him she loved him, which she definitely had once upon a time. No, it was nothing like that. All that had happened was that love had died. It had gone away and wouldn't be back. Love was in the grave and that was that, like it or lump it. Sure it was sad. Nobody was denying that. Indeed, from where Malachy was lying, it was just about the saddest thing you could get.

But I mean—what were you supposed to do? Slope about the place muttering to yourself "Love is in the grave and I don't know what to do. What am I going to do? Oh please God what am I going to do now that love is in the grave?"

That would look good. That would look good all right when you were going past the harbour and Alec and the lads were standing there waiting for you. He could just imagine it. The cigarette flicking past his face and Alec shouting "Hey! Dudgeon! Get over here to fuck out of that! What's this I hear about you and this love in the grave business? What are you on about? Are you out of your fucking mind or what? Are you out of your mind? Do you want us to get ahold of you and fuck you into that harbour? Is that what you want? Is that what you want? Do you hear me? Do you hear me, Dudgeon! Because if it is, that's what you'll get! That is what you'll get! Do you hear me! Do you! Do you, you fat little humpy little cunt!"

But of course he did. Of course Malachy heard him. He heard him loud and clear. Alec didn't have to worry about that. As a matter of fact, he wouldn't have to worry about anything from now on. From now on, everything would be A-OK and anytime they saw him he would make sure to have his head down and a shy little smile on his face that said to them there will be no more trouble from me ever again and if there is I deserve everything I get. He reckoned that would sort things out. That was what they wanted. That would keep them happy. "That's more like it," they'd say. "No more of this love in the grave bullshit. No more fancy shit-talk in this town! From you or anyone, Dudgeon! You just remember that!"

It was a trick of course. But he wasn't going to tell them that. Yes, now that Malachy was growing up fast, he decided that he had better learn some tricks. And this was one of them. "I wouldn't think about love in the grave if it was the last thing on earth," his face would say as he went shuffling past. Which was the joke of course because that was just about the only thing he was thinking about now.

One night he found himself standing by a graveside with the word "love" carved into the granite of the tombstone. He was just standing there, weeping away, when suddenly the earth broke open and his mother and father came bursting up out of it to the sound of organ music. His father was wearing his wedding suit and his mother her wedding veil and dress. They both hugged him and nearly broke his back in the process. "We love you," they said. It was just about one of the most beautiful things that had happened in a long time. Then he woke up, unfortunately.

Wee Cup of Tay

There was always a good bit of a laugh to be had down in the hotel. Malachy and Packie would come in and as soon as the door opened, someone would shout "Ah the bold Packie! Good man yourself there, Packie—what are you having?" Everyone liked when he came in and sat down beside them at the bar for then they could talk away and chat about the old times and how it used to be around the town and have a great laugh altogether when Packie went to the toilet. Best of all was that they were somehow under the impression that Malachy didn't notice any of this. No sooner would Packie be up off his stool than they'd be at it again. "I hear they were at it in the boathouse again last night" and "Fair fucks to the cowman—he's the man knows what they want!" and so on. Then, not a word as soon as they saw him making his way back to the bar. After that there would be great crack altogether. Singing and dancing and yarn-telling and the whole lot. Somebody'd say "Packie—how about you give us a song there? What about 'Wee Cup Of Tay'?" As soon as they said that, he'd be off, thanks to the couple of bottles of Guinness of course, hitting the air little thumps as he sang and everybody clapping as they sang along with him:

"When I am at my work each day
In the fields so fresh and green
I often think of riches and the way things might have been
But believe me when I tell you when I get home each day
I'm as happy as a sandboy with my wee cup of tay"

"A wee cup of tay is right!" they'd say and somebody'd mumble behind their hand "Plenty of tay to be had in Dudgeon's—if your name is Jemmy Brady anyhow!"

But sure poor auld Packie didn't hear that. Of course not. He was far too busy singing and having his Guinness and a bit of a laugh and a song.

Which was why one night when they were on their way home from the hotel, Packie put his arm around Malachy and said, with that old tear shining in his eye, "Son—if I die, promise me one thing. You'll never forget that I was once on this earth." Malachy said that no he wouldn't forget until the day he died. He wasn't sure at that particular time if what Packie said was intended as a warning but later on he came to the conclusion that it probably was.

Not that anything happened for quite some time. No, everything went on pretty much as normal—Cissie saying I love you to Packie when everyone knew it had been kicked into the clay long ago and poor old Packie smiling and saying I love you too.

Yes, that was the way it was back in those good old days. Roy Orbison in the charts, The Comancheros in the cinema, a dog off to space and every night stupid old Malachy Bubblehead blubbering away to himself like a half-wit, all because love was in its grave and there was nothing he could do about it.

There was no doubt it was a sad state of affairs. But you couldn't let it get you down. You had to look on the bright side. And then of course—there were always Sunday mornings to look forward to, weren't there?

Sunday Mornings

Sunday mornings—you just could not beat them. If there was one morning in the week young Malachy loved, it was that old Sunday morning. School was over, the Saturday night scrub in the zinc bath was history and there was nothing now only the Protestants across the way singing "The Lord Is My Shepherd" and every bell in the town ringing out to call the devout to their respective places of worship. Sunday morning was the best morning of the week, the best by a long shot. And Malachy wasn't the only one who loved it either. Another great fan of The Sunday Morning was Packie Dudgeon, who whistled a little tune as he made inroads into his white beard of foam in front of the shaving mirror and said "Man, Malachy, if there's one morning in the week I love, it's Sunday morning! Sunday morning every time!" He grinned when he said that, then wiped the razor with a towel and went on whistling his tune. Malachy was as busy as a beaver too, brushing his jacket and knotting his tie and combing his hair. Then it was on to the polishing of the shoes and as usual he had to keep at them until you could see your face in them. "I want to be able to see that old phizzog of yours in them!" Cissie would say. "And if I can't, don't think I wouldn't make you go and do them all over again for I would—and make no mistake about it!" But she needn't have worried. She didn't have to worry in the slightest for he was polishing away to beat the band and by the time he was finished, they were like mirrors the pair of them. Then it was off out to the scullery with her, rattling pans and breaking eggs and doing God knows what as she got the breakfast ready. The smell of rashers would make your mouth water. Was it any wonder they loved Sunday mornings? Bacon sizzling and eggs spitting and Cissie slicing away at her cakes of soda bread and making sure that you were going to have the breakfast of a lifetime. And so you would, once you were back from chapel.

But now it was time to get going, yes now it was time to hit the high road and off up the hill to say your prayers to Jesus. Packie squirted a bit of after-shave on himself and called into the kitchen "Are you right there, Malachy me son—I daresay it's near time we were making tracks. We don't want to keep The Man Above waiting now do we?" "Indeed we do not," replied Malachy, and fixing his nutmeg-knot tie just one last time, headed off out the front door, hand in hand with the one and only Packie Dudgeon, his father. Cissie didn't bother coming with them because she had already gone to early Mass as she always did. "To make sure I have a good big breakfast ready and waiting for my two wee men when they get home!" as she said. Boy, did Packie like that! On the way up the street, he rubbed his hands and turned to Malachy "What do you say, son? Isn't she a good one? Now when all's said and done you have to hand it to her. There's not many women in this town would have a breakfast like that waiting for you when you come home. There's times I think I'm not going to be able for the half of it, do you know that! Enough to feed a blooming army," he says! "Am I right, son?"

Malachy said that he was. No, he said he *sure* was, for he knew only too well from past experience just how hard it was to get through all the stuff she heaped on your plate. There were times when he was only able for quarter of it! Not that he was complaining of course! He most certainly was not! It would be a long time before you would ever hear a word of complaint out of Packie or Malachy Dudgeon about Cissie Dudgeon's breakfasts!

And so here they were on Sunday morning, strolling through the bright and colorful streets of the town with the warm breeze blowing and Michael O'Hehir the football commentator sweeping out of every window, getting so excited that you thought he was going to lose his mind: *"Yes! He's going through! Thirty yards out! Twenty yards out! Ten yards out! Oh my God! It's high! Yes it's high and it's—over the bar!"* Half the time you thought he was going to burst into tears or just go completely mad shouting "Oh Jesus! Oh fuck! Oh no! Oh please God no!" But he just kept on going, shouting out through every window in the town until he got hoarse. Malachy's father loved that—the sound of Michael O'Hehir's voice on a Sunday morning. "You always know it's a Sunday morning when you hear Michael," he said and smiled warmly as he squeezed Malachy's hand.

They always met plenty of people on the way up to the chapel. There was always someone to shout "There you are, Packie!" or "Good man, young Malachy!" or "That's a grand

day now, thank God!" Packie always made a point of acknowl-
edging every greeting saying "There you are now, Matt!" and
"A lovely day surely, Francie, thank God!" tipping his cap or
touching his forehead with his index finger.

Whether or not his father was the holiest man in the town,
Malachy couldn't have said for sure, but one thing was certain,
what with the way his lips were fluttering like the wings of a mad
butterfly and the huge gleaming beads of sweat that were appear-
ing on his forehead as he prayed to Mary the Mother Of God
and St Joseph and St Patrick and St Michael and every saint who
had ever lived to do something for him, if he wasn't Holy Man
number one, he was certainly trying hard.

When the praying was all over, off they went back down the
town again and into the shop to get the papers. Packie was a
great man for the papers. "Man, but I love the papers!" he'd say.
"There's great reading in them altogether!" Then it was across
the road and into the hotel where up onto the counter the bottle
of Guinness would appear and someone would say "Well, Packie
—who do you think will win the match?" Then Packie would
scratch his chin for a while. "Do you know what it is—I'd say
Cork!" "Now you're talking, Packie!" they'd say. "And of course
you're the man'd know!"

They'd smile when they said that and ask him did he want
another drink. It was good sitting there with him. For a long
time they'd sit there together and Malachy would try his best not
to think about what was behind his father's eyes. But somehow
he always seemed to see that day, when the sun was splitting the
stones and there were flowers and confetti and the organ was
playing glorious, holy music and Malachy's mother was saying to
his father "I love you" instead of "I used to love Packie Dudgeon
but I don't anymore. I don't anymore and I don't know why. If
only there was some way I could stop this happening but I can't.

I'm going to hurt you, Packie. I'm going to hurt you and there's nothing I can do. Oh Packie—where have they gone? Where have they gone, those days? When you held my hand along the seafront, when you took me in the boat out to the island where we thought we'd live forever. I don't want to do it, Packie! I don't want it to happen! Why can't I love you the way I used to? Tell me, Packie—please tell me!"

There wouldn't have been much point in asking Malachy's father that question for how was he supposed to know? All he could do was sit there nursing his Guinness and stare at something far away and try to stop the shine that was coming into his eye. Which even Sunday morning couldn't stop, no matter how good it was. It probably would have done Packie no harm at all if Malachy had gently tugged his sleeve and whispered "I love you," or something like that. But, with all his thinking about love in the grave, it had got to the stage now that he wouldn't have been able to say so if he tried. He was too afraid that the minute he opened his mouth, the words would wither up and die there on the spot. And he wasn't going to let that happen—oh no. It might have happened to Packie but it wasn't going to happen to him. Not to Malachy Dudgeon. No sir. Not in a million years.

And so, after three nice, tasty bottles of Guinness, it was time to go home. They had hardly turned the corner when they smelt the beautiful aroma of bursting sausages and heard the musical sizzle of frying rashers. "There you have it!" laughed Packie. "You have to admit it—she's a good one. I'll bet you a dime to a dollar there's not another pair of boys sitting down to a breakfast the like of what you and me are going to have right now! Do you think I'd be right there?" And Malachy grinned from ear to ear as he replied "I do, Da! I just can't wait to get home!" "Nor me either, son!" said his father and right at that very moment who should they see standing at the door only the bold Cissie, waving to them as much as to say "It's all ready!" As soon as she got them inside it was straight down to business, buzzing around them asking had they enough of this, had they enough of that and slicing up soda bread and pouring out tea to beat the band. "Have youse enough bacon?" she called from the scullery. "Don't forget now—there's plenty more where that came from!" By the time they were finished, they were as full as ticks and could just about move and no more. Then what does she do? Stands there with her hands on her hips and starts giving out! "You pair of rascals!" she said, "Youse haven't eaten a stitch!" But she was only joking and went away off out into the scullery saying she would make another drop of tea and laughing away to herself.

After breakfast, Malachy sat on the sofa for a while as his father read the papers. He was at it again this Sunday morning, chuckling away to himself at all the daft carry-on that was going on in "The Looneys." Of all the cartoon strips and comics and funnies that you could get in the Sunday papers, they were his favourite. "Boys oh boys, our Malachy!" he said. "I just don't know what we're going to do with these Looneys! As God is my judge I'll have a blooming stroke if I laugh any more!" They really were the bee's knees, those little Looney kids. Always playing tricks on their father—putting buckets of water over the door, leaving banana skins lying around for him to trip on—doing all sorts of things like that to try and catch him out. But it was OK because in the end they always had a good laugh. That was because they were a happy family and once you are a happy family that's all you need to care about. When he was finished reading, Packie would often say that. "Just you remember, Malachy—once you are a happy family, that's all you need," he'd say, folding the paper like he was about to deliver some really important fatherly advice, but it was no use, or at least it wasn't anymore, for unless you were blind right now you could see that if you jabbed him with a feather far from giving anybody advice about anything, he'd probably have gone and burst into tears.

Cork were leading Kerry by a point and Michael O'Hehir was really going out of his mind when Cissie came in from the scullery. It was the first time that Malachy had noticed her limping. Herself and Packie started talking then. It turned out she was having a lot of trouble with her veins lately. She said that the pain could be unbearable at times. As she described it, Packie held her hand. "You've no idea, Packie," she said, biting her lip. He nodded sympathetically. "I don't like bothering Dr Wilding on account of it being a Sunday but I can't go through another night with them, Packie—I just can't." "I want to hear no more of it, daughter. You're to go up that street now to Dr Wilding's and don't come back here until he's given you something—do you hear me now? And if you have to sit in that surgery from now till doomsday, you make sure he does that—for no wife of mine'll be put through the like of that while there's doctors in this town."

She smiled and gave his hand a gentle squeeze as she said "Thanks, Packie love." Then, in a low voice, she added "You're so kind" and went out into the hall to get her coat.

After she was gone, Malachy and Packie sat for a long time without saying anything. In the distance you could hear the Protestants still singing away as the Sunday morning bells rang out over the town. You could still hear Michael O'Hehir but he was far away now. As indeed were Malachy and poor old Packie, thanks to what had just happened. Maybe if she had said it was Dr Kennedy or Dr Hamill she was going to, they might have been able to believe her. But she had gone and made the same mistake again, as she had for God knows how many Sunday mornings lately. Maybe if she had never mentioned Dr Wilding's name, they might never have known. But she had, however. She had. And everyone—even the dogs in the street—knew that his surgery didn't open on Sundays.

The Detective

It was approximately twenty minutes later that Master Malachy Dudgeon, son of Packie who was now spreadeagled beneath the Sunday *Press* and snoring away with his mouth open and all the little Looneys running harum scarum across his chest, decided that he wanted to become a world famous detective. Now quite why he came to this conclusion I have not the foggiest notion, boys and girls, but one thing I do know is that if he had had any idea of the effect it was going to have on him for the rest of his days, he would have been more than happy to stay right where he was! But he didn't, did he? No sir, he had to go away off out the door, talking away to himself in an American accent and pretending that he was Tony Rome the famous detective he had seen at the pictures. Off up the town he went and down along the shore with the sea breeze in his face, then across the cliffs and away out the country on the trail of his mother. Which shouldn't surprise us because that's what detectives do, isn't it? Of course it is—and why should he be any different? After all, he was the big detective! Sure he was, stomping away there beneath the blue sky on a beautiful sunny Sunday morning, thinking he was Tony Rome, just about the coolest gumshoe in the business. "I'm Tony Rome," he said to himself and tipped his imaginary sailor's cap to one side. Tony lived by the sea too, in a little houseboat down by the marina. Tony was swell. He was just about the best detective going. One thing you did not want to do and that was mess with Tony. He hung out in all the cool joints, with women flocking around him telling him what a great guy he was. When he wasn't blowing away hoodlums and busting up cop cars, that is. Yeah—you name it, Tony had done it. Was it any wonder Malachy would want to be him? Especially now that he had arrived at the boatshed where he could hear some mysterious noises that needed investigating. "I wonder what this could be, guys," he said to himself in his American accent. But he needn't have worried. He needn't have worried his head. He was going to find out all right.

At first he couldn't see anything through the slats at the back of the shed but then he heard a clatter and when he looked again he saw someone just standing there in the gloom. At first he thought it was her but when he looked again he saw that it was Jemmy, standing there beside a pile of old nets with his cock sticking out in front of him. A sort of a faint hope leaped in him that maybe she wasn't there after all but then she appeared out of nowhere, coming out of the shadows and falling into his arms and running her fingers through his hair. The sound of Jemmy's breathing seemed to fill the entire boatshed. "I've been waiting days for this," he said as he ran his hands up and down her back. "Oh Jemmy! Jemmy!" she cried and then somehow they fell backwards onto the top of the nets and all Malachy could see was the whiteness of the cowman's body as he cried "Oh Jesus! Oh Christ! Christ Jesus but I love you, Cissie Dudgeon! I fucking love you!" Malachy covered his ears in case he'd hear what she'd say. But it didn't matter what he did because he heard it anyway. "Oh Jemmy! Jemmy darling! Come on! Come on!"

It was around four or thereabouts when Cissie came home. She said there had been a big crowd up at the doctor's. Of all the days that had ever been spent in the house, Malachy felt that that was the saddest. Mainly because he could tell by his father's eyes that whatever fight there had been left in him, there was certainly none now. If she had said "Why don't you go and drown yourself right now this very minute? Wouldn't it make more sense to go and do it now and be done with it?" he would probably have gone ahead. As far as Malachy was concerned, it would have been better if she had, instead of sitting there laughing and handing liquorice allsorts around, blowing shite about the doctor's.

That was the worst part of love dying and going into the grave. On its own it wasn't enough for people. They had to go and dig you up so that you would have to go to the funeral all over again. They had to press liquorice allsorts into your mouth.

Which was why Malachy didn't get so much as a wink of sleep that night. How could he, with Jemmy Brady and Cissie standing there beside a granite tombstone with Love on it, waving a pair of spades and falling about the place saying to one another "Let's dig the old bollocks up and put him astray in the head altogether. Yoo-hoo! Packie! Are you down there? Are you down there, Dudgeon? Are you down there, boy? Look what we have for you-oo!"

The Fishing Stand

So, as you can imagine, that little episode didn't exactly help things in the Dudgeon household, what with Malachy turning arctic on his mother and poor old Cissie at her wit's end to know what to do about it. I mean, it did pose a bit of a problem you have to admit. What was she supposed to do—turn around to him and say "Excuse me, Malachy—you weren't by any chance spying on me on Sunday morning were you?" Which, even if she could have done it would only have made things worse, considering she had no excuse—none in the wide world. Not that it mattered all that much in the long run anyway, as it happened, for events, as they say, soon overtook them.

To say that people were surprised when The Dummy who lived in Maguire's loft went out to the lake and threw himself in would be an understatement, because of all the people in the town who were likely to drown themselves, he was just about the last you would expect. As indeed was Packie, who did the very same thing no more than a week later, for although the whole town knew about his troubles and all the rest of it, they never really seriously considered that he might go that far. But he did. He went that far all right, as Malachy discovered one day when he was on his way home from school. One of the young Mc-Kiernans of Harbour Terrace came running up to him and said "Your father's dead! He was fishing on the stand out at The Dummy's Water. It broke and he fell in!" When he heard this, Malachy felt like laughing in the young fellow's face, for the McKiernans were well known for their mad yarns and tall stories. But, as he discovered when he got home, it was anything but a mad yarn or a tall story. He stood in the hallway for well over a minute as the world turned sideways. It was like being hit with a hammer.

Inside, the house was packed. The atmosphere was thick with despair and indignation. They were furious about the fishing stand, they said. They said there was going to be murder about it. Especially Nobby Caslin, who said he had written to the council long ago about it being a hazard. But had anything been done? Not at all. He took out his pipe and lit it with a trembling hand. Clouds of sweet-smelling blue smoke floated all around the room. Someone said "The bloody thing's been rotten this past eighteen months or more. There's not one in this town doesn't know that. Not one!" His cheeks reddened when he said that. Nobby nodded: "Isn't that what I'm saying? Isn't that exactly what I have been saying?"

It was a very sad occasion. Poor old Cissie was in a bad way. There was a mountain of Kleenex at her ankles and the tears were literally spewing out of her. "How will I manage without him?" she wanted to know. "How will I manage without my Packie?" When he heard that, Malachy felt like laughing. He had heard some good ones from her but this performance took some beating. The women told her it was going to be OK. God would look after her, they said. Then off they went and got more Kleenex. The cowman didn't show until quite late, looking like something that had been dug up out of the bog and decked out in a Sunday coat. He turned his cap around in his hands and said it was a bad blow. The women said they would get some more sandwiches, which they did. They said "Don't worry. Time is a great healer." The widow dabbed her eyes and appeared to agree that what they were saying made perfect sense. Then however she burst into tears again. There was another knock at the door and in came Father Pat. He had been a great footballer in his youth, which explained why he was blathering away about some match or other after only five minutes in the house. Just as he was running up the field to bury the ball in the back of the net, away went the door again and in came Alec and all his buddies, shaking their heads and remarking how cruel life was. That provided the cue for yet another philosophical discussion on the brevity of existence and so on, some half-wit friend of the cowman's observing wistfully "When you think of all the happy times we had in this house when he was alive," a comment which, if it didn't make Malachy burst out laughing right there and then on the spot, came perilously close. As far as everyone else was concerned however, it obviously was just about the most poignant and pertinent statement ever made.

Then came the time for Nobby to speak. When it came to funerals and sad occasions, there was no one to touch Nobby Caslin for the few words. He bided his time gravely until there was complete silence in the room, then he cleared his throat and began to speak. "It's always sad when someone dies," he said. They all looked at each other when he said that and agreed that that was right. Oh yes, there was no doubt about that. You just could not disagree with that, they said. Then he continued, going into a diatribe about the fishing stand and the state they had let it get into and by the time he was finished, it was all they could do not to march up en masse to the council offices and burn them to the ground right there and then. Which, of course, was the most hilarious yet, for as Malachy well knew, if there was anything in this world his father hated, it was the hobby of fishing, and if there was a reason he went out to the lake, it was one reason and one reason alone—to throw himself into the bloody thing. Not that it mattered to Nobby of course, for by now he was on to his pet subject, which of course was funerals. There was nothing this man didn't know about funerals. Mainly because he had been to more or less every funeral that had taken place in the town over the past twenty years. "I might be sticking my neck out here," he said, clearing his throat, "but I would not be one bit surprised if he pulls in over five hundred. He was a well-respected man and there's not one in this room or anywhere else can say different."

Everyone agreed with that and Nobby's speech would have been a good note on which to end the proceedings if some bollocks by the name Peter from the bog hadn't gone and decided to try and liven things up with a bit of a joke. "Just so long as it doesn't turn out like the McAdoo funeral!" he snorted and had to hold his sides in case he'd break in two with the laughing. It was only when he looked up and saw the face of Nobby Caslin glaring at him along with ten or eleven others that he realised he'd gone and stuck his big size twelves right in it. Nobby gripped the bowl of his pipe until his knuckles turned white. "If I ever hear another word about that funeral," he hissed through his teeth, "if I ever so much as hear another fucking word about it—!"

For a minute or two it looked like he was about to collapse or something but then, almost inaudibly, he continued "I swear to God as long as I live I never want to hear another word about it. Do you hear what I'm saying? It was one of the worst days I ever remember in this town. Every time I think of it I get sick to my stomach and that's the truth. So maybe now, Peter, maybe just once in your life you'd do the right thing and shut up about it. Do you think you could do that, Peter—do you? Mm?"

Peter did think that. Of course he could shut up about it. As a matter of fact, not only could he shut up about it but he hadn't the slightest intention of mentioning it ever again as long as he lived. Which was what he was about to say to Nobby before the latter pushed right past him and went off out the door without so much as another word.

After that, everybody started talking about something else just in case the subject of Mrs McAdoo and the funeral might somehow come up again. Which was interesting, thought Malachy, seeing as how not so very long ago, it was all anyone had ever wanted to talk about. You could hardly walk up the street then without someone mentioning Mrs McAdoo and what had happened in the graveyard that day. Now, by the looks of things, you daren't open your trap, for if you did Nobby Caslin or his ilk would be halfway down your throat shouting "Don't talk to me! You and Mrs McAdoo! Do you think we've had no other funerals in this town, do you not? Shut up about it! We want to hear no more about her or her carry-on! Do you hear me now! Shut up you and her!"

That, I am afraid, was what you could expect if you opened your gob about Mrs McAdoo. Which certainly made it clear in no uncertain terms just how important her forty years on earth had been.

Little Chubbies

What happened was she woke up in the middle of the night and heard her baby crying. Not just ordinary crying, but crying that would put you out of your mind. She wasn't really sure what to do because little Thomas was her first baby and that was why at the crack of dawn she went up to the doctor. "Don't you be worrying your head, missus—" the doctor said, "babies—if they don't get one thing they get another. You just make sure to give him this medicine and come tomorrow night he'll be right as rain, you'll see."

When she heard this she was as happy as Larry again and no matter who she met on her way down the street she said "I'm a cod to be worrying my head. The doctor gave me a tonic and he says by tomorrow night he'll be right as rain." By the time she got home she was so delighted with herself and so happy that she felt like having a party in the house to celebrate her son Thomas's visit to the doctor. Which would have been premature because by the time tomorrow night came around, far from being right as rain his crying was worse than ever and on top of that, he was white as a ghost. When she saw that, a spike of fear went shooting through her. "My baby is going to die," she thought to herself. But she pulled herself together. "What am I talking about or what is wrong with me? Didn't the doctor tell me there is nothing wrong with him. Nothing in the slightest. Run down—that's what he is. I know what I'll do. I'll take another walk up to the surgery just to be on the safe side."

Which is exactly what she did. The doctor gave her more medicine and no sooner had she said goodbye to him and gone off down the street than she was laughing and smiling away with the neighbours, just like old times. Wouldn't it be absolutely wonderful to say that that evening saw little Thomas back to himself? He wasn't however and the crying, bad as it had been before, was now very close to what you might describe as unbearable. So it wasn't really surprising when the neighbours said to Mrs McAdoo "Would you not think of bringing him up to The Canon? Don't you know that he can work miracles?" "Very well then," she replied, "I will." Because the truth was by that time she would have done anything. If the neighbour women had told her to feed the baby wood shavings she would have been glad to do it.

She put him into the pram and wheeled him off up to the parochial house. She told The Canon that there was something wrong with her child, that he had some kind of disease. "I see," he said to her. "Right—bring him out the back."

Of all the women in the town there was no one holier than Mrs McAdoo. She most definitely wasn't the kind who would speak back to the priests, especially not The Canon. But when he asked her to bring him round the back and put him down into the barrel of holy water she wasn't so sure after all if she wanted a miracle performed. In fact she was almost one hundred per cent certain that she didn't and although she was a little bit afraid she did manage to speak up a bit. "But, Canon, what if any of it gets into his mouth? There's all green stuff on the top of it there. It's just that I'm afraid it might make him sick, Canon, if you know what I mean."

When The Canon heard this he did not quite know whether to fall about the place laughing or just draw out there and then and hit her a skelp of his walking stick. He just couldn't understand it. He could not for the life of him understand what was the matter with her. Fortunately for her in the end he just sighed and said "Ah, daughter, will you come on now. Stop your cod-acting like a good girl and put him into the holy water, I have confessions at eight." When she started to sniffle a little bit, he said, somewhat more forcefully this time, "Mrs McAdoo, will you please put the baby in or what is wrong with you?" So then at last she put him in and when she took him out she hesitated for a minute or two. She wasn't so sure about putting him in the second time because he was, as she had said, all covered in the green slime. But The Canon was insistent that it had to be three times or nothing. He said the child was either to be immersed three times or the whole thing was a waste of time. So in went Thomas the third time and The Canon said "There now—that wasn't so hard was it? Good girl yourself."

Mrs McAdoo stuttered. Not very much. Just a little because she was confused. Then she composed herself and replied no Canon it wasn't hard Canon thank you very much Canon I want to thank you very much. And The Canon said that there was no need to thank him. He said never mind thanking me missus I'm doing no more than my job that's all I'm doing—no more no less. After that he said it was time for him to be off for his confessions.

On leaving the church grounds, Mrs McAdoo found herself in a state of near-elation and as she carried Thomas all the way down the hill towards the town she felt she was cruising at least three feet above the ground. And if she was sure of one thing it was that that day which was an ordinary misty-wet day in September was the happiest day ever in her whole life so far and it seemed to her that nothing would bother her ever again as she said to Thomas, tweaking his cheek in the pram, "Isn't that right, Thomas? Isn't that right, little chubbies? It certainly is, my little man!"

And it definitely did seem at that moment that nothing would bother her ever again. And went on being like that until around half-past eight or nine when she went into the bedroom to see if he was awake or did he perhaps need another feed. She was still so happy she was singing a little song which went *Mares eat oats and does eat oats and little lambs eat ivy!* and the words of it seemed so silly she was going to say to Thomas "Did you ever hear such silly billy words in your whole life—did you?"

That was what she wanted to say to her little man and if she had, she would have expected Thomas to give one of his big wide baby grins that said back to her "No, Mammy—I *didn't.*" But that's not what happened unfortunately and there was only one reason for that and one reason alone, the fact that he was dead.

And when she saw that, all that Mrs McAdoo could do was let out a howl, a howl that saw all the babies of centuries past flowing in front of her like a white stream.

In the days that followed, no matter where you went you would hear one set of people saying this and another saying that and others who did not seem to know what to say. Our old friend Nobby the Funeral Expert was quite firm. "Look—everybody makes a mistake," he said. "Are you going to sit there and tell me there's nobody in this town makes a mistake? I guarantee you this. For every ten tables knocked together above in the factory there's one doesn't come up to scratch. Am I right? And don't tell me the doctors don't drop the odd stitch either. There's men buried up there on that hill would still be walking the streets of this town if the doctors and surgeons had been minding their p's and q's. Mistakes? We all make them. And the boys above in the parochial house are no different. Of course it's very sad that the child was drowned. It'd be a hardhearted class of a man that'd say different. For there's no sweeter sight on this earth than the smile of a wee bonny baby inside in a pram. Of course it's sad—there's no heavier cross to be asked to bear. Poor Mrs McAdoo, Lord bless us and save us God knows what it'll do to her for what with her poor father passing away not two years back she wouldn't now be the strongest class of a creature if you know what I mean. But let's be honest now, when all's said and done what can you do about it? We're hardly going to go up to the parochial house and march The Canon down to McAdoo's to make the child come alive again. Jesus Mary and Joseph sure we're not going to do that. And if we're not going to do it then what are we going to do? I'll tell you what we're going to do—we're going to do damn all. Damn all, that's what we're going to do. Because there's nothing we can do. And why? Because The Canon is a very nice man—the best of a fellow. A gentleman that's what he is and no two ways about it. It's just unfortunate that whatever happened this time things didn't work out and I'm afraid when all's said and done that's all there is to it, no more, no less."

When he had finished his monologue, the men who were sitting beside him on the seat couldn't really think of much to offer by way of reply. They just sat there staring into the greasy bowls of their caps and dragging long and hard on pipes as they said aye and that's the way and true for you Nobby true surely.

The funeral took place a couple of days later and Nobby was proved right again. He had estimated that there would be an attendance of one thousand and his forecast turned out to be absolutely right. "The baby, you see! You can always be sure of a big draw when it's a baby. Do you mind the McMahon child? Close on the same, you'll find," he said.

They put the small white coffin on trestles in the chapel for all to see and anybody who saw it could not stop the tears coming into their eyes. The chapel was filled with beautiful flowers. Taped to the lid of the coffin was a small card edged in black reading "Thomas aged 6 months we loved you so much" with a photograph of the child on it. All the shops in town closed for the entire day as a mark of respect.

As the funeral cortege arrived at the cemetery everybody waited for The Canon to speak. Standing by the grave in his surplice holding his missal, he told the congregation that it was a sad occasion and when he said that everybody bowed their heads and stared at the grass. Although it was a sad occasion, he continued, it was also a beautiful one. And that was because there was always something special about a pure white unblemished soul returning to the welcoming arms of Jesus. Then what he wanted to know was who could deny or ignore the feeling of peacefulness that now pervaded the cemetery, the peacefulness of a community united as one in grief. He raised his arms heavenward and proclaimed it wonderful that at times like this everyone who gathered together as members of a community could put aside the small differences which it had to be admitted occasionally came between them, such as the unreturned spade, the hasty word, the broken promise. Today, he said, Christ walks amongst us on this happy occasion. Then he closed his eyes and went a step further: no on this happy *happy* occasion.

It was a great speech. It was a speech that had a marked effect on everyone present and there wasn't one person who was not close to a state of blissful contentment thanks to The Canon's beautiful, well-chosen words, words that effected a magnificent transformation on all present. Indeed, there would have been many happy, almost ecstatic people leaving the graveyard that day if The Canon had been allowed to continue in that vein and Mrs McAdoo had not thrown herself into the grave and begun to rant and rave like a madwoman. Not only that but tear away at the lid of the coffin with her nails shouting "Thomas! Thomas come back to me! I don't want you to die! I don't want you to go to limbo! I want you to come back to me so we can play building blocks!"

At first no one knew quite how to react. They hoped that she would somehow stop. She didn't however and the longer she went on, the less they seemed to know what to do about it. All they could hear was the scraping on the wood of the coffin. They simply weren't sure what they ought to do. The peaceful, harmonious, indeed almost magical atmosphere of togetherness and unity which The Canon had been talking about had all but disintegrated and they found themselves standing there trying not to hear, which was impossible because by this stage she wasn't shouting, she was roaring. Behind Malachy someone said "This is great carry-on. This is a grand how-do-you-do I must say. Or what in the hell is wrong with her? Jesus Mary and Joseph such a thing to happen on the day of a funeral."

Eventually the whole thing went too far and two men climbed in after her. "Come on now, missus, you can't be shouting like this," they said. "You'll have to come up now out of that." When they saw this everyone heaved a sigh of relief and said to themselves at last it's all over thank God but then, inexplicably, she lashed out and hit one of them. Whether it was by accident or not, no one could tell, but she was screaming "Leave me alone! Leave me alone!" The screaming was bad enough to begin with but by then it had become so intolerable that in the end there was no point in anyone pretending or even hoping that they could ever go away from that cemetery saying it had been a glorious day or a day of community solidarity or anything like it. An utter disaster would be a more honest and accurate description. Malachy was standing beside Nobby who lit another match, then tossed it away into the flapping wind as he said out of the side of his mouth "I seen a mongrel one time that had the rabies. That's what she reminds me of. I wouldn't get into that grave for love or money."

It looked like he was right because not long after he said that the two men came climbing back up out of the grave with nothing to show for their trouble only one bruised eye and a scratched face. There was a sort of last lingering hope that Mrs McAdoo would come up of her own accord and when she didn't a gloom began to descend and all anyone could think of doing was looking down at the toes of their shoes and producing something to examine in great detail—wallets, rosary beads, anything. The Canon did his best under the circumstances but he was only wasting his time trying to reason with her, for she swore at him too and told him yes there was something he could do for her, die in his bed that night. That comment alone put paid to any hope of sympathy there might have been for the woman, and after that everyone became very agitated indeed. As it happened, Nobby was the first to break the silence. "Ah this has gone to hell," he muttered under his breath. "It's about time someone did something. I'm supposed to meet Herbie Molloy in the hotel at seven-thirty. We're going to Longford dogtrack!"

Someone asked him did he think the guards would have to be sent for and he said "All I know is I'm supposed to be meeting Herbie and look at the time it is now."

An argument started as to whether the guards should or should not be called. Some were for and some against, but as it turned out, it didn't matter because Mrs McAdoo's head appeared out of the grave and she came climbing back out and walked off in the direction of the cemetery gate without a word.

When they saw her, a few of the women cried out and ran after her calling "Mrs McAdoo! Mrs McAdoo! I say! Mrs McAdoo!"

They were only wasting their time however. No matter what they called after her, she just ignored them and carried on walking towards the town with bow legs like she was after wetting herself or something.

After that the crowd began to disperse and drift homeward. There was a feeling of bitter disappointment that seemed to pervade the entire town like a drab grey sheet you could almost reach out and touch. And any time for years afterwards that the funeral was mentioned, Nobby Caslin would clench his pipe between his teeth and launch into his by now familiar speech: "Don't mention it! Don't mention it! It'd be a queer sort of a world if we were all to go jumping into graves every time a bit of trouble comes our way! Jesus Mary and Joseph does she think she's the only one ever suffered in the town?" Sometimes he would leave it at that but other times it would get too much for him and he'd shake his pipe bitterly and hiss "A sorry-looking sight now a sorry-looking bloody sight a sad pathetic sketch and no mistake." Then he'd add "He went off and left me standing outside the hotel—Herbie."

There was little else to say about Mrs McAdoo after that. By the looks of things there were only two people to whom it mattered now—Mrs McAdoo and her son Thomas, for all anyone had to say was that their stomachs turned over even thinking about it.

Malachy would often see her sitting there in the cemetery on his way home from school, just sitting alone by the graveside, which by now was covered in grass and weeds. The first time he saw her he didn't realise it was her at all. What was sitting there only bore a passing resemblance to her. She looked like she hadn't eaten for months.

Sometimes he went in and sat beside her but she rarely spoke. Perhaps an occasional moan but very little else. "Why are you waiting here, Mrs McAdoo?" he asked on one occasion. "I'll be joining him soon—my little fellow, Thomas," she responded. "Do you remember Thomas?" Other times she'd answer questions in ways that made no sense at all. "I won a book at school for never missing a day," she said once, and another time "Tide has gone up a penny." When she said that she was waiting to join Thomas, Malachy thought she must be joking. But sure enough not long afterwards he looked in on the way home and she was nowhere to be seen. Soon after, he was going past her house and saw that there was a black-bordered card on the door saying she was dead. On his way home he met Nobby on the square and told him the news. "Oh—is that right?" he said, and carried on walking up the street opening the lid of his tobacco tin.

So that was the end of Mrs McAdoo. She had been born in 1926 and lived for forty years. Not that it mattered much what she did, no more than it did an old schoolmaster dressed in what were little more than rags sitting by a window with moist eyes, waving to his mammy and daddy who were oh so proud of him, and had been ever since the day little Raphael Bell was born fifty-three years before in a tiny County Cork village that had nestled since time began at the foot of a mountain that rose majestically into the clear blue sky.

———————

Me Like Spheets

Approaching along a dirt track at the side of that mountain is a fat woman in a plaid shawl and her name is Mrs Evelyn Bell. She is fat because she is pregnant and inside her sleeps a tiny boy with tiny fists. The time is long ago in Ireland and we are in a quiet village where nothing much has happened for around a hundred years, and probably never will. Not that anybody minds. They are more than happy with the way things are, working hard in the fields, saying their prayers at night and being good for the Lord who looks down over all.

And where was Evelyn going on this warm summer's afternoon in the little town of Charleville, where the birds were singing and her neighbours called "Grand day, ma'am!" and "Did you ever see the beat of it?" as her skirt swished along the dusty road and she smiled and cried "Thank God for it!" She was on her way to the shop to buy some tobacco for her husband Mattie's pipe and a packet of pins for a dress she was making. That was what she was doing, at least until out of nowhere she emitted a cry of great pain and collapsed right there and then in the main street. The woman who happened to be standing next to her was of no assistance whatsoever, with neither rhyme nor reason crying "She fell on the ground, she fell on the ground!"

Fortunately however, Mrs Bernadette McAdam who was made of stronger stuff happened to be nearby filling a wooden bucket at the parish pump and she rushed over to Mrs Bell. "Get out of the way!" she cried to the distraught, mute bystander. Within minutes, Mrs Bell found herself effortlessly transported to a settle bed in a nearby cottage through the efforts of a number of sturdy females instantly recruited by the crusty Mrs McAdam who already had managed to rustle up a basin of steaming water and was applying herself industriously to the problem. "Quit out from that whinging now, ma'am," she ordered, "between me and the Sacred Heart we'll soon have this little baba out and about and right as rain."

Whether or not Evelyn heard what was being said to her was hard to say, but in any case she continued to howl and abuse all about her asking what she had done to deserve pain the like of this and why didn't men have to endure it for if they did they'd soon keep it in their britches. When they heard that, the other women present went pink and crossed themselves but they were not a little amused for they in their time had seen the walls of their stomachs come in for some serious abuse and would have liked nothing better than to inflict the same on their husbands. The beads of sweat on Mrs Bell's head were the size of thumbnails. "Is it ever going to come out that's what I'd like to know," remarked one of the women in exasperation only to find herself at the sharp end of Mrs McAdam's tongue. "Maybe you'd like to come down here and give me some help and never mind your moaning?" she said and after that there was no more complaining from anyone in the room. In the end their patience was rewarded when on the third stroke of the Angelus bell a wet wine head appeared and they shrieked with delight when it was followed by two chinky eyes and a pudgy face and two little fists ready to take on the world. "Well—what do you think now, Mrs Evelyn Bell? Wasn't it worth all the screaming and pulling and dragging?" beamed the impromptu midwife. Mrs Bell accepted the squirming moist bundle in her arms "God bless you and the Sacred Heart, Mrs Mac," she said, and that was how Raphael Bell first saw the light of day on a warm July afternoon in the year of Our Lord 1913.

Everyone loved Raphael. They adored the way he came up to them at the village pump and said "Me like spheets. Hab you got any spheets?" They made him say it over and over again they found it so amusing. "Say it again for us Raphael" and sure enough he would. "Hab you got any spheets? Hab you got any spheets? Me like spheets." He was the funniest little fellow in the village. And was his mother proud of him! As indeed she should be when her own husband informed her that Sister Camillus who was little Raphael's teacher had told him that in all her years teaching she had never come across a pupil who showed such promise. It filled her with great pride too when she was stopped in the square and the neighbours said "I hear great reports about this young fellow of yours."

She herself had to marvel at the neatness and tidiness of his schoolwork. In his copybooks there was never so much as a blot or a dog-ear and where other children might display reluctance when prevailed upon to attend to their books, Raphael spent hours upstairs in his room inscribing his exercise in a copperplate hand. What a diligent boy he was—and so good-mannered. Never once did she have to reprimand him. When she asked him to go to the shop for a message he always replied "Yes, Mother."

She was moved to tears when, having won a prize for best attendance in the school, he had used his prize money to make a small purchase in the gift shop to present to her, a little brooch which she wore to Mass, proudly displayed on her lapel. Whenever visitors came by, he was always on hand to sing a song or perform a little recitation. One that never failed to bring the house down was his Uncle Joe's favourite—"Wee Hughie." Whenever Uncle Joe produced the tobacco-stained penny from the depths of his pocket, out with Raphael into the middle of the kitchen, clearing his throat and closing his eyes as off he went:

> "He's gone to school, Wee Hughie,
> And him not four
> Sure I saw the fright was in him
> When he left the door

But he took a hand o' Denny
And he took a hand o' Dan
Wi' Joe's auld coat upon him
Och, the poor wee man!"

And the clapping that would follow that! As Uncle Joe said "You could hear it in three townlands!"

Then, with the penny proudly clenched in his fist, Raphael would tear off down to the corner shop and buy as many spheets as you could get. Always of course getting an extra one or two from the sweety man who just loved the way he said that word. He would hit the counter a little punch with his fist, repeating "Me like spheets! Me like spheets! Lord but you're an awful man, young Raphael!"

Back then to the house, out of breath and all excited and in your hand this time a lovely stick of barley sugar for your mammy!

"Now there's the good boy doesn't forget his mother!" said Uncle Joe.

"Our Raphael always thinks of his mammy, don't you, Raphael?" said his daddy.

"That's a sign of a good child," said Uncle Joe, packing baccy into his pipe while Raphael's mammy beamed and the happiest child in the world sat down by the window to think of millions more days when he would have money to buy spheets, and to look at the warm and happy navy-blue night coming down over the fields.

Eggs and Hairy Bacon

The yelps out of Raphael when the eggs and hairy bacon would start! "Well between the pair of youse with that old carry-on you have my head astray!" Evelyn would say and go off out into the scullery to peel the turnips or scrub the floor. Anything, anything but listen to them and their eggs and hairy bacon. "I don't know which of youse is the worst," she'd call and then smile of course because she was only pretending. Raphael even knew that. You could tell by the sound of her voice and the way her eyes twinkled when she said it. "Come on up here out of that, you wee divil you," Mattie would say then, and up young Raphael would get onto his lap and away they'd go with the eggs and hairy bacon song, clapping and jig-a-jigging and laughing their heads off at the funniest song that was ever made up in the whole world. "Good man!" Mattie'd cry, "Come on again now— louder!" and Raphael'd clap and sing "Eggs and hairy bacon, eggs and hairy bacon, eggs and hairy bacon for me and Da to eat!"

Was it any wonder Evelyn would give out to them? I mean —was it now? Or what sort of a pair of cods were they singing a song like that? Raphael didn't care what sort of a pair of cods. All he cared about was his daddy coming home after milking the cows so they could do it again. He'd wait for him in the doorway of the cottage and as soon as he saw him coming he'd tear off down the lane crying "Daddy! Daddy! Eggs and hairy bacon!" and Mattie would swing him round laughing "Wait! Will you wait till we get into the house, you little divil you!"

It was the best ever, that old eggs and hairy bacon. Raphael made him do it until he got exhausted and said "Will you go away out of that now, our Raphael, and let me have me tay!" Then Raphael would leave him alone and go off out into the fields to run about singing it to himself and the cows who looked over the fence chomped their big wet lips as if to say "Do you know what—I think that young fellow in there is gone mad!"

But he wasn't gone mad at all. He was just as happy as Larry, and there was nothing wrong with that. He picked daisies for his mammy, helped her carry the bucket to the well and spent all day chatting to her about what he was going to do when he grew up and went out into the big wide world far away. He was going to be a doctor, a priest, a soldier and a sailor, he was going to have a million jobs. "What am I going to do with you at all?" said Evelyn as she drew the needle in and out of the grey woollen sock, then stroked his cheek and said "I'll make some tea." Then they'd sit together sipping their tea, just Mammy and Raphael and Our Lady on the window ledge smiling over at them and saying "I am proud of this happy and holy family."

Then—whee!—off into the fields to sing eggs and hairy again and to play ball with Daddy who was coming up the lane with his coat thrown over his shoulder. "I'm the best!" cried Raphael, as he kicked the ball away into the trees. "I'm even better than my daddy!" "Oh no you're not!" shouted Mattie as he chased after him. "I'll soon show you who can kick!"

And you should have seen Raphael's eyes when the ball went sailing over the tops of the trees.

"My daddy's famous!" he cried ecstatically.

Reaping Race

And he was—didn't he win the reaping race? All the men for miles around came with their canvas bags and sickle hooks and beneath the burning sun moved like clockwork machines as they cut their way through the cornfield. "Oh please God our daddy'll win!" cried Evelyn as she squeezed Raphael's hand. By noon they were halfway and Evelyn and her son raced to him with the bottle of cold tea stoppered with a twist of cardboard and a warm cake of soda bread, dabbing his forehead with a cloth as they cried shakily "You can do it, Daddy! You can do it!" and as he said later when it was all over it was their words which had done the trick, for when the whistle blew once more he was like a man possessed and his sickle was a blur as he tore through the field for them and them alone, then at last his red arms triumphant in the air as he cried *"Críochnaithe!"* and it was over, over at last, and was it hard to keep the tears out of your eyes as you saw your daddy being lifted on high and all the men of the county crying "Mattie Bell has bested them all!" bearing him across the bridge and off down the road until they came to Clancy's bar and the doors were thrown wide open as Mattie called "Pull out a stool for Evelyn and the little man they call Raphael!"

A man with a nose like a sunburnt potato leaned over and said to Raphael "You must be a proud young buck this day" and Raphael smiled as he sipped his glass of lemon soda and then just looked up and beamed "I am."

She Lived Beside The Anner

Then afterwards in the flickering shadows of the tilly lamp, proud once more as Mattie held his wife's hand and looked into her eyes as he sang the song he had sung to her on their wedding day, a song that told the story of a love that had sadly gone away never to return. "Did you ever hear a tune that was sung so well?" remarked Pony Brennan to the man beside him. "I'm telling you now that man could charm the birds down out of the trees." "As well as show every man jack in this townland how to reap a field of corn," came the reply. His father's eyes were still closed as he sang:

"She lived beside The Anner
At the foot of Slievenamon
A gentle Irish colleen
With mild eyes like the dawn
Her lips were dewy rosebuds
And her teeth were pearls rare
And a snowdrift 'neath a beechen bough
Her neck and nutbrown hair."

In the window a giant moon with heavy-lidded eyes and outside the night so full of peace. The fire throwing out shadows that wrapped about you like shawls and in behind a cloud of perfumed smoke, Uncle Joe remembering faces from the long ago.

"Come on now, Mattie, that's the stuff! You're the man can sing!"

"Ah! cold, and well-nigh callous
This weary heart has grown
For thy helpless fate, dear Ireland,
And for sorrows of my own;
Yet a tear my eye will moisten
When by the Annerside I stray
For the lily of the mountain foot
That withered far away!"

It was the saddest song Raphael had ever heard. The girl who lived beside the Anner river went to America and was never seen again. She died far away among strangers, far from her little brothers or sisters. That night Raphael couldn't get her face out of his mind and that was why he said a hundred prayers, for her, but also in thanks because he wasn't faraway among strangers but being looked after by his mammy and daddy and surrounded by people who would never be strangers and who if anything happened to you would always look after you, like Pony Brennan and Uncle Joe and all the people who had been at the reaping race and everyone who said when you were going down the road "That's Mattie Bell's lad! That's young Raphael! There you are, son!"

All he wished was that the girl who lived beside the Anner could have been alive so that he could share some of them with her and tell her all about them and how kind they were but she wasn't alive. She was dead—she had died among strangers and would never be seen again.

Head Altar Boy

Raphael was eight years old when he was made head altar boy. Father Sean told his mother that he was the best little altar boy yet. "You want to hear the way he does the Latin!" he said. "Will you do a little bit of it for us?" Mattie and Evelyn asked their son one day when he came home from practice. "I don't know it all yet," said Raphael. "Just the tiniest bit," pleaded Evelyn and Raphael reddened. "All right then," he said and cleared his throat. "*Ad Deam qui laetificat juventutem meam,*" he said and Evelyn threw her arms around him. "My holy boy!" she cried aloud and Mattie shook his head in wonderment at the beauty of the world and the gifts they had been given by the Almighty.

The Latin Teacher

In the spring the crocus came and the young lambs tumbled in the fields. In the summer you climbed up a haystack and then came flying back down again. And then what did you do? You just turned around and climbed back up again. "I'm the best!" squealed Raphael and pulled the bits of hay out of his hair.

"Say some Latin for us!" the boys all pleaded because they couldn't remember it.

"*Introibo ad altare Dei!*" cried Raphael.

"Latin is good!" the boys said. "We wish we knew some."

"I'll teach you," said Raphael.

And he did. In a week they were all able to say it and off they went down the road chanting and clapping away to beat the band *Introibo ad altare Dei*.

It was good then. Of course it was. It was good being alive in those days.

Out In The Fields

Or at least it was until the War of Independence when people started getting shot right left and centre and sometimes even whole towns were torched and left to burn away to nothing. You never knew what was going to happen next. Just like the day Raphael was helping Mattie to fork the hay in the field when the Black and Tan soldiers came up and stood there smiling and saying "Turned out nice, didn't it?" They took off their caps and wiped the sweat off their foreheads saying "Bloody weather in this country. Like them what lives in it—untrustworthy, know what I mean?" Raphael didn't know much about the Black and Tans. He knew there was a war on all right and that Ireland was trying to win independence for itself. But apart from that he knew nothing and to tell the truth he didn't really care. At least not up until a couple of minutes later when the Black and Tan put his cap back on and hit his father across the face with a revolver.

What exactly happened after that, Raphael was never able to

say for sure. One of the others might have hit him with a rifle butt or something but anyway Mattie fell down and when he was on his knees the Black and Tan said "We know you're a rebel, Bell. We know all about you and if you don't tell us what we want to know you're going to be a sorry man. A very sorry man indeed, I don't mind telling you." Raphael knew it was serious now and started screaming but they told him to shut up or they would kill his father. So he shut up as best he could. Not that it mattered all that much anyway because the officer said he was fed up and told him to get up and then put the barrel of the revolver to his chest and blew a hole in it. Some of the blood from it splashed across Raphael's face. When they were going they said to him "You remember this day, son. That should keep you out of mischief."

His father wasn't dead yet and Raphael realised he was trying to say something to him. He fell to his knees and pleaded "Daddy don't die!" Mattie held his hand and said "Promise me one thing, son. You'll always look after your mother. She adores the ground you walk on, son. Promise me you'll be good to her no matter what happens."

"I promise, Daddy," said Raphael and then Mattie's head tilted to one side and he died.

Raphael stood up on the legs of a newly-born spring lamb and felt the fields were screaming.

Stranger

The sad part of it all was that Evelyn never really got over it. It doesn't really matter when all the preparations are being made for the funeral and so on and all your neighbours are there to comfort you. But they can't stay there forever, and that's when it begins to get hard. Although you're living in a lovely little cottage it's like you're inside a sealed metal container that lets in no light. That was what Evelyn felt when she broke down crying and it seemed to be for no reason just as it did the day Raphael came in the door and found her there in the middle of the kitchen weeping uncontrollably. Her hands were shaking and she was mouthing the word "Mattie" even though there was no sound coming out. Raphael went to her and threw his arms around her. Her nails bit into his wrist and he was afraid she would go hysterical. "It's all right, Mammy! It's all right!" he cried and hugged her.

Raphael was frightened. He didn't know what to do. Only for Uncle Joe he wouldn't have known what to do. The night he came he looked at him and, frowning under his big soft hat, said "You know, Raphael. You know don't you? You're going to have to be strong. Strong for her."

Raphael wasn't one hundred per cent sure what he meant but he had a vague idea. He nodded. "Because there will be times—and if you're not strong—there'll be nobody else there for her . . . do you know what I'm saying, son?"

Raphael said "Yes." Uncle Joe meant that if he didn't stay strong and keep a close watch on her something terrible might happen.

"You'll do that won't you, Raphael?" went on Uncle Joe. "You'll do that for her—and the memory of your dead father?"

Raphael felt a surge of pride as he stiffened and replied "Yes, Uncle Joe—I will! I promise!"

"For eight hundred years the likes of that animal that shot your father to death have been trying to break us. They haven't managed it yet and they never will. Not while we have young cubs like you coming up—am I right, Raphael?"

"Yes," replied Raphael and tried not to think of his father's mouth with the blood pouring out of it, and his terror-stricken eyes.

Then Uncle Joe put his arm around him and said "Come on, son. It's time we went to see the horses. I have the trap waiting outside."

If there was one thing Raphael loved more than anything else in the world it was going to Uncle Joe's stables to see the horses. And if there was anything better than that it was helping to brush them and comb them and run his hands along their lovely polished flanks. He was the happiest boy in the world as he sat beside his Uncle Joe with his mother in the back of the trap smiling for the first time since the death as Uncle Joe's pipe sent out a great big cloud of sweet-smelling smoke and he flicked the whip and said "Your father was a hero, son. You didn't know that. No one knew it. But he was. He died for Ireland. He's at one now with all the loyal patriots asleep in the ground."

Tears came into Raphael's eyes when he heard that. Tears of pride, tears of sorrow, tears of joy.

All that day he spent in the stables with the horses, looking into their guileless glassy eyes and stroking their noble, shining necks. He was so at one with them he didn't even realise he was talking to himself. He was saying "I'm going to make you proud of me, Mother. I'll make you the proudest mother in the whole of Ireland!"

Which were the very words he uttered the following day as he left for school except that it was different this time because the smile that had been on his mother's face all the way to Uncle Joe's farm in the pony and trap was gone now and the way she was looking at him wasn't the way he was used to, it wasn't the way you would expect a mother to look at a son. It was more like the look you would give someone you had never seen before in your life.

God Save Ireland

When Raphael heard the sound of laughter he was ecstatic and was standing in the kitchen before he realised there was no laughter at all. In the chimney corner armchair reposed a huge shadow. With blank eyes it considered him. By the window sitting at the spinning wheel, yet another, with a shadow-head that turned and whispered "Raphael!" It wasn't a bad voice. The voice meant him no harm. He knew that. But it made no difference. It was the voice of Nothing and it made tears come to his eyes. He wanted to ask "Why have shapes cut out of the dark come to steal my home?" More than anything he wanted to ask that question. But now there was no one to ask. You were afraid to ask your mammy because she might cry and more than anything you did not want that to happen. So you just lay there in the nighttime hoping they would go away. But they never did. They just sat there, people cut out of the dark, waiting.

Once, Our Lady came to you and sat there with you as the sweat glistened on your forehead and your heart beat so fast, laying her soft hand on your forehead as she told you that it would soon be all right because good boys who loved their mothers were always rewarded and to put your trust in Jesus Christ Our Lord. When you looked again she was gone, nothing but the night moths tapping at the window and the ghosts of her kind words still hanging in the air.

You would be standing by the river when the cherry blossom in full bloom sent out its intoxicating fragrance, where the children on the bank tossed a ball with frantic cries and cabbagewhites described great figure eights in the weighted air above the sparkling silver waters which slowly but surely started to turn red once again and the limp dead dummy of your father would go floating past again, downstream in the smoky haze of a dreamy summer.

And there were other dreams too, of the Black and Tan who had so cruelly done him to death, now swinging from a tree in that same field, pleading for mercy like the British coward he was, as Raphael in his rebel green gave the order for his men to "Execute!" as he slapped his wrist with the leather gloves and the Tan's eyes bulged as his neck snapped and somewhere Mattie smiled a wistful smile, now that he knew old Ireland would be free. All night long those dreams would go on, of a building aflame in Dublin, as it had been during the fateful week of 1916 seven years before, when the first blow was struck against the Saxon tyrant, perfidious Albion, the Commandant-In-Chief Patrick Pearse now calling out to Volunteer Raphael Bell "More ammunition! Over here, Raphael! Immediately! We're coming under fire from the Foresters!" But sadly, despite their valiant efforts, it was only a matter of time and when they were finally overrun, Raphael, on behalf of his father, defied them to the last and when the judge snapped impatiently "Do you realise your part in this foul rebellion has seen to it that you will most surely die?" Raphael clenched his fist and thumped the air, crying "God Save Ireland!" and felt the soul of his dead father enter his body as the bullets of the firing squad ripped it to shreds.

Tripping Over Himself With Brains

Tower Of Ivory
House Of Gold
Ark Of The Covenant
Gate Of Heaven
Morning Star

Those were the names. The names of Our Lady the Mother Of God. The Cedar Of Lebanon whose pearl-white foot crushed the head of the serpent. A crown of golden stars adorned her head. At her feet in his surplice and soutane, Raphael each day intoned the words:

> *"To thee do we cry poor banished*
> *children of Eve*
> *To thee do we send up our sighs*
> *Mourning and weeping in this*
> *valley of tears."*

The air was heavy with the scent of candle-smoke and incense. He prayed for his mother, that the sadness might leave her.

That the flickering fire would once more return to dance in her eyes.

That the words which he knew she wanted to speak to him would not wither on her lips and her eyes turn again to glass. He prayed that even one old day would return. The day of the reaping race! Oh! If only it could be!

The Lord works in mysterious ways, the priest whispered to him, proud of him as he watched him pray. "Your father would have been a happy man had he lived to see this. His young boy growing to be a man and the country he loved soon no more to be a province but a nation once again!" There were tears in the priest's eyes as he spoke the words.

When in the year 1925, at the age of twelve Raphael was awarded a scholarship to St Martin's College, he was sad because he knew his mother would be all alone. "Now," said Uncle Joe, "I have to ask you to be stronger than ever before. You pass up this opportunity, my son, and your father would turn in his grave. Never fear. We'll keep a close eye on her. She'll be a proud woman when you come up that lane the day you finish, Raphael. That's what you have to think about—the day you come walking proudly up that lane."

Uncle Joe stood over him and looked into his eyes. "There's times I look at you and I think to myself you're the spit of him. And he was one of the bravest men that ever walked this earth. To see you the way you are now, son—it would have made him a happy man!"

Uncle Joe hugged him then and the next time they saw one another after that was the big day, with Pony Brennan waiting in the trap outside the cottage as Evelyn smoothed the hair back from his eyes and said, almost in her old, Mammy voice, "The day you were born I remember Mattie saying—he said you had the face of a scholar. That was what he said the day you were born, our Raphael." She tried to smile but she could smile no more. "You will write to me, son!" She cried out "Please tell me that you'll write to me!"

A tear glistened in the corner of Raphael's eye as he choked —"Every day I'll write to you, every day for five years I'll write to you!" and then it was time to go, Pony chucking the reins as the horse's hooves clip-clopped in the summer afternoon and bloating with pride because he was the one to drive the scholar to school. "I always knew it, me bucko!" he cried. "I always said that any boy of Mattie Bell's would be tripping over himself with brains," and what could Raphael do when he said that but grin from ear to ear.

Head Prefect

But how, oh how could it be so frightening when you thought it was going to be the most wonderful place in the world, with its shadows twice the size of those at home, when you woke up in the menacing silence of the giant dormitory with its steel beds in military formation and the dean of discipline moving like a ghost among them, hungry for a misdemeanour, many thousands of miles away now the warm glow of the embers in the kitchen fire, the freckles on the wrinkled hand of Mammy to whom you felt like crying out "Please come to me! I cannot stand it here without you!" And without the smell of soda bread, the slow tick of the clock that marked each passing peaceful day and the heavy sighs from the chimney corner that let you know she was always there. But now she was not. Now there was nothing but the smell of older flesh, the flap of the wind as you walked alone through the vast oppressive grounds with their harsh, enclosing granite walls and vigilant, looming towers, the strange, impenetrable tongues of the half-boy, half-man students who circled you and triumphantly handed you an ominous warning—"Make no mistake—the first five years are the worst!"

Oh how he cried those first few months. Even for Raphael Bell the intricate codes of Greek and Latin, the brutal symbols of trigonometry and calculus uncompromising in their obstinacy as nightly in the big study he struggled to best them, at times their icy logic too much for him who wanted only to be there with her and hear that voice again, comforting in his ear as outside the huge night settled over the fields. And that was why he wrote daily, wrote "Dear Mammy I miss you so much the new college is nice there are so many things to do—geometry, Latin and on Wednesdays we have a half day I am looking forward to Christmas when I will see you again, The school team is in for the Munster Cup I think we will win. I am having a trial on Friday for the junior team so here's hoping D.V. I hope you are well and I will write soon—your loving son, Raphael."

And indeed he did have a trial for the junior team that Friday, Raphael Bell, and not only secured a place for himself but was the talk of the whole school with not only his tough, wiry steadfastness in defence impressive beyond all expectation but also, because of his height, his ability in the air, being described as second to none. As the President, who trained the team, said to him in the dressing rooms after the game, "I can tell you are going to do well in St Martin's. You can tell a lot about a fellow by his performance on the playing field."

Raphael beamed when he heard that and as the days went by, the puzzles of Pythagoras and Homer and Ovid ceased to be quite so daunting. In the nights the vastness of the dormitory did not seem so oppressive and soon Raphael was first out of his bed every morning, rubbing himself with a rasping towel, eager to embrace the day that lay ahead of him.

"I am so happy here," he wrote to his mother some months later. "I got ninety-five per cent for my history essay and Fr Bourke says it was one of the best he has ever had. Well that's about it for now. I have no more news so will end here. Please write soon. Your loving son, Raphael."

On his first visit home that Christmas, he was the talk of the parish in his big suit and his hair combed back like a real scholar and as Uncle Joe pressed a note into his hand, he heard him say "A few bob for the young fellow who is a credit to his father's name." And when they went to see the horses this time, he found himself on the back of a beautiful black fellow, clearing ditches with the greatest of ease. "I never seen a fellow grew up so quick!" smiled Uncle Joe as he puffed on his pipe. "What a pity himself is not alive this day!"

It saddened Raphael more than anything to see his mother failing, which undoubtedly she was now. But he vowed to redouble his efforts at college during the coming term to make her prouder than any mother had ever been of her son.

When he scored two goals and three points and took the team into the Munster Colleges Finals, it came as no surprise to anyone. "Bell is the best by far," the other juniors said. "He scored that point from sixty yards out!"

By the time he reached his third year he had excelled in just about everything. The freshfaced first years followed him around and wanted to be him. When, at the Halloween party, which took place in the Big Study in 1928, he strode to the top of the hall and stood still and dignified upon the podium before one hundred and eighty fellow students to sing "God Save Ireland," the spirit of his father momentarily passed him by as if it had floated in from the fields to be with him, and together they brought tears to the eyes of everyone there present with the words:

> *God save Ireland said the heroes*
> *God save Ireland said they all*
> *Whether on the scaffold high*
> *Or the battlefield we die*
> *O what matter when for Erin dear we fall!*

In his fifth year, Raphael was unanimously elected Head Prefect. Each night he took his place at the desk overlooking the study hall, and checking his watch, signalled to the mute, respectful assembly that the main study period was to begin. It was his duty to maintain discipline and to ensure that the rules of the study hall were respected at all times and, should punishment for misdemeanours such as whispering, distracting other boys or interfering with the silence which prevailed in any other manner whatsoever be deemed necessary, then Raphael would present the offender with a "yellow card" upon which his name would be written, to be presented to the Dean of Discipline after night prayer, and a suitable punishment meted out. It was generally acknowledged that in the administration of this system, Raphael was "tough but fair."

Even by the way he walked you could tell that Raphael had principles. It was clear to him that students did not respect weakness in a prefect. In any position of authority, be it captain of a football team or anything else, equivocation or uncertainty was as nothing. If you made a decision you stood by it, no matter what; an aspect of his character which revealed itself in no uncertain terms when, in his second term as prefect, he encountered the well-known bully Lally, mistreating a junior. Not only mistreating him in fact, but brutally assaulting him and then humiliating him by ducking him in the senior grade toilets.

Raphael had chanced upon the incident purely by accident but as he watched it, he paled. His heart went out to the poor unfortunate youth as Lally's rough hands manhandled him while a gaggle of coarse compatriots mocked him mercilessly. It was the first time Lally had perpetrated so despicable an act, although his reputation was well known. The juniors in fact, more or less lived in terror of him. Raphael knew that if he were to report him to the Dean, he would, possibly, manage to talk his way out of it by giving some muddied alternative version of events and perhaps receive nothing more than six or twelve slaps with the leather. Such he had received on previous occasions, obviously to no effect. Which was why Raphael stood up to him there and then and said "Leave the boy alone." Lally, like all cowards, appealed to his fellow bullies, scoffing "Well well if it isn't Mr Suck. Mr Suck-Up-To-The-Priests Bell. Who's talking to you, Bell?"

Raphael hit him one blow and the blood ran from Lally's face. The junior freed himself and ran off and Raphael lifted his fist again. Lally swore. "You made a mistake hitting me, Bell!" he snarled. "I'll fucking creel you!"

Raphael stood his ground. In his mind he saw his mother sitting in the chimney corner and in the same moment his father dying in the fields as a coward with a smoking gun laughed above his head. A coward of a Black and Tan with a smoking gun and Lally's face.

"Go on, Bell—hit me!" snapped Lally. "Mr Big Head Prefect! You're too afraid! He's too fucking afraid!"

Raphael realised that there was really only one thing he could do as already an inquisitive crowd had begun to gather. "Meet me in the back handball alley today after dinner. We'll see then who's afraid," he said softly.

Lally realised just then what he had let himself in for but it was already too late. "Go on, you cunt you!" he shouted after Raphael who kept on walking, stiff, upright, with his head held high.

A junior was dispatched to keep watch for the Dean. There must have been up on one hundred students gathered in the alley that day. Raphael and Lally were stripped to the waist. Cheers rose into the sky. "Bell! Bell! Bell!" Then: "Lally! Lally! Lally!"

Lally was first to strike, a solid blow to Raphael's left cheek.

But Raphael remained steady. A few more blows went wide of the mark. Then Raphael struck home, a fine punch directly on the nose which began to bleed instantly. Lally was shaken by the impact. He stared in horror at the blood on his hand. Raphael's next punch hit him on the side of the head and the one after that, the left eye. Lally, can you believe it, began to cry.

The cheers became deafening. "Bell! Bell! Bell!" A surge of pride ran through Raphael as his father's cheers merged with those of the redcheeked, triumphant students. The Black and Tan cried helplessly, his bottom lip trembling "Don't hit me! Don't hit me!"

By now Lally was on his knees, his legs having buckled beneath him. Raphael punched him mercilessly until his nose was nothing more than a bloody pulp and then dragged him by the scruff of the neck over to the junior he had treated so badly. "Apologise!" he demanded. "Apologise to the boy!"

"I'm sorry!" blubbered the bloody Lally.

Raphael hit him again. "I'll never do it again!" he instructed.

"I'll never do it again," choked Lally.

"Let that be a lesson to you!" snapped Raphael as he pushed him out of the way like the piece of dirt he was and then, buttoning his shirt, took his jacket from an admiring junior and walked off alone in the direction of the main building.

Bye Bye Love

It was exactly thirty-nine years later, the day after Neil Armstrong took a small step for himself and a giant one for mankind, that a thought struck Malachy Dudgeon as he was walking past the grocery shop thinking about Cissie. It would have been won-

derful if he had grown to like her again. If somehow it had
become even remotely like the way it used to be between them,
walking along the shore and staring out at the yachts bobbing on
the horizon and so on, but it hadn't, for the old boatshed days
were still with him and to tell the truth, if he had arrived home
to hear that she had had a stroke, it wouldn't have bothered him
very much. Of course he was aware that it was wrong to think
the like of that about someone who was supposed to be close to
you—but so what? She should have thought of that before she
threw herself on the nets in front of the cowman, shouldn't she?
She ought to have given that some thought before she started to
make up her little visits to Dr Wilding. Sadly, however, she
hadn't and now it was too late. "Way too late, my friend," as
Malachy now said to himself in his recently remodelled American accent.

As for Cissie herself, she was more or less at her wit's end as
to know what to do about the way things had gone between
them. Once he looked up to see her standing in the doorway of
the bedroom with her voice shaking, pleading "Please, Malachy
—I don't know why it happened. Forgive me for God's sake—
please!" He looked at her for a long time but he didn't say
anything. There wasn't a muscle moving in his face. And his eyes
—well they were just about the coldest she had ever seen. It was
sad of course. But then, as he had discovered some years before,
there were lots of things that were sad weren't there?

In the end it did get so bad that Malachy began to feel a bit
sorry for her. I mean she was so pathetic. Sitting there going
through her tenth or eleventh box of Kleenex, practically throwing herself at his feet. One day she broke down at the kitchen
table and began to weep uncontrollably. She told him she had

met Jemmy Brady up the town and sworn at him and told him that it was him had caused all the trouble and she never wanted to see him again. "It will be all right from now on won't it, Malachy," she wept. "Everything will be the way it used to be in this house now that all that's over." For a split second he felt so warm towards her that it was indeed like old times but it was only that—a split second and when it had passed it might just as well never have happened at all.

Which suited Malachy just fine. For if on a Sunday morning in the hotel long ago, he had been afraid to whisper the words "I love you" to his father in case they would wither and die on his lips, he knew one thing for sure and that was that he wouldn't be having that problem ever again, for from now on it was bye bye love as far as he was concerned, be it with his remorse-eaten mother or anyone else. He had more sense than to let himself go down that road again didn't he oh yes but of course he did.

He Said Nothing

Not that it was all bad back in those days—indeed in many ways Malachy was happier now than he had ever been. For a start, Alec and his crew were no longer a problem, having long since lost interest in him and now directing their attentions towards some other poor stuttering unfortunate whose mother with a bit of luck was making mysterious Sunday morning visits to boathouses. Jemmy Brady was still to be seen about the place but sad to say he was a shadow of his former self and if someone had told you that once upon a time he had been considered something of a whiz kid in the prick department, all you would have been able to do was laugh your head off. Nowadays just about all Jemmy was able for was falling about the place with an old brown coat on him and a bottle of whiskey in a paper bag, muttering and raving to himself. Not that Malachy gave two fucks what he did, for he was too busy enjoying himself. He spent long days in the café listening to Donny Osmond and looking at women. Women who were never going to mean anything to him because of course he had too much sense for that. Sunny days on the fairgreen with the blue sky over you and your whole life stretching out like a highway. "So—what's the story?" his buddy Kevin Connolly from The Terrace would say "Where are we headed tonight?" and Malachy'd reply "Let's go hear Horslips in Carrick!" Horslips were jigs and reels on speed as you boogied all night long and went half-crazy shaking your head and Kevin Connolly yelled over at you "Shakin' All Over!" and man were you shaking all over or what! Then it was out into the warm air and an open field with the dawn coming up as the Carrick women called "You will come back and see us won't you?" and you both cried "Sure, girls—see you next time OK?" as you roared off into the morning.

In many ways it was the Summer Of Dreams and when the exams were all over and the call came to teacher training college you just could not believe it. "Can you believe it?" you said to Kevin Connolly who flicked the cigarette and said "You gotta be kidding. You a teacher? Man, it's crazy. Now why would you want to do a thing like that?"

Malachy didn't know. And man, did he care! It was just another of those exams he'd done and if they were dumb enough to ask him to join the club, well then who was he to argue. As long as it got him out of the town once and for all, that was fine by him. He sailed through the interview the following week but, man, did he feed them some bullshit about being devoted to a career of teaching children. "Whee-hoo!" laughed Kevin Connolly as they fell out of the pub that night, "I gotta hand it to you—you sure can bullshit your way into things—Master Dudgeon!"

The summer drifted by. In the café Donny Osmond smiled at you from the wall, a row of gleaming teeth. "Now why would you want to do a thing like that?" asked Donny. And did you know? Of course you didn't. At seventeen you didn't know and didn't care. Why should you? You just wanted to climb the highest peak in town and cry out across the rooftops "It's over, man! I'm gone!" and so you would be, a puff of smoke into the future and the past all bundled up and buried, kicked into the grave where it belonged. Kevin Connolly and you got drunk, man, you got so drunk and when you embraced he said "It's all yours now, man! You've got it all!" and the tears, man, they ran down your face.

The last days, maybe they were the saddest when Cissie tried her damnedest to raise it from the ground, what had once been between them. She sat there looking at him, knowing there was nothing she could do now for she had done everything. She stared at him with her eyes so raw and red and said "Do you remember the way it used to be, just you and me, the pair of us shopping up the town. Do you ever think of them days now, Malachy?"

He said nothing.

The day he left, Kevin stood in the town square by the purring bus and handed him a copy of *Midnight Cowboy*. Malachy leaned out of the window and said "Looks like it's goodbye, kid!"

Kevin shot him with a gun-finger and said "Yep! You make sure and write me all about those Dublin chicks now—you hear?"

"You better believe it," grinned Malachy.

The bus pulled out and Malachy strained to hear as Kevin called after it "Master Dudgeon—can you believe it!" and then that was that, goodbye town forever I'm gone and that's the way it's gonna be as trees and shops and other towns by the score sped past and Midnight Cowboy Joe Buck Malachy Dudgeon flipped open the battered pages of the novel and sailed on down the freeway of his mind into the heart of the midday sun with the sound of Harry Nilsson singing "Everybody's Talking" ringing in his ears.

St Patrick's Training College

Way back before Harry Nilsson was a gleam in his father's eye, on the fifth of October 1930 at the age of seventeen, Raphael Bell climbed out of the hired car that had taken him from the station and, waving goodbye to the driver, turned and took his first look at the grounds of the training college which was to be his home for the next two years. As he walked up the avenue listening to the birds singing in the sycamore trees, he felt he would faint with excitement. He could not believe that it was actually happening and he was at last embarking upon the career that he knew now without doubt to be his true vocation. He registered at the main desk and was shown to St Brigid's Dormitory, not unlike the one in which he had spent five years in St Martin's. When he found himself alone, he slipped to his knees and said a silent prayer to Our Lady. He felt like weeping he was so happy.

Outside the birds twittered in the twilight as bicycles sped homeward all along Drumcondra Road.

The Philosophy Of Education

Malachy had arrived there too of course. But what he was look-ing at in the year of Our Lord 1973 was not exactly what had met Raphael's eyes way back in those good old days. He would have had a heart attack if he had seen what was going on; the place was swarming with women and all you could hear was rock music blaring out of the canteen. If the bursar who had been in charge in Raphael's time had seen them at the like of that, he wouldn't have been long putting an end to it. He'd have run the lot of them out of the college, the whole bloody lot, for if they weren't prepared to dress and act like people who were in charge of children, and to attend to their Euclid and Ovid, then they weren't worth having. That was what he would have said. But there wasn't anyone saying that now. As a matter of fact, there didn't seem to be anybody saying anything about anything. By the looks of it, the place had gone like everywhere else in Ireland these days. You could do what you bloodywell liked. Which in-deed appeared to be the attitude of one Malachy Dudgeon who right now was doing exactly that, sitting in the lecture hall chew-ing a pencil and staring off out the window watching the world as it made its way on by.

The lecturer paced up and down with his clipboard and fixed his glasses on his nose once more as he tilted his head to one side and said, frowning, "Rousseau says that children are not vessels to be filled." Malachy didn't really care what Rousseau said. Outside two girls with folders and their hair tied back with flowery scarves sat on the steps. Their sweaters were knotted about their waists and they were laughing. The mature student sitting next to Malachy took a dim view.

"Drug addicts," she said, "for that's all they are."

She went back to her scribbling and Malachy took a look out at the addicts. They were leaning against the flower beds, clutching their folders to their chests, still laughing away. The way they nodded said "I'm cool. I'm just about as cool as you can get." Of course they were. They were second years. Of course she was. She was a second year. Part of the cool bunch who draped themselves around the record player and looked around the canteen at everybody else as if to say "We're second years— OK? We've done just about everything there is to do. All you got to do is make sure and remember that. You just remember that and you'll be fine. Meanwhile let me get on with smoking my drugs if you don't mind." All day long they kept that record player going, just sitting there and listening and looking cool.

It wasn't that easy looking cool you know. It wasn't just any old bollocks who could do it. You didn't jump up and shout "This is a fantastic song!" or "This is the best song this year!" Oh no—you couldn't be seen doing that. What you did was hide in behind a big pile of hair and emerge every so often to remark "Nice drumming that" or "Like the guitar break there." Then you vanished back into your haystack for another hour or so. Another thing you could do was peer over your shades now and again and take a look around you like everyone in the place apart from your mates was some kind of human garbage. Then you chuckled to yourself as if to say "What a sad, pathetic bunch of miserable little people!" before flopping back into your chair, and picking up an album sleeve and starting to investigate the back of it for interesting facts about the bass player or perhaps some cryptic clues to something mysterious hidden inside the lyric sheet.

Meanwhile back at the notepads, the mature students were scribbling away like madwomen as the lecturer gave out some gen about Paulo Freire and a few other heads who reckoned they had the lowdown on schoolkids. Malachy considered the blank vastness of his page and wondered should he stop chewing his pencil and get started. It seemed too late to bother now however so he decided to draw some instead. He drew some addicts talking to mature students. "I hope there's no drugs in these sweets," they said, "because if there is—we're telling! Aren't we, Annette?" Annette nodded and said, "Yes! Yes we are!" as her word balloon spread away out all over the page.

"Oh no," the addicts said, "there's nothing in them—they're just ordinary sweets."

"Thank heavens," Annette said as the top of her head came flying right off and her friend went racing off down the road shouting "Help! Help! They gave us drugs!"

Yes, there was no doubt about it, said Malachy to himself as he put the final touches to his work of art and the Philosophy Of Education lecturer thanked everyone for coming. Drug addicts or no drug addicts, this college sure was one swell place to be on this brilliant, leaf-kicking, sun-streaming autumn day.

Conker Men

I mean just what was going on or who in the hell did Malachy think he was now, Jack Nicholson coming in the college gates sporting a pair of shades he'd just bought in the Dandelion market in Grafton Street? Clicking his fingers and puffing on his rollup well now, man, wasn't he just the cheese. "Where's that Joe Buck?" he laughed aloud. "I said where's that Joe Buck!" Hell I am one crazy motherfucker he said to himself and felt like jumping ten feet in the air as he made his way into lecture hall fifteen for today's lecture "Conker Men In The Classroom."

Conker Men were little people made out of matchsticks and chestnuts. As the lecturer said, kiddies loved them and they were easy to make and of course very economical. All you needed to get your little conker family going were half a dozen chestnuts and an ordinary box of household matches. That was all you needed and you were away. You used the bigger conker for the body, the little one then for the head, you put in your matchsticks and hey presto—Daddy Conker. The lecturer beamed with pride as he held him up. "Doesn't he look good?" he said. Everyone agreed that he did and the lecturer moved on to Mammy Conker. When they were all finished, he put the whole family up on the windowsill along with all the other little people they had made this term so far. Then he adjusted his spectacles and said "I'm sure you'll find that a great activity, particularly those of you who will be taking infants and the younger classes for teaching practice. The little ones always get great enjoyment out of it. Anyway, that's our Conker Men more or less finished with. Now let's see. Yes—I think now we'll move on to the Bead People."

What next, thought Malachy, as he wrote "Bead People" in his folder, and started that old dreaming again, wondering where it was he was gonna be headed tonight.

Chirpy Chirpy

As if he didn't know of course, considering they'd spent the last thirteen nights in the pub across the road where all the first year women hung out. By the time eleven o'clock came, Malachy's head had just about gone AWOL and all he could think was "If only Alec and those assholes could see me now!" He was completely gone, man. He could do anything. Any woman in the bar, he could have had her. He knew that. They were there for the taking. They were as far gone as he was. What were they on about now? Music? "I'll tell you about music, man!" shouted Malachy as he took off his shades. "You want to know something about music?" They told him to shut the fuck up or the barman would throw them out. "So—he throws us out—he throws us out!" shouted Malachy in Pacinospeak as he nearly fell off the seat. "No—the best single of the last two years!" someone was saying. "What was it?" "Maggie May," someone said. "Don't talk bullshit!" said somebody else. "Brown Sugar" was the next suggestion. It got the thumbs down too. After that they came thick and fast. It was going hot and heavy when could you believe it, what do they hear then only this voice saying "No—it was 'Chirpy Chirpy Cheep Cheep'!" Well when they heard that, they just about went and exploded right there on the spot. "You have got to be kidding, man!" someone laughed. "I mean you really have got to be kidding!" The laugh was that she wasn't kidding at all. "No—I'm not!" she said. "I really do like it." They all stared at her in amazement. She was small with blue eyes and short strawberry blonde hair. "No—I really do!" she had to insist as they kept on staring at her, waiting for her to retract. But she didn't and in the end they got fed up waiting and started laughing and talking about something else. Someone told Malachy her name was Marion. Not that he was pushed one way or another what her name was, as he lit a rollup and said "Where are we headed after this then? Into town?" and then hit the bar for the last drinks of the evening. It was fantastic. It was the best night yet and that was saying something! He was on top of the world!

A Fading Voice

He met her a few times after that by accident, at lectures and stuff and always said the same thing to her: " 'Chirpy Chirpy Cheep Cheep'—huh?" and so what if he reddened, what difference did it make, it wasn't as if he was going to ask her out or something, even if he had been thinking about her ever since the night in the pub for some reason. I mean it wasn't as if he was going to fall in love with her or something Miss Chirpy Chirpy Cheep Cheep, she'd be waiting a long time if that was what she was expecting, which explained why when he overheard her saying she was going to the first year dance in the hall in Parnell Square that he happened to be standing where he would be able to see her. She was wearing a stripey tank top and a shirt with blue flowers on it. The band was playing "Killing Me Softly With His Song" when he finally plucked up the courage to ask her to dance. As he was crossing the floor he could hear "What? Dance with you? A son of Packie Dudgeon—that humpy cunt whose wife made a cod of him in front of the whole town?" and was about to turn back when he heard her say "Sure."

There wasn't much room to dance so they just more or less stood there. He could smell her perfume as he held her hand. He felt like he was going to drop down dead on the spot. Her hair lightly brushed his cheek as she said "How are you enjoying the college so far?" He was so busy thinking about the feel of her hair that he nearly said "What college?" But he managed to get it together just in time. "Oh—it's fine," he said, "it's cool," as he tried to figure out just when would be the best time to ask her would she like a drink or something like that.

The first night he kissed her he didn't know what to do with himself. He thought the top of his head was going to come off.

He ran his fingers through her hair and whispered "Oh Marion!" He really couldn't believe it was happening. She said she would meet him in the canteen after English the next day. They drank coffee and argued about Hedda Gabler. Marion said that Hedda was right to do what she did. Malachy said she wasn't. But he didn't give a shit whether she was or not. He just wanted to keep the argument going so he could sneak looks at Marion's eyes. Blue eyes. Blue eyes, strawberry blonde hair and small hands.

The first night they made love he thought he was finished altogether. How many explosions were going on inside him, he did not know. It was the night they went to the end-of-term party in Phibsboro. They went mental, dancing to the twelve bar boogie of Status Quo and twice as mental hugging one another to the slow blues of Eric Clapton. He wanted to kiss the mouth off her.

They were half-drunk as they came up Drumcondra Road. They went into the Perki Chick for chips and the notorious gang leader Philly Fuckface, head of the Drumcondra skinheads, laid it on the line for Malachy. "You tell those country fucks up in that college that I'm onto them. You hear what I'm saying? You better because you want to know about those assholes—they're history. You got that, Mulch-Head with the glasses?"

Malachy took off the shades and gave Philly the thumbs-up. "I got it," he said. Philly flipped a chip into his mouth. "Bleedin' right you got it," he said. "And don't you forget it."

He loved kissing her stomach and then her breasts and then her arms. Then it was off up to her mouth which he could kiss till he died. Running his fingers through her hair and hugging her like a madman. By the time they were finished it was dawn. That was the end of lectures for that day I'm afraid.

Occasionally a tiny voice would whisper at the back of his mind: "But what about your promise? What you said about love?" He heard it all right but each time it came, it grew fainter and fainter until he could no longer hear it at all.

Midnight Cowboy

There was a double bill of *The Graduate* and *Midnight Cowboy* on at the Adelphi. Marion had her head stuck in a big box of popcorn as she said "When you said it was your favourite movie you didn't tell me you knew the whole thing off by heart." But he did, he knew it all right. And just like Joe Buck in the movie he did not give a shit as Ratso Rizzo slapped the bonnet of the car and tossed a cigarette butt at the windscreen shouting "I'm walking here! I'm walking here!" Man, it was crazy. Then who does Joe Buck meet only this prostitute with a poodle. He's got it all worked out—she's worth at least fifty dollars sure as hell. Yeah sure she is until he's standing there shaking her perfume into his boots and she's gone apeshit shouting "You thought I was gonna pay you?" Like a bat out of hell that Joe Buck gets on out of the apartment and doesn't stop running till he reaches Times Square. Malachy reckoned the prostitute's outburst was just about the funniest thing he had ever heard. He was still saying it when they were coming out of the cinema—"You thought *I* was gonna pay *you*! You big Texas longhorn bull!" Marion hugged his arm. "I love the way you do that—it's amazing!" she said. "Do it again. Do some more."

"Can you tell me where the Statue of Liberty is please, ma'am?" he said then twisted up his face and said "Sure. It's up in Central Park taking a leak. If you hurry you might catch the supper show."

He did most of the movie and still she wanted to hear more. "How about *The Graduate*? Can you do any of that?" "I've had it," said Malachy. They went to The Shakespeare Bar in Parnell Street. There were a few of the other heads from the college but Marion and him stayed on their own. They sat in the corner and didn't say much after that.

What would you want to say anything for?

The Dutch Catechism

Sister Ken The Yank had eyes like a hawk. "What you gotta do is make your own choices, your own decisions in life. That's what it's all about, buddy—believe you me." She said that every week in her Yankee accent. That was why they called her The Yank. In fact she had never been anywhere near America in her life. She had been drafted over from a convent in England for a term or two and put in charge of Religion for the whole college. As well as being Sr Hip. Yep, as far as she was concerned, she was just about the hippest thing on the planet. She was the next thing to a drug addict. You wouldn't catch her wearing a dowdy old nun's habit. Not at all. She was too busy hanging out and discussing sex before marriage. "Yep, the church was going through some mighty big changes," she said, "and we gotta ride along with them." That was why she had brought in the Dutch Catechism. She reckoned everyone in the seminar group should read it. "Some people tell me they find it difficult," she said. That was when Marion chipped in with her "psst psst" to Malachy. Now if Ken The Yank was pretty cool when it came to matters religious, things weren't quite the same when it came to interrupting her seminars. Which was why she was staring over at Marion with mad eyes and every blood vessel in her head about to burst. It was no use Malachy even beginning to try—he just couldn't keep in the laughing and that was that. It might have been OK until Marion lost it as well. "May I ask what you find so amusing?" The Yank said. "Perhaps you might be so kind as to share the joke with the rest of the group?" Marion wiped the tears from her eyes and tried her best to get herself together. A few of the mature-moustaches pulled their cardigans about them and glared at her with glacier-eyes. "I'm not surprised they find it hard, really," she chortled. "If it's written in Dutch, I mean." That was enough for Malachy, whose essay on The Dead Sea Scrolls went flying all over the floor. "Some students have a rather idiosyn-cratic sense of humour," said Sr Ken as Malachy's glazed eyes welded themselves to the pages of his catechetical masterpiece for which he was now without a doubt destined to get—0 marks.

All the way down the corridor, they couldn't stop laughing. "The big mad eyes of her," said Marion.

"Shee-it, that Sister Ken," said Malachy. "She is gonna blow us right outta the water, pardner."

"I guess there's nothing for it now only the poob," Marion said.

"What are you talking about—poob?" he said.

"It's Dutch for pub," she shouted, and then tore off across the grass as he ran after her, with at the very least half a dozen pages of meticulously annotated biblical Hebrew fluttering in the breeze behind him.

Snowmen

They hung out in the park behind the college. The day the snow came they were supposed to have a Philosophy Of Education seminar but the way they were feeling they couldn't have cared less if every Philosophy Of Education lecturer in the place had been rounded up and shot. They were off to make snowmen. They rolled a huge big ball down the hill and stuck a tiny little head on it. "It's Mr Conker's Snowman Brother," Marion said. She knew it was stupid to say that, but she didn't care. Neither did he. They stuck a stick in its face for a pipe.

The park was an unbroken blanket of snow. She was sitting on a swing listening to Neil Young on her portable cassette player, wearing a black knitted woollen cap and a duffel coat. There were flakes of melting snow in her hair. Neil was singing "Out On The Weekend." He sang away as Malachy gave her a few pushes on the swing. "What do you think of our snowman?" she asked. "He's good," Malachy said. "I love him," she said, "I love our snowman. His little head." They were supposed to go back for tea but they didn't bother. They stayed there for hours. Then they started firing snowballs. One burst on her back and she roared "I'll get you for that!" Unfortunately he fell against the snowman and knocked off his head. "Now look what you did —look what you did to our snowman!" She tore after him again. By the time they had done all that, they were completely exhausted.

Malachy sat on a bench as she just stood by the frozen river, staring at something far away. He was drawing in the snow with a stick when he looked up and saw her turning towards him. He didn't know what she was going to say. But then she looked into his eyes and her lips parted as she smoothed back her hair and said "I love you."

Zero's

Not long after that came teaching practice and Malachy was steeped in luck. They gave him just about the easiest class imaginable and he sailed through it. Marion was well on top of it too and to celebrate they went to a club called Zero's. She was wearing a cheesecloth blouse with a big knot tied in it, a brown corduroy skirt and knee-length boots. She had some eye shadow on but not much. Not that he minded. Eye shadow looked lovely on her. She could have worn a bucket of it if she wanted. She had earrings with little golden shoes hanging from them and a necklace with her name in silver letters. Her cheek touched his as they danced. He held her tight and as her hair brushed lightly against his cheek he smiled at her and said "You don't really like 'Chirpy Chirpy Cheep Cheep' do you?" She didn't say anything. Just hit him a pretend punch as they went on dancing in the same spot for over an hour as Jimi Slevin and Peggy's Leg tried their best to blow every amplifier they had.

Bring Me The Head Of Alfredo Garcia

The head honcho was in no mood for games. Someone had violated the honour of his daughter and would have to pay. The reward was to be a million dollars, no less. You bring me the head of Alfredo Garcia and the million dollars is yours, he said to Benny, alias Warren Oates. Benny was cool. He was even cooler than Joe Buck. Malachy decided he would be him now. He wore a beat-up linen suit and shades and no matter what way you looked at it he was just about the coolest thing going. Benny played "Guantanamera" in a Mexican bar with chickens running across the top of the piano. Benny didn't care. All he cared about was bringing Alfredo's head home and collecting the million bucks. But what a job he had doing that. He tracked him halfway across Mexico and when he did eventually get him and the head, every hood in the place was trying to get it back off him. It got so bad Benny kind of went off *his* head. Started talking to the head and all this kind of stuff. Not so good. Talking to a head in a muslin bag ain't so healthy, just like it ain't healthy to share a station wagon with maybe half a million flies. Like Benny was crazy. Him and Alfredo.

After following Benny halfway across Mexico they decided to hit the Mayfair Grill in O'Connell Street. "So maybe you like to eat some of zees food, señorita?" Malachy said as he flipped the menu open. Marion was getting in on it all now. She shrugged her shoulders. "Maybe I do, maybe I don't. Maybe I don't want to eat any of your steenking food, you pig!"

"I theenk maybe you keep it a leetle quiet because zee woman—she come."

"Do you want the burger in the bun or outside the bun?" asked the middle-aged waitress.

Benny Dudgeon lowered his shades and said "I theenk maybe inside. What you say?"

Marion shrugged again. "I theenk maybe inside."

"Right you be," said the waitress and stuck the notebook in her pocket.

Malachy twined his fingers around Marion's. Then he kissed her on the lips. "One million dollars—that ees what I pay for you señorita," he said. "You're a headcase," she said and shook her head. "Do you know what I say to you Meester Dudgeon—you are crazy in zee brains. You see—in here? Crazy! Pah!"

Outside the buses groaned like they were on their way to the wrecking yard. Beneath Daniel O'Connell's statue a skinhead kicked the air mercilessly with his Doc Martens as a bunch of Skin Girls urged him on, clapping and singing. Outside The

Ambassador the hippies queued up for Pink Floyd at Pompeii. A tramp looked in the window and played a few bars of a song for them on a busted harmonica then went off laughing and giggling to himself. Malachy kissed the back of Marion's hand, hardly realising he was doing it. It was 1974 in Dublin and it was good to be alive.

Horslips

The Stadium was packed to the door. All you could hear was "Horslips! Horslips! Horslips!"

If they didn't show soon the place would be torn apart. Marion was going mental. She was up on the seat cheering "Horslips!" She pulled him by the sweater. "Come on!" she cried. "Get up here!" Up he got. The screams were unbelievable. Then out of nowhere appears Eamon Carr the drummer with a giant shamrock on the backside of his satin suit. He starts pummelling the drums like a madman. Before you know it the band are into "Johnny's Wedding" and the place has gone absolutely apeshit. Charlie O'Connor's mandolin is like something possessed. It's like it has a tiny music demon inside of it and is away off on little silver legs never to be caught by anyone ever again. "It's good to be back in Dublin!" cried the bass player. A thousand scarves and woolly hats went into the air. "This one's called 'The High Reel'," he said and Marion fell off the arm of the seat right on top of Malachy. "Come on," she said, "let's dance!" and dragged him out into the middle of the floor, shaking her strawberry blonde hair like a wild thing.

The Scarecrow

Come the holidays, whenever they were apart, they wrote every day. "Dear Marion," he wrote, "I love you so much. I am gone fuckways in the head I am so in love with you. I can't wait to get back to college to see you again." Half the time he didn't sleep at all thinking about her. She sent him a picture of herself and he kept it in his pocket. Sometimes when he'd be drinking with Kevin Connolly he'd take it out and say he was going for a piss just to have a look at those eyes.

Every day himself and Kevin went to the café. Donny Osmond was still there, flashing his teeth and singing away about how them older folks just didn't understand him and his poor old Puppy Love. But they didn't know, you see. No sir. Not as far as Donny was concerned. They could say what they liked. "Damn right," said Malachy as he took a drag of his cigarette and nearly shit himself when he realised he had just agreed with Donny Osmond.

After a couple of dozen cups of coffee, Kevin Connolly said "You're fucked—do you know that? You're out of your mind over this woman. It's going to come to a bad end." He was joking. Of course he was. He was laughing when he said it. But little did he know just how right he was. Malachy sure had come full circle. Those hotel Sunday mornings when he was afraid to utter a word about love in case it would wither and die on his lips seemed like a thousand years ago now. It was as if they had happened to a stranger.

Relations between him and Cissie didn't improve any however. He was civil to her but that was about it. Sometimes she'd plead with him and turn on the tears but he didn't want to know. Not that it mattered because most of the time anyway he was either in the café or at the movies, dreaming of the day when he'd be heading back to college. When he'd come home she'd still be sitting there in the chimney corner, going through old memoriam cards and trying to pretend that it had all been so beautiful way back in the old days when Packie and her were so much in love. She looked sad and broken sitting in the chimney corner where she spent all her days and it was hard not to feel sorry for her. But then he came to his senses and thought to himself "Well too bad ain't it—that's what you get when you make your bed. You have to lie in it don't you?" Which is absolutely true of course as he was going to find out himself, and a lot sooner than he thought, standing there in the kitchen coming on like a preacher and passing judgments on a helpless, choked-up wretch who, with her stick fingers and wizened skin and rapidly disappearing teeth, was beginning to look more like a scarecrow than someone you would be inclined to call your mother.

Tell Me I'm Dreaming

The first sign that old lover boy might be in for a little bit of a surprise came when the inspector on his second teaching practice said to him "I see where you received a B-plus for your earlier teaching practice. To be quite frank I can't understand it. Perhaps it was because you had second class. Sixth class as you can see are a different kettle of fish altogether. There were times, Mr Dudgeon, when I felt you were seriously out of your depth." Malachy was dumbstruck. He stared at him in disbelief as he clicked his briefcase shut. What was he talking about—out of his depth? Sure there had been a little bit of a problem getting one or two of the boys to sit at rest during the geography lesson but that was no big deal was it that was no big deal for Christ's sake. I mean—come on! As he was leaving the inspector paused and said "I would suggest you pay careful attention to discipline and related areas. Much of your teaching is good but classroom discipline is of paramount importance. Unless that is taken care of everything else suffers. A good rule of thumb is—firm but fair."

When he was gone, Malachy felt like laughing. What did he care—he would get a job anyway. There were hundreds of jobs. Thousands. He didn't care what the inspector said. Fuck him! He had it all worked out and nothing was going to stop him! Of course he would get a job. They were crying out for teachers all over the country. Everyone knew that. Soon as you left college, all you had to do was walk right into one. Which was exactly what he was going to do. And just as soon as he did, Marion and him would get married. It was all worked out. It was all worked out and nothing on earth could stop it. Nothing.

He said it to her that night after they had made love.

"I want to get married," he said.

"Me too," she replied. "But let's live together for a while first? See how it goes."

"No," he said, "let's get married. Who wants to live to-gether?"

"Right in, Malachy Dudgeon. Right in at the deep end every time."

"I want you all to myself," he said and kissed her neck and face.

She was wearing a T-shirt with a big red number 99 on it. Even the sound of her brushing her teeth in the bathroom was enough to drive him mad.

Marion was first to get a job—teaching in a convent on the south side of the city. The night she received confirmation of her appointment, they went out and got plastered. They kissed outside the gates of the college just like that first time after the dance in Parnell Square. Malachy was ecstatic. "I just can't believe it," he said. "Moving in with the woman I love more than anyone in the world. Wake me up—tell me I'm dreaming!"

"You're dreaming!" a faint voice echoed at the back of his mind. "You're dreaming." But he didn't hear it. With his tongue halfway down Marion's throat, he never heard a word.

———

Two Happy Men

In the year of Our Lord nineteen hundred and thirty-one, when Raphael was eighteen years old and in his first year at St Patrick's Training College Drumcondra, he found himself one evening sitting under a laburnum tree with javelins of light sailing toward him through the autumn leaves. As he looked up from the Hall and Knight's *Algebra* opened on his knee, he saw standing in front of him the blocky figure of a youth in a grey suit with a great big smile.

The youth leaned against the tree and ran his fingers through his blackberry curls, shaking his head at the boundless wonders of the world. "Boys," he said to Raphael, "but that was a powerful game you played against St Bartholomew's. As true as I'm standing here you could have put them from here back to Bartholomew's all on your own." Three priests floated by as Raphael smiled to himself and closed the book. In the trees the birds sang, a tram clanged along Drumcondra Road. "Once I knew where I was with the fullback, it was plain sailing after that," said Raphael.

His name was Paschal O'Dowd and he was from Athlone. He had been on his way to Maynooth College to become a priest when he changed his mind at the last minute and headed for

Drumcondra. "Raphael," he said as they walked the playing field together, "I think the church of Rome can soldier on for another while yet without the likes of me."

A good man on the football field too, the same Paschal, well able to rise into the air as gracefully as any man, plucking the ball from nowhere and sending it high and over the bar for yet another point for St Patrick's.

A devout man. Many times Raphael would quietly enter the college chapel, perhaps after tea or before study period, and find him there, deep in contemplation at the foot of the cross or beneath the pale feet of the Blessed Virgin Mary to whom he too had a special devotion. For it was she, he said, who had helped him along the road to the decision he had made to serve as best he could the children of Ireland. The first free generation of a country for centuries in chains. Free at last to take its place among the nations of the earth.

"We are a proud and noble people," he remarked to Raphael on one occasion, "for too long kept upon our knees."

But that all belonged to the pages of history now, there consigned because of the courage of men like Raphael's father, brutally done to death by a cowardly commandant in a bloody field. There were nights when his face, a mask of terror, would return to Raphael, he would call on her, the Mother of God, and she would yet again come to his assistance as the calm once more descended and sleep drifted down upon him as a gossamer veil from her very own brow.

"We have been given so much, Raphael," Paschal said. "Much is expected of us."

A sea of fresh and hopeful faces, of children whose names as yet they did not know, swept into the future before them. In the nights they saw themselves with chalk in hand, pacing polished classrooms, league-stepping into infinity.

Both, happy men. In the afternoons they chased the football wildly with the enthusiasm of young colts, then afterwards a silent prayer in the incense-perfumed stillness of the chapel.

The musical evenings were held in the college assembly rooms, occasions rarely missed by either of the two men. When Paschal would excel himself with his rendition of "Macushla," with its sad tale of a husband's yearning for his dear departed love who was now cold in the ground. He sang it with such feeling that it would wring tears from a stone. "Now who," Raphael was heard to remark on every single occasion it was sung, "could follow that," as he himself would shyly take the stage to begin his, as he described it himself, "humble rendition" of his father's favourite song, the story of a young girl who died far away among strangers—"She Lived Beside The Anner."

Visiting The Sick

Part of their work in the Legion of Mary which they had joined on the same day was to visit the sick. One of their charges was a distant relative of Paschal's, Mrs Ellen Malloy, who had never recovered since her husband's death. Raphael stood by the bed-side and took the sick woman's hand, looking into her eyes as Paschal intoned a decade of the rosary. You could see she had once been a lovely girl, with happy smiling eyes and everything to live for. But that was all in the past. Now she could barely breathe and all the flesh had fallen off her. The hand Raphael was holding was like the skeleton of a bird. She looked at Paschal and tried to say something, but she hadn't the strength and just fell back onto the pillow. Her groans were pitiful as, defeated, she turned her face away. Paschal was not an overly sentimental man and had seen many harrowing things in his day, but on the way home that evening Raphael could see that he was upset, and when he turned to him and wiped a tear from his eye, saying "Sometimes this world—it's a sad old place, Raphael—do you know that?"

Raphael understood.

The Eucharistic Congress 1932

It was like the city had risen up out of the ocean. As far as the eye could see—banners that would dazzle your eyes with their fluttering colours. Everywhere you looked—a flag, the Papal Keys in yellow and white flying in the breeze. "Get your Congress badges here! Get your Congress badges here!" the old women shouted. It was like the country was about to burst with pride. Out of all the Catholic nations of Europe, Ireland had been chosen to host this, the thirty-first International Eucharistic Congress, when once again the Church of Rome had chosen to summon the Catholic nations together to celebrate and proclaim their faith to the world.

Already, houses that hadn't seen paint for over twenty years were every bit as bright-looking as Duffy's circus. No matter where you went, the smell of flowers followed you. And children. Little girls in flowing lace veils, little boys with starched white shirts and red ties. Hands joined, heads lowered, rosaries laced through fingers. Raphael overheard one woman say "They're walking saints," and it was true. Nearly every child in Ireland was expected to turn up. Those who could walk at any rate. The colonnade which had been erected in the Phoenix Park would take the sight from your eyes.

But there was just so much to be done, and so little time to do it! Where would all the faithful stay? Would there be enough accommodation in the city for them all? Upwards of a million people were going to attend, for heaven's sake!

The people of Ireland knew that the good Lord would not let them down however, and that all would be well in the end, as indeed it was, and more, a triumph perhaps, with thousands sleeping in the open air, or in their cars along the quays, those that were fortunate enough to have cars, as out in the bay the lights of the pilgrim ships twinkled and powerful searchlights beamed their sacred messages across the night sky through massive lettered screens: *Laudamus! Glorificamus! Adoramus!*

For Raphael and Paschal, the highpoint was The Children's Mass, for in those eager eyes, so innocent and unblemished, they saw their whole lives reflected back at them. And as they sang "Jesus Thou Art Coming" with one voice, they were many present who wept openly and saw no shame at all in doing so.

As Raphael did not when, on the final day, after the consecration at the High Mass, Count John McCormack the world famous tenor, stood up and, as the host was elevated, began to sing, in a voice that surely no angel could ever hope to emulate, César Franck's "Panis Angelicus."

Raphael neither knew nor cared about the moistening of his eyes, for already his mind had been taken away by the sound of a military command which snapped out as the troops on the altar steps whipped out their swords to present arms, followed almost immediately by the tinkle of the fifteen hundred year old bell of St Patrick, now sounding once again throughout the land, as the multitude there gathered in the Phoenix Park, with a mesmeric hush, fell devoutly to its knees.

When, that night, exhausted, his eyelids at last closed over and he saw them again with their holy rosaries and white shirts and red ties, Raphael knew that he had indeed made the right decision in coming to St Patrick's so that he might serve them, and what he wanted to do more than anything else in the world was to put his arms around them, each and every one, and pray to God that he might die there on the spot and bear them all to heaven with him.

Valediction

On the day they were to leave the college for the last time, it was sad saying goodbye to Paschal, but, as he said, "It's not as if we're off to opposite corners of the earth, Raphael. I'm only going to Athlone for God's sake!"

Raphael nodded. Then Paschal smiled that mischievous smile and said "I've something for you."

"Glory be to God but you're an awful man!" replied Raphael, reddening a little.

Raphael was deeply touched as he read the title on the beautifully illustrated songsheet—"She Lived Beside The Anner." The charcoal drawing was of a young girl with flowing hair standing at the water's edge as she stared out across the sea towards her home in Ireland and the little brothers and sisters she would never see again.

"Spending your good money on me," said Raphael.

"I thought you might like it. Anytime I hear it sung now, it will remind me of the nights we had in the assembly rooms," smiled Paschal as he lifted his belted suitcases.

"I'll treasure it all the days of my life," said Raphael as he embraced his friend and said goodbye.

Chin Up, Chest Out

Raphael's first position was as assistant teacher in St Anne's in Fairview. He was, as the headmaster said, "a credit." His classroom was immaculate. Every evening, the blackboard wiped clean, the floors swept. Not a peep out of his boys. "How does he do it?" his colleagues often wondered. There was of course nothing to it. Not as far as Raphael was concerned. Once they knew you meant business, your boys would respect you. That was all you had to remember. If you remembered that, you would have no problem in a classroom. But there could be no half-measures. Children could be very easily unsettled. And that was where bad behaviour and poor schoolwork came from— insecurity and uncertainty. Of that there was no doubt. No doubt whatsoever in the wide world.

Every morning at exactly 8:55 A.M., his boys filed in one by one without so much as a word, with their white shirts and red ties, which was a strict stipulation made clear by Raphael to the mammies and daddies at the beginning of each school year, with their little heads held high and their fingers to their lips. Then they would stand in their desks, ramrod stiff and not move a muscle until their Master was finished speaking. Then they would be allowed to sit and, at 9:05 on the dot, begin the lessons of the day.

"Today we are doing the Battle of Kinsale and the subsequent Flight of The Earls," Raphael would say as he paced the room like a colossus. "Would you like to begin reading, Michael Noonan?"

"Yes, sir," the boy would reply and take up his book.

"Chin up, chest out!" Raphael would caution and young Noonan would smile and lower his head shyly, then continue reading as The Master paced and the boys listened and through the windows the sun streamed in and everything seemed possible.

A Visit From The Monsignor

The days passed into months and the months into years and Raphael might well have remained in St Anne's until the day he died, so contented was he with both pupils and colleagues, and most likely would have done had not a knock come upon his door in the month of September 1937 and the principal of the school, apologising profusely for the intrusion as he introduced him to the clergyman who accompanied him, saying "Raphael— I'd like you to meet Monsignor Cassidy. The Monsignor is in charge of things below in St Anthony's. Do you think maybe we could have a word?" Raphael nodded and silenced the class with a click of his fingers.

"The first boy who talks while I am out of the room . . ." he intoned darkly. He had to say no more.

The door closed behind him and he stood in the corridor facing the two older men, saying "So then, gentlemen—what can I do for you?"

The Interview

Raphael could not believe his ears. He stared at the three men sitting before him and wondered was he indeed hearing things. But he wasn't. What he had indeed heard Monsignor say was "I am prepared to offer you the position of principal here at St Anthony's, Mr Bell." This seemed ridiculous. He had of course been flattered to be invited along for the interview at all and had been glad to attend because it would give him experience. But he had never seriously considered the possibility that he might actually be offered the position. To begin with he was much too young for such an offer. An older man, perhaps an existing member of staff, must surely be in line for the job.

Directly above The Monsignor's head was a picture of the

Holy Family. On the wall opposite, the framed proclamation of Irish independence. Beside that a St Brigid's cross fashioned from bullrushes. Raphael was so taken aback by the offer which had just been made to him that he spent a ludicrously long time staring at it. The cross had long since turned yellow thanks to the sunlight and the passing of the years. He realised that he ought not to be giving it all his attention for such abstraction was hardly appropriate in the circumstances considering he had just been offered the principalship but try as he might he simply could not help himself, oscillating as he was between euphoria, astonishment and utter disbelief and would probably have meekly accepted his lot if The Monsignor had lost his temper and slapped the desk crying "What are you staring at, boy? You've wasted enough of my time! Now get out of my office before I take the strap to you and really give you something to think about!"

What he did instead was clear his throat and say again "Well, Raphael—do you think you might be prepared to accept the position? I can't tell you what it would mean to have you as head of our staff. I have heard so much about you and your excellent work in St Anne's from Father Curran. I have no doubt whatsoever in my mind that you are the man for us. Well, Raphael—what do you say?"

For no explicable reason, a ball went sailing high over a bar in his mind. There were cheers from vague, unformed crowds. A tall-hatted cardinal in full livery extended a solemn hand. A little boy whispered "That's our Master." Raphael felt himself flush with pride and embarrassment. The words shrunk in his dried-up throat. Only with a great struggle did he manage to free them at all. "Yes, Monsignor," he replied. "May I say how grateful I am."

"No," said The Monsignor, as he rose from his desk, "may

I say how grateful I am," a warm smile illuminating his face. "Am I right, gentlemen?"

"Yes," said Mr Cunningham, the outgoing principal, and "Yes," said the young freshfaced priest whose name was Desmond Stokes, who would one day be almost insanely loathed by the man whose hand he now shook, and whose heart was also destined to break.

Brothers

Not that it seemed like that back in those days of course, oh no. Back then there was nobody like good old Father Stokes who in a couple of years would be taking over from The Monsignor as boss of the school and who just could not do enough for Raphael to help him get settled in. "Have you enough of this?" and "Have you enough of that?" was all you ever heard out of old Stokes, tearing up and down the corridors like a blue-arsed fly with boxes of chalk and maps and kettles to make Raphael cups of tea during his break. Raphael of course was as bad. If you didn't know better you'd have said the pair of them were having an affair. But of course they weren't. They were just the best of pals, that was all. In fact they were more than that. It would be more accurate in fact to say they were like brothers. There simply was nothing Raphael wouldn't do for Father Des and nothing Father Des wouldn't do for Raphael.

Rarely a day went by but the classroom door would open and in the young priest would come—"Ah howareye, Raphael, and how are things? Did you see where Cork won again yesterday by God do you know I think they're going to take the Munster Final!" or some similar observation.

Pacing the playground together each and every lunchtime, if there was a subject they didn't get around to discussing then you could be sure it wasn't worth wasting your breath on. One minute it would be the horrific events in war-torn Europe and the next it would be the latest antics of Clarke, the rapscallion in fourth class who had poor Mrs Galligan driven astray in the head. Raphael shook his head and chuckled softly.

"Boys, she says to them, why did St Peter say 'Thou shalt never wash thy feet'? Why did he say that now, boys, do you think? And what does Clarke do, sticks the hand up and nothing will do him but he gets to answer it. Well, Clarke, says Mrs Galligan, why do you think now St Peter might have said that? Because, missus, because he says—his feet were clane!"

Tears came into Raphael's eyes—"Because he says, his feet were clane!"

It took them nearly five minutes to get over that and was it any wonder the young lads in third class were looking at them and whispering "Look—The Master and Father Stokes is laughing!"

Raphael shook his head as he handed the brass bell to the young Kelly boy from fifth class—"Well I swear to God, Father," he said, "if I hear any more of that Clarke fellow's spakes I'll be carted off. I'll be carted off now and that's a fact!" Then he went off smiling across the playground to his boys who were already lining up in single file, straightening their red ties and fixing up their white shirts after the boisterousness of their play just in case The Master might decide to do an on-the-spot inspection. Which he didn't. Not today. He was just too busy thinking about that bloody rascal Clarke and the carry-on of him!

Sundays

Nearly every Sunday Raphael would call to the presbytery and together they would listen to the wireless. There was nearly always a good match on and afterwards, a bit of a play or something to keep you amused. Father Stokes was a great man for the plays. His room was filled with books and plays. One day he handed Raphael a copy of Charles Kickham's novel, *Knocknagow —The Homes Of Tipperary.*

"Do you know Kickham?" the priest asked.

"Know him?" replied Raphael with a tinge of sadness in his voice. "Wasn't his masterpiece "She Lived Beside The Anner" my father's favourite song, God rest him?"

"Do you know," said Father Stokes, "there's songs would break your heart."

Songs like "Panis Angelicus" and "Macushla" to which they listened sometimes in the evenings and Raphael would recall fondly the day he had heard that very same Count John McCormack sing it in the Phoenix Park, the pure notes trembling in the air as the Sacred Host was elevated and you thought you would faint such was the love you felt for Jesus Christ the Son Of God and for all those about you.

"As long as I live I will never forget that day, Raphael," said Father Stokes, "for I was there too."

The cries of children echoed in the failing light of a Sunday evening as the haunting strains of "Macushla" filled the parlour and Raphael cradled a small Jameson whiskey in his lap and mused softly "I wonder will I ever see him again—Paschal. My old friend Paschal O'Dowd."

The Souls Of Newborn Babes

There were trips to the Abbey Theatre to see the plays of Yeats and Teresa Deevy and Paul Vincent Carroll. To marvel at the abilities of the great F. J. McCormick. To see Jimmy O'Dea in pantomime at the Royal Theatre. There were outings too to the countryside with the Ballsbridge Literary and Historical Society. There was even a trip to the lakes of County Cavan where the pair of them stood together on the lakeshore, two silhouettes by the bending reeds in the autumn twilight. Was it any wonder the mammies said "Inseparable, missus. Inseparable, the pair of them. Whenever you see one, you can be sure the other's not far away."

Not that they minded one bit, the mammies, as indeed why should they, for by now they realised that their sons were under the care of one of the most respected headmasters in Dublin. Only two years after his appointment, with the Monsignor retired and Father Stokes now at the helm, St Anthony's underwent a general inspection of the whole school, the results of which were beyond their wildest dreams and the rating "Highly Efficient." An evaluation which became common knowledge, envied by colleagues throughout the city. As were the inspector's comments on the wonderful work being done in the school as regards training in good habits, the formation of character, and the pride clearly being taken in all things Gaelic and Irish, the evidence of which was visible no matter where you went in the school, from the neat displays of handwritten poems by the executed insurgents of 1916 to the framed photographs of balladeers and martyrs long since passed away and on every wall, The Mother Of God, Mary Of The Gael looking down upon each and every little boy who passed through St Anthony's as if he was hers and hers alone.

And so it was a proud Raphael Bell who stood at the door of

St Anthony's Boys' National School the following day and
watched his boys filing in with their heads down and their rosaries twined about their fingers, without a doubt their young souls
unblemished as those of newborn babes.

Headless

All of which doesn't mean of course that there weren't occasional
difficulties which Raphael had to face, as any headmaster must in
the day to day running of a school. One such being the incident
with Donnellan the bully who, despite repeated warnings, had
continued to tease and torment young Matthews, whose mother
had been recently widowed and who had quite enough on her
plate without having to come up to Raphael's office every five
minutes to complain about the likes of Mr Donnellan. Standing
there in his office, a fragile, sticklike thing practically wasted
away by sorrow since her husband's death, she reminded him so
much of his own dear mother Evelyn, now sadly confined to a
nursing home in Cork city, her mind no longer her own. Mrs
Matthews fiddled with the strap of her handbag and stared at the
floor. "He wets the bed at nights, Mr Bell, and I don't know
what to do."

"You can put your mind at rest, Mrs Matthews," said
Raphael, "for you'll have no worries after today, I promise
you."

"God bless you, Mr Bell," she said, adding "He loves you,
you know, my little Martin."

Raphael smiled as he put his arm around her narrow shoulders and escorted her to the door.

Donnellan denied it of course. Raphael knew he might
as well be talking to the wall. "Did you take his marble?"

he shouted at him again, their noses almost touching. "Did you?"

The brat denied it again. And then would you believe it—again. There were beads of sweat on Raphael's brow.

"I'm going to ask you one last time," he said. "Did you?"

"No," muttered Donnellan sullenly.

Raphael was having no more of that. He opened the cupboard and took out his stick and gave the insolent wretch three slaps on each hand that were so hard that the tears leaped instantly to his eyes.

"Did you?" he snapped, and a vein started ticking just above his right eye.

"No!" he cried defiantly.

It took another eight slaps to get the truth out of him. Raphael himself was exhausted. But it was worth it.

"Let that be a lesson to you," he said. "And if you go near that boy again by God I can tell you it will be God help you. Do you hear me?"

The boy said nothing. Blood rushed to Raphael's face. He bawled "Do you hear me?"

"Yes," the brat squeaked. For that's what he was. A brat.

Raphael glared at the pathetic wretch clutching its raw hands.

"Get out of my sight before I really lose my temper!" he snapped and Donnellan slunk off like a dog.

The instant he closed the door behind him, Raphael felt as if his head was lifting off his body, lightweight drifting into air. It wasn't a pleasant feeling. For a second it terrified him. He clung onto his desk. Far away in the world there were tiny sounds that had somehow become stars, glittering like lights in a night city as they tried to send him some kind of signal but knowing they never could because he was lost to them now. He was on the verge of crying out to them, but then the moment passed and he realised it was the sound of the children laughing and playing directly outside his window.

A Phantasmagorical Galleon

Then there were the choral competitions. Every evening now you could hear them beavering away after school, with Raphael walking up and down past the window, mouthing the words along with them and every so often spinning on his heel to cry "No! No! No! For the love and honour of God how many times do I have to tell you! Right—from the beginning again!"

It was Father Stokes who had first suggested the idea of a school choir. Much as he adored music, Raphael had never considered himself much of a practitioner, but Father Stokes's confidence in him give him all the encouragement he needed. "You wait and see, Raphael," the young priest said one day. "Between the pair of us we'll knock a few notes into these crows," as Raphael grinned mischievously and reached in his top pocket. He held up the brand-new tuning fork which he had purchased that day in Walton's music shop in North Frederick Street. "Just what I was thinking myself, Father," he said.

They could not believe it when they were awarded the prize in Belfast the following year. "As beautiful a rendition of 'The Lark In The Clear Air' as I have ever had the privilege to listen to," the adjudicator had said.

St Anthony's Boys' National School had been somehow transformed from a drab old battleship ready for the breaking yard into a phantasmagorical galleon soaring towards the future at full sail across the skies.

The Scaredy Cat

Now, if you had said to any of the boys in sixth class, or indeed to any of the classes in St Anthony's "Boys, I'm sorry to have to tell you but I'm afraid your teacher is a scaredy cat," it would have been as if you had cracked just about the funniest joke that was ever invented in the world. The idea of Mr Bell ever being afraid of anything was enough to bring tears to your eyes. What —the man who had stood up to the docker Byrne when he came down, as he said himself, "to bate The Master" for what he had said to his son? Not only stood up to him but sent him off home with his tail between his legs after getting a promise out of him that he would never darken the school door again until he was prepared to show a little bit of manners. Yeah sure, Mr Bell a scaredy cat. You'd have had your work cut out for you if you tried to put that one over on the loyal warriors of St Anthony's School, I'm afraid. They'd have made a laughingstock of you, for God's sake! Which was even funnier again because the laugh of it all was that it was in fact true. The bold Raphael was a scaredy cat. Oh he wasn't scared of boys who squared up to him and snapped "I won't do it!" or "You can't tell me what to do!" or for that matter, whiskey-swilling dockers or irate mothers or anyone else. But he was a scaredy cat when it came to women. Oh he was a silly old scaredy cat then all right.

One day a young woman had called to the office to inquire as to whether there might be a place for her son in his school and when she crossed her legs, Raphael flushed to the roots. When he heard the swish of her stockings his eyes went everywhere but in her direction. He looked at the map of Ireland on the back of the door, at the Pope conferring his blessing on the multitude in St Peter's Square, at Maura and Sean who were playing ball with Nip the dog. Nip has the ball. Maura has the ball. Sean has the ball. Wuff wuff says Nip. Eventually there was nowhere else to look. He knew his face was the colour of a tomato, but there was nothing he could do about it because the more he thought "My face is the colour of a tomato. I must look ridiculous. I must do something about it," the worse it got.

That was exactly what happened the very first day he met Nessa Conroy, at a meeting of the Legion Of Mary in a hall in Mountjoy Square. When the meeting was over there was tea and sandwiches for everybody. Raphael was chatting away to another teacher from the south side of the city when Father Stokes took his arm and said "This is Nessa, Raphael. She's only just joined us recently." He smiled as he introduced them. "Nessa's from the Wee North," he said and as the blood rushed once more to his head, Raphael tried not to spill his tea all over himself.

The next time he met her was in the churchyard of the Pro-Cathedral when High Mass was being concelebrated by Father Stokes and two of his colleagues. It wasn't easy this time either but at least he didn't have a cup and saucer rattling away in his hand, showing him up. They talked about the weather and the Mass and how beautiful it had been. When Raphael told her he was hoping to enter his boys in the Belfast Schools Choral Festival again this year, her eyes lit up and she said that she herself was very fond of music. She loved the nocturnes of John Field, she said, and just about every song Count John McCormack had ever recorded. "Do you know a song called 'Macushla'?" she said shyly. "I love it so much." When she said that, Raphael almost felt tears come to his eyes, not just because she had said she loved the song Paschal O'Dowd had sung so beautifully all those years ago. It was because he had just at that moment realised he had never talked to a woman like this ever before in his life. Usually his topic was his pupils, Johnny or Pat or Mickey or Tom, and how they were getting on in school. In fact the only woman he had ever really talked closely to was his mother. His mother whose mind had now finally been irrevocably lost to her and who, when he visited her in the Cork nursing home, searched in vain for something in his face that might bring the name of Raphael Bell her son back to her once more.

It was only when the young woman had finished talking that he realised the churchyard was empty but for the pair of them. He could not take his eyes off her, her twinkling eyes, her pink cardigan and the white blouse with little forget-me-not flowers on the collar. When she said goodbye, Raphael's heart was thumping and his head was light all over again. Something was happening to him and he did not know what it was. He was excited in a way he had never been before in his life.

The next day he went into a record shop and bought the nocturnes of John Field. He played them all that evening and for the life of him couldn't sit still. Even his pupils remarked on it the next day when, having given them six algebra sums to do before dinner, he went and completely forgot all about them and didn't even correct one of them, which was not like Mr Bell at all!

As indeed the following statement wasn't either: "On account of you being such good lads this past week I'll let you off homework. What do you have to say to that?" The boys didn't know what to say. They were completely dumbfounded! Belly Bell letting you off homework—it was unbelievable! Just unbelievable!

They ran off out the gate that day cheering and when they told their mammies and daddies they couldn't believe it either. "Mr Bell letting you off homework? You're fibbing aren't you? Give me a look inside that schoolbag till I see if you're telling the truth or not!"

But, as the parents found out, they were indeed telling the truth, and the reason they were was as pure and simple and uncomplicated as they come: The weekend before Raphael had been on a trip to the "Wee North" as Father Des called it, with the Literary And Historical Society, all the way to the Giant's Causeway in County Antrim and would you believe it, who was on the bus along with him? When Raphael saw her this time, he nearly fainted right there and then on the spot. But he was getting a little bit cheekier now and wasn't quite the old beetroot-faced Bell that he had been before and would you believe it, it was no length of time before he was helping her across rocks and taking photographs of seagulls and buying her ice cream and laughing away and telling her jokes to beat the band.

As he lay on the sand and watched her paddling in a rock pool, her blonde hair tied back with a scarf he suddenly couldn't believe what he was doing. He might as well have been standing on a cliff pointing down to the pair of them and saying "Look at that fellow down there in his shirtsleeves with the beautiful young girl. He's the lucky man, isn't he? I wonder who he is?" But you see he wasn't standing on any cliff. He was lying right there beside her. Beside Nessa Conroy. And not only that but now he was carrying her sandals and taking her small, cool hand as they made their way to the hotel. Out of nowhere came a whiff of her perfume on the salt breeze. They were supposed to be taking notes on the locality, wandering around noting the age of various buildings and important landmarks. They were taking no notes however. They had forgotten all about buildings and landmarks. When she had her sandals fastened, she tucked her knees up to her chest and as she spoke her voice sort of hypnotised him. He was so busy listening to the sound of it that he only heard half of what she said. She worked in the civil service in Dublin and shared a flat with two nurses on the North Circular Road. "Is that right?" Raphael found himself saying and wondering did she know he was hypnotised. It didn't matter whether she did or not, for he knew there was nothing he could do about it anyway. She was speaking again now. He loved it. He loved her speaking. He loved it so much. Especially the way she said "Och now" and "Aye surely." He loved that.

That night he thanked Jesus and his Blessed Mother for his good fortune. He was so lucky to be alive. He knew that. In the school, his boys loved him even more now. Anytime Father Stokes met him, he had a twinkle in his eye too, for he knew a lot more than he was letting on.

Ave Maria

The following summer they went up to Belfast together and Raphael marvelled at the accents and the sights that were to be seen. She clasped his hand in hers as they wandered together through Ann Street on a Saturday night, with the smell of fried steak wafting on the warm air while the fruit-sellers peddled their wares in sharp-edged tongues and the excited cries of children lifted to the sky as the carousel circled in a colored blur. What a night that was. Out of nowhere leaped a melodeon player, confronting them with demands for money and the sad relic of what had once been a respectable march melody. "Here," smiled Nessa as she opened her purse and took out a sixpenny piece, "More," as she said later with a wry grin, "in pity than in payment." A grizzled woman caught hold of Raphael by the coat sleeve and waved a card of collar studs and tie pins in front of his face. "There!" she cried. "These'll dazzle your eyes for you! Surprised are you, mister? I'll bet you are! Six simulated gold tie-pins and six gent's studs. A tanner for the lot—what do you say?"

A tanner indeed it was as they pressed onward through a crowd gathered to hear "Springtime In The Rockies" being played on a saw by a dirty-faced youth. "He's good," murmured Raphael as the boy astonished all about him with his performance, his grubby cap filling up with coppers. "In all my living days I never seen the like of this Belfast," said Raphael as he put his arm about her shoulder, and as if to prove his point found himself almost eyeball to eyeball with a tiny man in a battered stovepipe hat who shoved a doll-sized trapeze artist complete with swing into his hand and shouted "Get your somersaulting wee men here!" and then, as if that wasn't bad enough, twirled what looked like a giant green worm in front of his nose, exhorting him to not miss this, the last opportunity he might ever have to treat his lady friend to a "wriggly snake in Ann Street." And what could the schoolmaster do but agree, as he pocketed the painted rubber toy, thinking to himself what a surprise that would give his pupils on Monday morning.

After the Royal Cinema where they spent two whole hours laughing themselves sick at the lunatic carry-on of The Marx Brothers, it was into the Genoa Café to treat themselves to a pair of ices topped with cherries, and as Nessa mushed up hers with her spoon, he caught her looking at him out of the corner of her eye and if he had been the happiest man on earth earlier on when they were watching Harpo and Groucho wrecking half of New York, well now he didn't know what he was.

Sometimes now he didn't even notice the boys at the back of the classroom talking. That was because he was writing "I love you" in his letters to Nessa.

The day of their marriage was a truly joyous occasion. Partly of course because the service was being celebrated by Father Des but also because Paschal O'Dowd had managed to make it and had had a great day along with all of Nessa's relatives, who were wonderful people. They made it the party of a lifetime. When Raphael took the floor and recited "Wee Hughie" in what can only be described as a ramshackle Ulster accent, it nearly brought the house down. But not nearly as much as Nessa when she got up and sang "Ave Maria." Nobody had ever heard anything like it. When it was over, Raphael had to look away from her, he was so overcome by emotion. There was a part of him that wanted to die there on the spot and he understood why. Because he realised that as long as he lived, he could never, possibly, be as happy again.

At least not until that night when they lay together in bed and he ran his fingers through her long blonde hair, her body warm against his. The moon shone on her ivory-pale face and Raphael was so overwrought, the words he wanted to say got all clogged up in his throat. But it didn't matter. She said them instead. "I love you," she said and her lovely soft fingers traced a line across his cheek as delicately as a webstrand falling through the air.

Scones For Father Des

Father Des was a regular visitor to the house in Madeira Gardens. There he'd be, coming up the road with his jacket over his shoulder, already licking his lips at the prospect of some of Nessa's scones—for boy could she bake scones!

Raphael would have him spotted just as soon as he turned the corner. "There he is—the man himself!" he'd shout and Nessa would look up from the rock garden and shade her eyes as she smiled and waved. Then it would be into the politics of the day and what they were going to do with this rascal McKeever in third class and that terrier O'Callaghan in fifth class and how much money they were going to need for the new playground extension and would the numbers go up next year so they could get a new teacher and who was going to win the match on Sunday as John Field came lilting out the open window and Nessa arrived with a tray of scones and a pot of hot strong tea and Father Des, as usual, made on to be the most surprised man in the whole of Ireland. "Nessa!" he'd say. "Where do you think you're going with all this?"

Then, off they'd doze, the butterflies waltzing in the weighted air as passersby stopped to gaze in wonder at the garden and its riot of colour which took the sight from your eyes. At the bottom of the pond, a constellation of pennies tossed in admiration. The wooden sails of a windmill turning. Sweetpea climbing skyward on a trellis. And out there by her beloved rock garden, come rain or come shine, was Mrs Nessa Bell, née Conroy.

"That woman," said Father Des as he licked his lips and crossed his palms over his black-clad tummy, "is a wonder."

"Don't I know it," replied Raphael and lay back on the rug beneath the hot burning sun.

The King Of All Headmasters

How Raphael did it the other headmasters did not know and would have given anything to be able to find out. Everyone knew that the inspectors considered St Anthony's to be something of a light upon the hill as far as primary education in Dublin, and indeed in Ireland, was concerned. Anytime you met the parents from that school, they were falling over themselves telling you how good it was. And of course, if that wasn't enough for Raphael Bell, he had to go and win the Junior Schools Football

Championship three years in a row. Not to mention his own class broadcasting on Radio Eireann, singing to the whole of Ireland if you don't mind! It wasn't fair! Why should St Anthony's get everything?

The other headmasters didn't say that of course. They were much too professional to do that. But they thought it all right. Sometimes things got so bad that they wanted to burn the school down. St Anthony's that is. Yes—burn it down! No, blow it up! Who cared what the hell you did with it as long as everybody stopped going on about the dump being the best school in Dublin and that big lanky galoot Bell being the King Of All Headmasters.

A Single Word Whispered

It was well past ten by the time they all got home. Young Phibbs and Carson were out for the count. Their eyes were hanging out of their heads. "Wakey! Wakey!" cried Father Des, tugging their ears. All the other boys laughed when the two red-cheeked lads woke up with a start. Nessa was standing in the doorway watching proudly as they clambered out of the cars. She hugged a few of the little fellows. "You were wonderful," she said. "Aren't you a credit, the whole lot of you! Singing on the wireless!"

Father Des stayed behind after all the boys had been collected by their mammies and daddies and Raphael and himself helped themselves to a little Jameson whiskey as they went over all the events of the long day. "Panis Angelicus," said Father Des. "That song would melt the hardest heart."

"And after Count John, you would be hard pressed to find it sung better than those lads did today, Father," said Raphael.

"You never spoke a truer word in your life," said Father

Des, swirling the whiskey in his glass as his eyes shone with pride.

That night Raphael stroked Nessa's hair and whispered a single word into her ear. The bold Count McCormack was behind that too, for the word he spoke was "Macushla."

"Macushla," he whispered into her ear, "Macushla, my darling. The one I love more than any other in the world."

Maolseachlainn

Yes, the happiest days that were ever known were lived by Raphael and his beautiful wife way back when the sun shone on the garden, the little boys sang for Jesus and each and every other night they offered up the rosary for the conversion of Russia and all the pagan peoples of the world and then repaired to bed to join together in a pure and wholesome union which they prayed to Jesus would result in a special gift being granted to them; a little boy called Maolseachlainn perhaps, whose tumbling golden curls would be the envy of all and to whom his daddy would tell stories of the hated Black and Tans and the Eucharistic Congress and a day in Belfast with the gentlest creature in the world.

Or perhaps that gift might be a red-cheeked smiling girl called Brigid who they would say was so like her mother and who would tend the garden and plant little flowers all of her own and look at you with twinkling eyes that would melt your heart and the world would be so wonderful, it would be like all those beautiful marvellous things which had already happened taking place all over again, like a brilliant light that bathed the world and made you want to cry "I love my little boy! I love my little girl! They have made the world live all over again!"

Those were the thoughts that were going through Raphael's

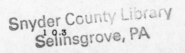

head as he paced the floor of the hospital waiting room and got himself into a right old state asking himself "Will it be Maolseachlainn?" and "Will it be Brigid? Glory to God will you hurry up nurse!"

Those were the exact words he was saying to himself as he wiped the sweat off his forehead with a big sheet of a handkerchief, when the door opened and the nurse entered, accompanied by the doctor. Raphael could tell that it was all over and he was so giddy his eyes were as big as golfballs. "Well is it to be Maolseachlainn or Brigid?" he cried like a young fellow.

"Neither," the doctor said. "I'm afraid your son is dead."

Well actually he didn't say that but he might as well have for unless you were blind you could tell by the way he looked at you. Raphael couldn't believe it. He had been so sure. That was why he kept repeating it to himself as they all moved about him like phantom people. Maolseachlainn. Then he would say nothing for a while. Then—Maolseachlainn again. Maolseachlainn.

Why Me?

So there you are—that certainly took the wind out of Raphael's sails, boys and girls. And it didn't help either when he was walking along O'Connell Street and heard someone shouting "Hee hee—there goes Bell. That soon shut him up!" For a split second he was sure he had heard it. It sounded like Lally, his defeated adversary from the handball alley days of long ago. But how on earth could it be? God knows where he was now. Lally belonged to the dim and distant past. He listened again and then realised that he was imagining things. Of course he was. People didn't shout at you on the street. It was just because he was upset. That was why it had happened. Because he was upset. Because he was heartbroken. Heartbroken thinking of Nessa's tearstained face.

It had been almost raw from crying, that face. Every time he thought of it, he felt like hitting someone. He felt like shouting "Why? Why? Why me?"

But then of course, when you think about it, why anyone? I mean there are people in the world who have never had anything.

Which, I am afraid I have to tell you, was about as much as Raphael was going to be left with when it was all over, not so much because of the death of little Tumble-Curls Maolseachlainn—which as time went on he reluctantly came to accept —but rather the one and only Malachy, who some sixteen years later arrived on the doorstep with a great big bright and happy face on him asking for a job. In the best school in Dublin. Which —can you believe it—he was given! Actually given a job by Mr Raphael Bell, father of the dead Maolseachlainn and husband of Nessa née Conroy Bell. The laugh of it is he thought Malachy was quite a nice sort of chap. He considered that he had done a very good interview indeed. Which of course he had—being actor of the year, thanks to all that practice with his Joe Buck and Alfredo Garcia voices. When Raphael turned to Father Des and said "I think this is the man for us," he really meant it. So did the priest. He said "Welcome aboard, Mr Dudgeon," as he held out his hand. Malachy was surprised. But not that surprised. He knew he had fooled them up to the two eyes. To have heard him, you'd have thought he was just about the most dedicated teacher on earth. When he was leaving, Raphael shook his hand and thanked him for coming along for the interview. "I look forward to a long and happy association together, Mr Dudgeon," he said and went off then as happy as Larry with himself, relieved now that the staffing problems for the coming year were resolved, and not for a moment considering the possibility that he might find himself at some time in the not-too-distant future once more returning to those two familiar words: "Why Me?" by which time of course it would be quite clear that what he'd done that fateful day in July 1975 was to employ a person who not only would prove to be a hopeless inadequate where teaching was concerned, but was also going to prove instrumental—along with a little, unwitting help from the aforementioned Father Stokes—well, in more or less destroying him, I suppose you could say.

Laurel and Hardy

"I can't believe it," Marion cried down the phone when Malachy said he had got the job. "What was it like! Tell me what it was like!"

He could hardly talk himself he was so excited. "Oh it was just this old baldy guy and some priest called Stokes. You want to hear the questions they asked me: Do you think the teacher has a moral responsibility to his pupils and the community? How important do you think neat dress is for the teacher? Man, it was priceless! Anything they asked me I said sure. If they'd ask me did I think the teacher should work twenty-four hours a day I'd have said absolutely. Such an amount of bullshit! But I got it! I think, says the sky pilot at the end of it, that this is the man for us! Man, you want to see those two guys, they're something else!"

That night in the pub he told them the whole story. Raphael looking at him over the rims of his big thick glasses and trying to put the wind up him with stories of how hard teaching was in the old days. "The pair of them," laughed Malachy as he shoved another pint down him, "Laurel and fucking Hardy."

Rathmines

Rathmines is a suburb to the south of Dublin City, regarded as something of a Latin Quarter. Students and self-styled bohemians abound. Kentucky Fried Chicken boxes flutter in the breeze. There is a huge clock with Roman numerals. Weekends the place goes crazy as the plateglass smashes and the discos thump. Young people reckon it's the place to be. Parties erupt at the drop of a hat. Rathmines is the East Village of Dublin. Or so Malachy and Marion thought. Not that it made a blind bit of difference what they thought, considering the way their lives were about to go. But of course they didn't know that then. How would they when they were still madly in love, twining on the floor almost every night until they could hardly walk.

Which was the way it was destined to go for the next four or five months anyway. Before his life started to fall apart and Malachy began to realise just how beautiful those first few months living together had actually been, as it slowly became clear that Marion, even though it was the last thing in the world she herself wanted, couldn't bring herself to love him anymore.

Cup

The first sign that there was trouble ahead came the day Malachy took Mr Boylan's cup. Mr Boylan taught sixth class and didn't like people taking his cup. It was a white one with two blue rings and he had had it for twelve years and did not like anyone touching it never mind taking it. Malachy didn't know that of course. He thought you could take any old cup. He thought you could just walk over to the cup-tray and help yourself to the first cup that took your fancy. But you couldn't of course. You most certainly could not. Which he knew now all right because Mr Boylan was glaring at him like someone possessed. He didn't have to say anything. He didn't say "That's my cup! Give me back my cup, you unmannerly wretch! That's my cup! I've had it for twelve years and you, you ignorant little upstart, you come in and you take it for yourself right there in front of my nose! Well—you'll not! You won't! You just wait and see! You might do that in that so-called college you've just come out of—but you won't do it here! I'll soon see that you won't! And the rest of the staff too! That's not the way we do things here—as you will soon find out, my impertinent friend!"

He didn't have to say any of that. He didn't have to because the look said it all. When it dawned on Malachy what he'd done, he went all red. He stuttered a bit as he washed it and put it back on the tray. He could see that no one else liked him taking Mr Boylan's cup either. But once he had put it back, everything settled down a bit and got sort of back to normal. Mr Keenan licked some crumbs off his lips and said "The forecast's good for the weekend."

Mr Boylan replied "That's something anyhow."

Mr Keenan shook his head and said "Would you believe it, I was hardly in the door of the classroom and Corcoran was out of his seat again. He can not get it into his head!"

"Who are you telling?" frowned Mr Boylan as he sipped his tea.

Then the door opened and in came Mr Malone who taught fifth class. He was wearing a safari jacket and you could see Spiderman looking out over the top pocket.

"I'll break his back," he snapped, "if I catch him up on those windows again!"

"Is it McCreesh?" asked Mr Boylan.

"Cassidy! Cassidy! Who else! I swear to God I'll not be held responsible!"

He ran his fingers through his curly hair and rinsed out his cup.

"A cur! For that's all he is!" he hissed again.

"The brother was the very same," said Mr Boylan just as Mr Bell came in. Mr Bell took off his glasses and shone them with a great sheet of a handkerchief. His cheeks were reddish-purple as he replaced his spectacles. Suddenly he bellowed "I told him! I told him not to go near the pipes but do you think he'd listen? I didn't hear you! I didn't hear you Master Bell, he says! Well by God, boy, I said if I ever catch you up on them pipes again it'll be straight up to that office as fast as your legs can carry you and we'll see how much you'll hear then. We'll see how much you'll hear then!"

He shook his head and fiddled with the jangling bunch of keys in his hand then all of a sudden turned to Malachy and cried "There you are! I was wondering if I could have a word with you in the office?"

The next thing Malachy knew, the door was closing behind the headmaster and Mr Boylan was staring into his Tupperware box with a sort of grin on his face because he knew that Mr Bell was cross over something. You always knew that he was cross by the kind of voice he used. And he was cross now. Mr Boylan wasn't annoyed that he was cross or anything like that. He was happy actually. Very happy in fact. That was why he looked over at Malachy and said with his eyes "You see? Now you see, don't you? None of this would have happened if you hadn't taken my cup."

In Loco Parentis

Behind the door hung a map of Ireland and upon the wall stood the Pope blessing the multitude in St Peter's Square. Over the window rested a St Brigid's Cross fashioned from rushes and beside it the charcoal heads of the seven men who had taken on the might of the British Empire and struck for Ireland's freedom. And looking down over all, little St Anthony standing on his plinth with two chipped fingers upraised and sadness in his eyes as Mr Bell shone his glasses and looked away from Malachy. There was a slight tremor in his right arm which he steadied by gripping the edge of the table between his finger and thumb. It seemed an age before he spoke. "Just what the hell is going on?" Malachy thought suddenly. "Why is he calling me up here like a bloody seven year old?" He received his answer almost immediately. "I am sorry to have to say this but it is my duty to tell you that there have been a number of complaints from parents."

Malachy was dumbstruck. The headmaster continued, "I want you to know that it gives me no pleasure to say this and I would much rather it did not have to be said at all. But now that these complaints have come before me it is my responsibility to deal with them. Quite frankly, some of the parents are concerned about your, how shall I put it . . ."

He faltered in mid-sentence and turned his back on Malachy and stared off out across the playground with his fingers now laced behind his back, gathering his thoughts. A lone seagull was battling with a breadwrapper beside the toilets. He cleared his throat as he turned. "The way you dress yourself," he continued, "—many of them find it—inappropriate. And, I am sorry to have to say, so do I. At the interview you did indicate that you felt these things were important. I can only conclude that you did not mean what you said. I appreciate that certain standards may not apply in other schools. That these days there is a flexible attitude to matters such as this. I can only be honest with you and say that I fully understand the parents' views." He paused and said, almost in a whisper, "St Anthony's has always upheld the highest standards. That is why, Mr Dudgeon, they continue to send their children to us year after year. It is important that we maintain those standards."

He said nothing for a long time and then told Malachy that he was genuinely sorry he had to say these things. He too had been a young teacher once, believe it or not. He knew what it was like. "We are in loco parentis here, Mr Dudgeon," he went on. "We have duties. A relaxed attitude may be perfectly fine in college. But not here. Children need consistency. Firmness. They need someone they can look up to. Do you understand me?"

This was the test, of course. If Malachy had really been Joe Buck or Benny or any of these headbangers whose antics he spent most of his college days aping trying to impress Marion, he would have grinned from ear to ear and drawled laconically "Hell—you are quite a guy, ain't you, Mr Bell? You sure are one hell of a crazy guy. You know who you're talking to here?" But, as he knew more than anyone, he wasn't Joe Buck, was he? He was Malachy Dudgeon, that's who he was, son of Packie the biggest bollocks in the town. Which explained unequivocally why it was that he stood there like he had gone and pissed in his trousers. He could hardly hear the headmaster as he began again "Oh—and another thing. I should tell you that Mr Boylan had that class last year and Mr Keenan before him and they really have been excellent all the way through the school. Don't spoil it, Mr Dudgeon. All it takes is a firm hand. You'll get no thanks for being lax with kiddies, believe me."

The headmaster squeezed the desk with his finger and thumb. "Mr Dudgeon," he said, "there has never been any trouble whatsoever in this school right from the very first day I left St Anne's to come here in 1939. I perfectly understand the teething troubles that we must expect all young teachers to encounter. Rest assured I will give you my full support. But I must ask you for your total cooperation in the matters we have just spoken about." He cleared his throat once more and smiled. "I know we won't have to have another meeting like this. Thank you, Mr Dudgeon."

Malachy waited for a minute or two, fiddling with his fingers and looking out the window. Then he realised Bell was waiting for him to leave so he stuttered a barely audible "Thank you," then more or less fell out the door into the clattering corridor with its heady aromas of stale urine and sour milk. He stood there for over a minute not knowing what to do with himself. Then he looked up to see Mr Boylan smiling at him as he closed the door of his classroom behind him without so much as uttering a single word.

For the rest of the morning, Malachy didn't know where he was. He might as well have been hit with a hammer. All he could hear was "Teacher! Teacher!" as the little voices of the kiddies went through his head like piercing drills. By the time 3:30 came, he was just about exhausted.

He wasn't the only one of course, for hardly had he left the room before Raphael slumped into his chair with his head in his hands, desperately trying to ignore the nerve that was beginning to throb over his right eye. Yes, by the looks of things, the son of Packie Dudgeon had taken more out of Mattie and Evelyn Bell's little fellow than you might have expected, for right at that particular moment he did not seem to be quite the unshakable tower of strength that he would like you to believe. Of course it might never become common knowledge, and no doubt he would do everything in his power to ensure that it didn't, but, as he sat there with a blank sheet of paper before him, endeavouring to make a beginning to the task of applying to the Department for Class 4's visual aid grant, that, I am afraid, is unmistakably how it appeared.

Bra

Not that poor old Malachy should have to take the blame for it all, mind you. There's no point in letting Terry Krash off the hook. He has to shoulder some of the blame too.

Terry arrived on the scene in 1965, long after little Maol-seachlainn was put into the ground never to be seen again. The doctors told Raphael that there would be plenty more Maol-seachlainns but there never were. Raphael and Nessa didn't mind. They loved one another and put their trust in God. He would provide and everything would be OK. They knew it would. Then one night Raphael turned on the wireless and heard a chirpy voice saying "Hello good evening, come on in! You're very welcome to *The Terry Krash Show*, the show that's different!" The audience was laughing their heads off. One woman said to Terry—"You're shocking!" but you could tell that she didn't mean it. What she really meant was that he was great fun. And Terry knew it. That was why he said more cheeky things. The topic tonight was ladies' underwear. The sort they would wear for their boyfriends or husbands. It was the word "bra" that rooted Raphael to the spot. He felt as if someone had slapped him right across the face. Every time Terry turned to the women and asked them something, they chuckled like little girls. "Sure what is a bra only an ordinary old item of clothing—isn't that right, ladies? There's no harm in talking about that now, is there? Ah sure not at all!" They chuckled again. "You can't beat a nice bra on a girl, I always say!" he laughed. Just the sound of the word made needlepoints of sweat break out all over Raphael's back. Terry Krash might as well have been shouting "Are you listening out there, Mr Bell? Did you hear it? You didn't? Very well then, I'll say it again, just for you! Ha ha! Come on now, everyone. Bra! That's it! Bra!"

Over an hour passed before Raphael could bring himself to mention it to his wife. "I don't know what to say" were the words that came to his lips. Nessa nodded.

"I read all about it in the paper. Apparently it's going to be on twice a week. They say he's become very popular, this Krash, whoever he is."

Raphael couldn't taste the bread in his mouth. He looked at his fork as if it had stopped being a fork and he didn't know what it was now. Then he just left it down beside his untouched plate.

That night in bed, he almost cried. He thought of his mother, the lovely Evelyn, now interred in a lonely Cork grave-yard, and he thought of his father lying dead in a field as his Black and Tan murderer wiped blood off his hands with a rag.

Peyton Place

But that of course, although Raphael didn't realise it, was just the beginning. There were a hell of a lot more than Terry knocking around inside that old wireless and once that bunch got started, it sure was going to be some job trying to stop them. Not that Raphael had any intention of trying. If that was what they wanted to do, that was their own business. Their immortal souls belonged to them and no one else and who was he to try to tell them they were in danger of damning themselves for all eternity or any of the rest of it. They knew that. They knew it only too well. Obviously it saddened him but there was nothing he could do about it. All he could do was look after his boys and make sure they were kept on the straight and narrow. The last thing he was going to do was run after the likes of Terry Krash and tell him he was corrupting the youth of the country. Of course he told his boys not to listen to him and have absolutely nothing to do with him. Above all he implored them not to watch his new television show. To have nothing whatsoever to do with it. In fact he went so far as to implore them to have nothing to do with television, full stop. He told them it would poison their young minds. Television was full of false promises and dreams that could never be realised. It promoted a lifestyle that was alien to the Irish people. More and more he had come to see this.

On one occasion, in a hotel bar, he had been asked to switch it on, and found himself confronted by a young, very beautiful woman who had not only left her husband for another man but was openly boasting about it. She tossed back her hair and laughed as she described the man with whom she had taken marriage vows as a "silly old fool." As he stared at the screen, the woman slowly faded and a nerve began to tick over his right eye. He got a pain in his head. He had to go home and lie down. Nessa came into the bedroom and asked him was he all right. "Yes. Yes I am of course," he replied. But he wasn't. He wasn't right at all.

When he came back downstairs, he thanked Nessa for the cup of tea she had made him and found himself leafing through the TV pages of *The Irish Independent*. Another woman looked out at him. A woman wearing heavy eye shadow and a nightdress that barely concealed her body. Directly beneath her, the words *"Peyton Place*—the sensational, saucy secrets of suburbia." He felt sick.

That was why he shouted at the Clarke boy the following day. Because he knew that if he did not pull himself up, that was the loose sort of filth he would end up watching. "You must have respect for yourself, Clarke! Do you hear me? Apply yourself! Sloth has no place in this classroom—in this school! Do you hear what I am saying to you?"

Clarke lowered his head and bit his lip as he tried to stop the tears that came to his eyes.

"Yes, sir," he replied hoarsely as Raphael licked the chalk and, telling him to go back to his desk, wrote the names of the nine counties of Ulster on the blackboard.

Coyle

Perhaps the saddest day of Raphael's life—after Maolseachlainn's death—was the day he met young Coyle in O'Connell Street. He had been in Marlborough Street ordering some new books and was on his way to Walton's music shop to purchase the sheet music of "Has Sorrow Thy Young Days Shaded?" which he intended to begin with the class the following week, when a wildeyed figure appeared out of nowhere with its hand stuck out and saliva literally dribbling from its lips. Raphael's first inclination was to push past and go on about his business for he was in a hurry anyway, but then something happened. Wild as the youth's eyes were, something flashed in them and the moment he saw it, Raphael felt the blood drain from his face and it was then that he recognised Donal Coyle. Or what had once been Donal Coyle, for what he saw standing before him bore no resemblance to the happy, brighteyed little boy who used to do the savings stamps with him on Friday afternoons. Raphael fumbled awkwardly for money and then it dawned on him that Donal Coyle had recognised him too. The youth began to stammer. "I'm sorry," he said and turned away. Raphael could not believe it but there was a smell off him. The straggly beard was dirty and matted. "I'm sorry," he said again as he backed away and by the time Raphael called out "Donal! Donal Coyle! Come back here!" it was already too late for he had been swallowed up by the teeming crowd.

That night, he didn't sleep a wink. He kept thinking of the young boy sitting there at the back of the class, third from the left with his head down and his tongue out as he clasped the wooden pen in his right hand, working away like a little beaver. He was a great little fellow. "How many nines in seven hundred and thirty eight, Donal?" "Eighty-two, sir." "Excellent. Very good indeed. If you were all like Donal, you pack of lazy scoundrels!"

Another night, he dreamed about him. Donal was sitting in that same desk, dragging a razor blade up and down his arm. He looked up at Raphael with his eyes still wild and his scraggy mane of hair worse than ever. Then he just went on drawing ragged bloody lines along his arm as if the headmaster wasn't in the room.

The Walton Programme

There was nothing Raphael and Father Des liked better than *The Walton Programme*. Every Saturday afternoon the priest would drop by and he'd have a cup of tea and a scone and listen to the bold Leo Maguire introducing the ballads of long ago with "This is *The Walton Programme*, brought to you by your weekly reminders of the grace and beauty that lie in our heritage of Irish song—the songs our fathers loved." One day they played "God Save Ireland" and Raphael nearly hit the roof. "Man, but I love that programme," he'd say. Sometimes Nessa joined them. But she was more for John Field and the classical stuff.

When they played the songs of old, it was hard not to think

of the reaping race and the day they carried his father shoulder high across the fields. It was hard for him to stop his eyes misting over when he thought of all those good times that were gone. But when they played "The Boys Of The Old Brigade" and "The Rifles Of The IRA," he smiled again. Smiled because he was proud. The Black and Tans had tried to make his father bend the knee but he wouldn't and didn't because his name was Bell. A proud and noble soldier who died a noble death in an Irish field beneath an Irish sky.

"What would we do without it every Saturday?" said Father Des one day as he was leaving. "Leo Maguire and *The Walton Programme.*"

"And now it's time for Charlie McGee with *The Homes of Donegal,*" laughed Raphael as he got up out of his chair and added "Are you sure you won't stay for another drop of tea, Father?"

"No," replied Father Stokes, "I'd be as well get back to my duties for if the boss hears I was gadding about here again he'll have my life."

"No rest for the wicked," chirped Raphael as he led him to the door.

"Goodbye, Nessa!" called the priest as he pulled on his overcoat. "See you next Saturday!"

Raphael noticed that Nessa's gladioli were coming on great as he hummed the programme's signature tune absentmindedly to himself and smiled at a neighbour who was waving from across the road.

Bomb

Two years after Neil Armstrong came back from his travels, a young boy went into a shop. "I want two penny chews, a packet of wine gums and a bottle of lemonade please," he said and was blown to bits. Raphael read about it in the paper. The shopkeeper got blown up too. There was a photograph of them both with sheets over them. You could see the young fellow's shoes and socks. Underneath the photo it said the IRA had done it. Raphael went crazy. He said they couldn't have done it. He said to Nessa "They couldn't have!" But when he mentioned it to Father Des, the priest replied "Oh they did it all right. It was on the news. There's no question about it."

After that, Raphael just stood there because he couldn't think of anything to say. He just stood there scraping the top of his index finger with his thumbnail.

Atrocities

Raphael was telling his boys the story his own uncle Joe had told him about the day his daddy went off to blow up the British soldiers. They hid the bomb in a culvert and went off up the fields to watch and wait for the convoy. They waited for over an hour and then glory be to God what happened, didn't a couple of little lads like yourselves come along and start playing right beside the culvert where they had put the bomb. And the convoy about to arrive at any minute! But do you know what they did, boys? Do you know what those men did? They called the whole thing off. They called it off right there and then and went home. And do you know why, boys? Because those men would not stoop so low as to kill children. Do you understand me, boys? Do you understand me!

With one voice, the boys replied "Yes!" and Raphael stood

before them, as he always did now when he had read of some new atrocity in the papers, which seemed to be practically every other day now, with the eyes in his head nearly as wild as young Coyle's, or should I say old Coyle's, because of course young Coyle was dead wasn't he, or at least the young boy he had once known, and all the big plans he had for himself, and Raphael too, no more than dust blown away by the breeze.

Horses With Melting Eyes

Which was deeply troubling of course, just as the dream about Uncle Joe's horses was the night Raphael woke up with the sweat hopping off him crying "Nessa! Nessa!"

It was a strange dream into which Uncle Joe had come once more, inviting young Raphael—that is, the Raphael of the old pre–St Martin's altar boy days—over to his house to help him look after his beloved horses. When he said it, little Raphael nearly had a heart attack on the spot and pleaded with his daddy who had never ever looked so happy and alive and smiling as on that sunny day in the dream. "Oh please! Please let me go with Uncle Joe to help look after his horses!" When his daddy saw how excited he was, a twinkle came into his eyes and he started teasing Raphael saying "Oh no I don't know now. We'll have to ask your mother about this!" But then Evelyn hit him a sort of pretend slap on the arm and said to him "Would you go away out of that, Mattie Bell, and not be teasing the child. Of course you can go, our Raphael!"

Well what a happy day that was with Uncle Joe chucking the reins and sucking his pipe and the blue smoke floating in the air as the pony trot-trotted along and Uncle Joe whistled a little tune and said "Wait till you see the new fellow I have, Raphael.

Sounder Man; a lovely shiny black coat on him and as good a horse as ever I paid money for."

Raphael smiled. He liked the way his Uncle Joe talked about his horses. He loved them you see. That was why he talked like that about them, calling them by their first names as if they were his children. Once Raphael heard his father saying "If a wife got half the attention he gives them horses, she'd be made up." Uncle Joe knew he said things like that, but he didn't mind. "I have no time to be tricking about with women, Mattie," he said. "I have enough to do looking after these beauties of mine."

And was he right about that for if ever horses were beauties, these were. Their manes combed to perfection, their flanks glistening and polished as they stood erect and stately in their spotless stalls. At least until the night the scream came and Raphael shot up in his bed to hear Uncle Joe thundering down the stairs and crying hysterically "My horses! My horses!"

By the time they got out into the yard, it was already too late. The flames were leaping into the sky and the pitiful neighing of horses that knew they were going to die shrieked out into the night. Uncle Joe was wandering around in circles crying "What are we going to do? What are we going to do?" You could feel the heat on your face. Tiny stars of soot went floating by. The roof caved in with a crash. "What are we going to do?" wept Uncle Joe, still turning round in circles. Raphael tried to say something but found that he was suddenly, inexplicably mute. The head of a horse appeared in the half-door. Its eyes gleamed silver. They gleamed silver for a split second and then they were gone. Literally gone because they dribbled down its face like water. Raphael prayed oh please God because he could not bear to think of them all inside with their shiny eyes melting in their heads and their flesh burning up, cooking away like meat on the stove as they helplessly pawed the air with their hooves.

It was hard to believe it but Uncle Joe was laughing now. He was looking over at Raphael and pointing to the stables, repeating "Meat! Cooked meat—can you believe it?" He'd mutter for a bit, then start laughing again, going on about cooked meat and melting eyes. He shook Raphael. "My beautiful horses —can you believe this is how they ended up? Can you believe it? Dear oh dear!"

When the burning was over, it was hard to know which was worse, the piercing silence that followed, or the relentless choking pleas of dying beasts. Raphael didn't know what to do, where to go or where to look and was still rooted to the spot five minutes later when he looked up and saw a man in a mask emerging from the charred shell of the barn. He was like something from another world as he walked towards them humming a tune and stood in front of them saying "Well—what do you think of my handiwork? Impressive, eh?"

What made Raphael go cold all over was the fact that he recognised the voice. It had a pretty bad effect on Uncle Joe too because he just stood there with his lip hanging and trying to get his tongue around words that wriggled like eels in his mouth. He was still stuttering and stammering when the mask came off and Raphael found himself looking into the eyes of his own father. One of the eyes winked as he said "Well—what do you think, Raphael? Not bad, eh?" A coil of smoke rose slowly and a lump of masonry fell to earth. Mattie smiled then winked again. "Wait," he said, "I have something for you."

He put his hand in his pocket and extended his closed fist to his son. "Close your eyes and open them again to see what the good Lord will send you!" he said and so petrified was Raphael, he did exactly that. And, why, he found a piece of burnt meat sitting in his hand when he opened his eyes again. Mattie was laughing his head off now. His laughter was even louder than the death-cries of the horses. "Cooked fucking horse!" he shouted.

Raphael had never heard his father cursing before. That was how he knew it wasn't his father. Somehow Mattie knew what he was thinking and that made him laugh even more. "Oh but I am your father," he taunted. "I'm your father all right and I always will be, forever and ever, little Raphael, my boy!"

When Raphael looked again he had the mask back on and all you could see were two dead eyes staring out through the slits in the black wool. Behind him all was quiet now except for Uncle Joe laughing and muttering to himself "First you have horses and then you have none! First you have horses and then you have none!"

When Nessa awoke she was astonished to find her husband shouting into her face "My father never hurt horses! My father never hurt horses!" She tried to calm him down. It took her a long time, mind, for he was in quite a state. He kept complaining of a pain in his head and there was sweat all over him. She made him a cup of hot cocoa and they sat in the kitchen together until the fever or whatever it was had passed. Then they went back to bed and he hugged her like a baby.

Another night he dreamed of the Black and Tan and his father in the field. The Black and Tan had a gun in his father's mouth, "You murderer! You fucking murderer!" he was snarling. "You and your murdering Shinner mates crippled my best friend! You blew his legs off! He can't walk, you bastard! He can't even shit by himself! And *you* did it!" Raphael waited for his daddy to say "No!" To cry out "It's a lie!" But he never did. All he did was smile at the Black and Tan. All he did was smile and the smile didn't mean "No, I didn't. You've got it all wrong!" It meant "So what if I did?"

Raphael did not like those dreams. He did not like them at all. Without Nessa he wouldn't have known what to do. He might have gone out of his mind.

A Groovy Way Of Thinking

Which of course wouldn't have bothered Terry Krash and the rest of them one bit for by the looks of things that was what they were hell bent on doing. It wasn't enough for him to be on the wireless. Now that he was on both the radio and the television and you literally couldn't move without him squawking at you. The latest was sex before marriage. According to Terry, this was great altogether. He had two girls on the show and they were all for it. "Oh yes," one of them said, "as far as we're concerned, marriage is for the birds. We like to play the field, know what I mean? Travel the world and have a good time—that's our motto! Oh sure marriage is OK for other folks maybe—but not for us!"

Well isn't it a wonder Terry doesn't give them a medal, thought Raphael, he's so excited. "Good girls!" cried Terry. "You certainly got a groovy way of thinking!"

One day Raphael picked up the paper. By all accounts they were having good fun in the midlands. There was a big festival on down there. A motorbike had been thrown through a window. And what was this? An old lady assaulted and beaten? And all her money taken? Hmm. And what's this? The offender gets off with a caution. Raphael knew what he'd have done with him. What he did with Lally all those years before. Then by God we'd see how many old ladies he'd rob. And the same with the murderers who were slaughtering and maiming in the name of Ireland. He knew what he'd do with them too. "I'd horsewhip them, Nessa!" he cried. "For that's all they deserve. Murderers —for that's what they are, Nessa!"

Nessa smiled and said they weren't worth bothering about. When he relaxed he realised that she was right. Then he said "That bloody pain in my head, I can't seem to shift it." Nessa stroked his forehead. "Whereabouts is it?" she asked. He showed her the spot. Just over his eye. She kissed it softly. "Oh Nessa," he said and touched her on the arm.

A Letter Of Complaint

Raphael getting pains in the head was all very well but if he thought that was going to stop Terry Krash and all his buddies then he had another think coming. When he came home for his lunch one day, he switched on the wireless to hear them all laughing about *The Walton Programme*. They were saying that the songs on it were a load of rubbish. "Who wants to hear a bunch of old songs about bogmen sitting by turf fires?" said one young whippersnapper. "What would be your favourite programme then?" asked Terry. "Oh—*Pick Of The Pops!*" said the whippersnapper. "It's just terrific!" "Indeed it is," cried Terry. "And now we have our own pick of the pops with the fabulous Roy Wood and Wizzard—take it away, Roy!"

When he went back to school that afternoon, he told Father Stokes and they decided there and then to act. It wasn't as if they were furious or anything. They just didn't see why someone should be allowed to insult the programme over the airwaves. And not only that but be encouraged to do so, which they plainly were. After the schoolchildren had gone the two of them spent well over an hour writing a letter of complaint to RTE radio, which Raphael himself posted on the way home.

They expected some sort of acknowledgment but none ever came. They might as well have thrown the letter into the river for all the difference it made. This upset Raphael. He had wanted some sort of reply. Someone to say that maybe it had been a bit insulting or at the very least, insensitive. But I'm afraid he'd be waiting a long time if he was expecting a few words of apology from Terry. In fact, not only did they receive no apology but the following week he made another scurrilous remark about the programme. Referring to some outdated appliance, he said that it had "Gone out with the ark—like *The Walton Programme*!" Everyone in the studio thought this was the funniest thing out.

Which I'm afraid Raphael didn't, as you can imagine. In fact he got quite depressed. Nessa noticed. For quite a while afterwards he was gloomy and withdrawn. He remained in his study much longer than usual—two hours at a stretch was as much as he had ever spent in there before—and Nessa knew well that he wasn't correcting homework or preparing lessons all that time. This state of affairs caused her some concern and that was why she mentioned it to Father Stokes. "Let me talk to him," said the priest "—worrying his head about the likes of those people." The two men were pacing the playground together some days later when Father Des said "If you let them annoy you, Raphael, sure what are you doing only playing into their hands?"

When Raphael had given it some thought, he could see that the priest was indeed right and he began to cheer up considerably. He had more to do with his time than worry about the likes of them. Hadn't he a school to run, for God's sake, a school full of boys whose futures he had to mould and whose characters he had to build, a school which was, and acknowledged as such, a light on the hill, a fortress buffeted by the winds of change and caprice and modish fancy, against which it had, no more than if it had been fortified by walls of concrete three feet thick, always remained firm and resolute, and would have continued doing so until the day the Good Lord decided to call Raphael Bell to his eternal reward, but for the arrival not so very long afterwards of Evans the Abortionist and Dudgeon the Incompetent who between them took everything he had and, with the same callous dedication of a torch-bearing saboteur who had once visited the midnight stables of a dream, burnt to the ground.

Trouble For Dudgy

The ridiculous thing is that Malachy fully intended to do what Raphael said. He really did. He knew that things had been getting on top of him a bit in the class and if dickeying himself up and coming the heavy a bit would do the trick well so be it. It was just a pity that Marion couldn't seem to understand what he was up to at all, practically laughing her head off when she saw him in the new suit. She thought he was joking. She said he had to be. "You can't be serious," she said, "Joe Buck goes straight— it's just too much." Then she went off into the kitchen laughing away to herself. But then of course, it was easy enough for her to laugh seeing as she had been lucky enough to land herself a job in a great school with a staff who had a ball and kids a monkey could discipline. Which was a lot more than you could say for Class 3 I'm afraid, especially Kyle Collins and Stephen Webb and Pat Hourican who went out of their way to get Malachy going. One day he even heard Pat saying "Let's make trouble for Dudgy."

Dudgy—that was what they called him. "Here comes Dudgy," they said. When he was writing on the blackboard, he often heard Pat sniggering. He knew it was him beyond all shadow of doubt. But he was very hard to catch. When you'd turn around and shout "Hourican!" he'd just go on sitting there as sweet as pie, writing away. Then he'd smile and say "Me, sir?"

Hard to believe that you could wake up in the middle of the night with sweat all over you, thinking about something like that. If someone in the college had told him that six months before, he would have laughed at them. He would have laughed his head off. He would have said it could never happen. He would have gone further, in fact. He would have said "You're out of your tiny mind, my friend," or worse. But it did happen. Oh yes. And not just once or twice either.

Realistically of course, it would have been far better in the long run if he had been straight with Marion and told her what was happening to him, that the class was getting out of hand and the place was on his mind all the time. But he didn't. Mainly because he was afraid she might say "You must be kidding. Joe Buck's worrying about a bunch of kids? You don't expect me to believe that, do you?" So he just kept his mouth shut about the palpitations and night sweats and went on grinning like it was a great old joke every time she said he was turning into a right old fuddy-duddy schoolmaster.

So what if that's the way it looked—just so long as he could get things back on an even keel. Sort out the class and keep the parents and Bell off his back so that everything could be the way it was before. When he was cool as a breeze and didn't give a shit, when the sun shone down as he lay on the grass and Marion laughed at some stupid thing he'd done somewhere, her head tilted back and her eyes twinkling the way they did, his fingers running through her soft strawberry blonde hair as they both laughed until they just weren't fit to laugh anymore.

Evans

Unfortunately however, as time went on, laughing came into the picture less and less I'm afraid, for the son of Mr and Mrs Bell as much as Malachy. I mean if someone in training college in 1931 or '32 had said to Raphael "You're going to work your back off for the children of Ireland and it's all going to be destroyed on you by a woman who had an abortion," he would have laughed himself sick. If he had even known what an abortion was, which he didn't. If there were such things as abortions in 1932, then Raphael Bell didn't know about them. He was too busy saying the rosary with Paschal O'Dowd and running around the place visiting the sick. But he'd find out soon enough what it was. He'd find out soon enough surely, like on the day when Evans came breezing into his office swinging a bag if you don't mind, and tossing her hair and going "Hi-yah!" to him, like he was some kind of a go-boy she might meet at a dance. The minute he saw her he disliked her. You couldn't blame him. She made him! What did she think—she owned the school or something?

Once she started talking, you couldn't stop her. Plans and schemes and ideas came spewing right out of her mouth like mad tickertape. It was unbelievable! By the time she'd finished, Raphael was drained. He had a pain in his head. "Well, what do you think?" she said, and tossed her hair again. Raphael's mouth dried up as he stared at the woman in front of him. She was wearing huge golden hoop earrings and flared blue jeans. In her lap, a leather handbag. With native Indian markings on it. Raphael felt sick all of a sudden. It was bad enough a Parents' Committee being set up in the first place, thanks to ridiculous, newfangled Department Of Education regulations, but to send this—*this!*—as their representative—he quite simply couldn't believe it. He felt dizzy. "Some of the parents at the meeting thought it would be a good idea," she said. She was talking about noncompetitive sport. She wanted it introduced to his school. She wanted compulsory games banned. That was what she was saying to Raphael. Out of nowhere he heard the cheer as the referee blew his whistle and the boys of St Anthony's lifted their captain up on high, in the All-Ireland Junior Schools' Championships of 1955. That was what came into his head as she sat across from him, smiling, the smell of her patchouli perfume filling the office. And as she sat there in silence with her big inquisitive eyes looking him up and down as she waited for his answer, he realised that her smell, and what she had just said, upset him so much he felt like punching her in the face.

Frogspawn

What was Malachy doing now for God's sake, Marion wanted to know. He said he was doing the life cycle of the frog. Kneeling on the floor colouring in little dots in the middle of circles. Frogspawn—lots and lots of it on a big chart for all the kiddies in Class 3. Who can tell me how long a tadpole stays a tadpole? What about you, Michael? Come on now—good boy! And you, Thomas—can you tell me anything about our little friend the tadpole? What about his legs for instance? How many has he? Good boy, Thomas—you can do it when you want to. Up with you now to the top of the class like a good boy!

"You've been at it for the last two hours," Marion said. "I know," said Malachy, "but if I haven't it prepared he'll be down on me like a ton of bricks." "Who will?" she wanted to know. "Bell," said Malachy. "Oh for God's sake," she said "—Bell. Come on, Malachy, wise up. You're overdoing it." "You don't know what he's like," he said. "Oh I do," said Marion, "or I should at any rate, considering he's all you ever go on about these days. Him and that school of his and that bloody class."

He didn't like it when she said that, and grunted. She didn't like his grunt much either and snapped at him. "It's only a job, Malachy," she said. "I mean it's not the end of the world if they don't know where the tadpole eats and shits, you know what I mean?" Malachy knew what she meant. He wasn't stupid. And she was right—of course she was. But then she didn't have Bell coming in and out of her classroom every minute of the bloody day hoping to catch her on the hop. Which was all he did now, ever since he had decided that there had been no sign of real improvement since their office meeting. You never knew when the tap would come on the door and you'd look up and there he'd be again, shining up his specs and glaring at you like you were fucking handicapped or something.

Maybe if Bell had left him alone for a while and let him get on with it, he might actually have been able to turn the situation around, or at the very least, stopped everything from going down the fucking drain. Sadly however, he didn't, and that was exactly what happened. Half the time, Malachy didn't realise he was shouting at the kids at all. But he was. He was shouting all right. At times, you could hear him roaring away like a man possessed. "Sit down!" he'd bawl, and "Shut up!" or "For the last time do you hear me!"

Not that the kids objected, mind you. They didn't object at all. They thought it was great fun. In the playground, they said to their pals "All you have to do to drive Dudgy mad is go 'psst! psst!' If you do that he goes all red and starts shouting at you."

All the kids were jealous of Class 3. They were jealous because they wanted a master like that too. They wanted one who would go mad every time you did something, not like Mr Bell or Mr Boylan or any of the other teachers who could scare the life out of you with just one look. They were no good. Dudgy was the best. One day Class 3 came in and some boy had written "Dudgy is stupid" on the blackboard. You should have heard the laughs of everyone! It was fantastic! Dudgy didn't know what to do. He got all red and wiped it off—then told everyone to take out their sums. This was the best ever because you could see everyone laughing in behind their desk lids and Kyle Collins making the words "Dudgy is stupid" with his lips and then chuckling away into his hands.

Yes—perhaps if Marion had been forced to spend a couple of weeks with that kind of behaviour, she might have started to see things a bit more clearly. Why barely six months before, Malachy was one kind of person and now he was another. Why it wasn't so easy to go out on the town every bloody night of the week drinking vodka when you were going to wake up with a hangover and then have to go in and face all that bullshit. He tried his best to explain it to her but it was no use. "Oh for Christ's sake, Malachy, I'm working hard all day—I don't want to stay cooped up in this bloody place!" she said.

She went on asking him for a while but he always had some excuse so in the end it didn't really come as a surprise to either of them when she said she was going to a gig with some of the staff from school and wouldn't be home till very late that night. She asked him did he mind. Of course not, he said. And he didn't. That was what he wanted her to do, because he knew all this was temporary. Of course it was. It had to be. In a couple of months time, it would be all sorted out and things would be back to normal. Before she went, she said one last time "Are you sure you don't mind me going out?" Maybe she was half-hoping he would say "No—don't go!" or "You're not going without *me*!" or something like that, anything that might ignite the old spark. But he didn't of course. His head was too full of frogspawn to do something sensible like that. Which was a pity, because it was never really the same again after that night.

"You go right ahead. You do that," he said. So she did. She went off to The Baggot Inn to meet her mates. They were with a band called The Electric Strangers. One of the girls knew Paddy Meehan the guitarist, a big guy with a mane of curly hair and an earring. Everybody loved Paddy. He was a real character, and, as they said, could he play that "axe." He was great fun to be with. After the gig, they all went to The Granary, a restaurant beside The Project Theatre in East Essex Street. Marion had a whale of a time. It was the best night she had had in months.

When she came home in the early hours, she was in flying form. "Pissed as a newt," she said, tearing off her blouse. She let a yelp out of her, climbing in beside him and covering him all over in kisses. "Make love to me the way you did the night we met Philly Fuckface. Make love to me the way you did that night, my darling Mal oh my darling Malachy Dudgeon." Malachy smiled when she said that. He felt good remembering that night. And he turned to her and took her in his arms but it was no use. It didn't happen. All he could think of was "Eight o'clock. Eight o'clock I've got to get up and go into that fucking place." She touched the hairs on the back of his neck and said that it didn't matter. But it did, of course. Of course it mattered. Outside a broken burglar alarm started up, needling mercilessly into the night.

Mammies

All the mammies were busy as bees chatting away and talking about all the little kiddies as Malachy came trotting in the school gates with his big briefcase under his arm. There was Kyle's mammy, Mrs Collins, and Stephen's mammy and Pat's mammy and young Nicholson's mammy. Lots of mammies. "Hello," they all said to Malachy as he went past. "Hello," replied Malachy with a big smile. They all smiled back and off he went again with his big case and his smile. Then Mrs Webb called "Oh—Mr Dudgeon—could I have a word, please?" Malachy said OK yes but of course he wondered what it's about this time? You like words don't you, Mrs Webb, you're very fond of them aren't you, you and your words. He didn't say that of course—I mean he didn't want her running off to Mr Bell now did he, getting him into more trouble. No. What he said instead was "What can I do for you, Mrs Webb?" at which point Mrs Webb took out Stephen's copybook and said "It's this sum here." Malachy didn't know what she meant. Which was why he said "Yes?"

Mrs Webb looked incredulous. "You've marked it correct." "Yes," said Malachy again. The other mammies smiled and laughed and looked away. One mammy looked at her shoes. "It isn't correct. It's wrong."

As indeed it was. Poor old Malachy—that was another thing that hadn't been so good lately—the old concentration. Because of the noise in the class you see. Even when it was quiet at home in the flat he could still hear the shouting and the banging of desks and the clacking of rulers. And of course the "psst pssts." That was what made him make mistakes. It wasn't that he was stupid or anything. Oh no. Just that he was a bit shaky and jittery and absentminded, that's all.

He probably would have been able to talk his way out, if a certain person hadn't happened along. If Bell hadn't gone and stuck his big nose in, blustering across the playground with his keys and his big bald head. Webb had to go and blab to him, didn't she, she had to go and open her big mouth she had to go and open her big fucking mouth.

"It's this sum of Stephen's," she said to Bell as she showed him the copybook. "It's wrong you see. But the teacher has marked it correct."

Malachy got a look that would take paint off a gate. Mammies galore staring at him and Bell glaring like a madman. Now wasn't that a nice little interlude with which to begin your day's work?

Not to mention having to face the little cur who had caused all the trouble in the first place, Mr Smart Alec Webb. His interfering mother would make a fool of you when you made a tiny mistake, she'd do that all right, but where was she when Webb was trying his best to destroy the class, where was she then oh no she wasn't to be seen then, Webb fucking Webb and her stupid son butter wouldn't melt in his mouth well by God let him try any of his tricks this morning and we'll see how far he'll get. We'll see how far he'll get this morning, said Malachy to himself as he unzipped his briefcase and eyeballed at the class as they filed into their seats.

"Take your hands out of your pockets!" he barked as he clicked his fingers. "Do you hear me?"

"Me, sir?" asked Stephen Webb.

Oh for God's sake. Malachy felt like bursting out laughing. Me, sir. Could you believe it? I mean, could you even begin to believe it?

"Yes, sir—you, sir!" snapped Malachy. "Stand up when I'm talking to you!"

The way he stood up—real slow, to drive you mad! And then that stupid, sickly sweet voice. And the big innocent face with its angelic kiss curl falling down over his stupid big eyes.

"Take your hands out of your pockets I told you!"

"Sir, my hands aren't in my pockets," said Stephen.

"I see. Not in your pockets."

Malachy was grinning now. What a little spoilt brat Webb was when you thought about it!

"No, sir," said Webb as he twiddled with his fingers.

"Of course they're not," laughed Malachy. "Sure how would they be in your pockets? God bless us, Stephen, sure a good boy like you would never put your hands in your pockets now would you?"

Stephen smiled and dropped his eyelids like he did when he wanted to say "I'm mammy's favourite!"

"No, sir," he said and Pat Hourican chuckled behind his hands. Very well. Chuckle, Pat, Malachy said to himself, I'll deal with you in my own good time.

Then he went back to Stephen. "And I suppose you're going to tell me that you weren't laughing when I came in?"

"Laughing, sir?" replied Webb.

"Yes, laughing. You know—laughing."

"Sir, I wasn't laughing."

"Sir, I wasn't laughing."

"No, sir."

"Oh but you were you see."

"No, sir, I wasn't."

"You weren't laughing?"

"No, sir."

"You're going to tell me you weren't laughing?"

"No, sir. I wasn't."

Malachy could see Hourican giggling away behind his hand with his shiny black imitation Beatles hair hanging down in front of his face.

"You really do think you have got an answer for everything, don't you, Stephen?" Malachy said.

"No, sir," Stephen said.

"Oh but you do, sir."

"No, sir."

Malachy spread his fingers on the desk.

"Sit down please," he said, staring right into Stephen's eyes. Then he grinned again. He grinned right at him. It was hard not to laugh aloud. It really was. The little upstart really thought he could best him. He really did. What an idiot! "I mean—what an idiot!" Malachy said to himself. "I mean just how stupid can you get!" He shook his head and if there weren't tears in his eyes it wouldn't be long before there were. Then he said "Marion!" What did he say that for? He didn't know. Who cared? He could say what he liked. It didn't matter. Phew. Oh boy. What are you looking at, Webb?

Webb was looking up at him with big stupid eyes. Oh Webb, you stupid fool. You useless little good for nothing fool. Do you know what? I'm an idiot for even wasting my time talking to you. Kiss curl! Ha ha ha! Don't make me laugh, Mr Kiss Curl! Ha ha ha! Dear oh dear oh dear.

Sandwiches

Disaster had struck and there seemed to be no way out. Mr Boylan had forgotten his sandwiches. The night before, his wife had made him a packet and put them into his briefcase. What kind of sandwiches were they, Mr Keenan wanted to know. Mr Boylan went "Hmm" and thought for a minute or two. Then he said "Ham." Then he changed his mind and said they were egg. Then he changed his mind again and said they were beef. Then it was salad. Then it was back to beef again. He settled for beef. Then on with the story.

What happened was that after breakfast he decided he didn't want beef, took out the packet of sandwiches and made himself some new ones—this time tomato and cheese. Because there was a football match on that evening, he made himself some extra. "I think I made six altogether," he said. "Six?" croaked Mr Keenan. "Yes," replied Mr Boylan and continued. "So anyway I had them all prepared and wrapped in tinfoil and everything and when I come in this morning—what do I find?" He upturned his Tupperware box. It was completely empty. Mr Keenan's jaw dropped. "Nothing!" he gasped.

Mr Boylan shook his head.

What had transpired was that his own car was out of action, and he was expecting a lift, but as soon as he heard the toot of the horn outside, he had found himself in such a state of confusion, between saying goodbye to his wife and grabbing his coat, that he had left not only the beef behind but also the tomato and cheese. He shook his head again and stared wearily into the desolate nothingness of the Tupperware container. "What class of a cod am I at all?" he wondered.

Everyone sighed. It was a dreadful thing to have happened. But they all sympathised with him. Many's the time the same thing happened to ourselves, they said.

After that, they all shared their lunches with him and he cheered up considerably. "All's well that ends well," he said.

Malachy didn't say anything. He was too busy staring out the window thinking about Webb and Collins. He was eating a sandwich too. Not that it made any difference what he was eating. He might as well have been eating a slice of cardboard for all he could taste of it.

Snowflakes

The kiddies were lined up in the playground, all neat and tidy with their starched white shirts and their red ties and their rosary beads.

Mr Bell paced up and down with the bell covering his hand like a big brass boxing glove. The silence in the playground was immense. Cranky seagulls hobbled about fighting over crusts and crisp bags. Mr Bell was waiting. Even though everyone was quiet, it still wasn't good enough for him. He waited one minute then two minutes then three minutes. It was hard to say for certain how many minutes he waited. Then he cleared his throat and seemed to look into everybody's eyes at once as he said "Do you realise what I have spent my morning doing? Do you realise I have spent my whole morning down on my hands and knees scrubbing the boys' toilets? Do you realise that! How many times have I told you that you are not allowed to do wee wees on those seats! How many times! Are you animals? Is that what we have in the school—animals? I don't know the culprits now but by God if I ever find out life will not be worth living for those boys! It will not be worth living—do you hear me!" Suddenly he roared "Pick up that paper!"

A boy out of Mr Boylan's class picked it up and dropped it into the wire wastebasket. Mr Boylan glowed with pride.

Then Mr Bell said they could go inside. He was looking at Malachy's class like a hawk of course but the joke was on him because they filed in as good as gold. After they had said the prayer, the boys sat down as quiet as mice. It was time to do some spellings so Malachy said "Take out your spelling books." He always gave them twenty spellings in the test. He started off with the easy ones first, getting harder as they went along. The last word on the test was "incident." That would fox them for sure. Then he said "Turn your books face down" and started correcting them one by one. Some of the boys got very good marks indeed. Tom got fifteen. Eamon got sixteen would you believe and Pearse and Seamus a terrific nineteen each!

Kyle Collins was "pssting" over to Webb but Malachy just

ignored him. He had about had it with Collins. If he wanted to waste his time at school, why should he worry? So when he had Kyle's marked, he beamed and said sarcastically "Well done, Kyle—five marks!"

After Kyle he marked Joseph Hanratty's and then Stephen Webb's. Was there no end to the boy's impertinence? Looking over at Collins trying to make him laugh when his teacher was correcting his spellings. It was hard to believe. Trying to make another boy laugh while his teacher was standing right beside him! With that stupid smirk of his. Oh for God's sake! laughed Malachy to himself and threw the copybook down on the desk. He clicked his pen and said "My, my, Stephen, you have worked hard haven't you?"

"Oh yes, Mr Dudgeon," replied Mr Kiss-Curl-Butter-Wouldn't-Melt In-My-Mouth-Oh-No.

"You have indeed," continued Malachy. "I mean your work is so neat isn't it?"

"Yes, teacher," said Stephen.

Malachy chuckled. You should have seen Stephen's face when he did that. You didn't expect your teacher to chuckle when he was talking about spellings, did you? You certainly didn't! Stephen was taken so much by surprise that he was at a loss for words—and that was something you didn't see very often! Malachy smiled and then chuckled softly again.

"Your work is definitely neat and no mistake, Stephen," he said. Then he lifted up the copybook and showed it to the children.

"Look how neat it is, everybody! Look!"

They all looked up to see and then Malachy tore off a little piece at the corner of the page. Just a tiny piece. It fluttered down and landed on top of Stephen's head. Then he tore off another piece and another piece and they all landed on Stephen's head like little paper snowflakes. He could have gone on doing that till doomsday but he had far more to do than waste his time on the likes of Webb so he told them to take out their maths books. "Right," he said, "who can tell me how many sixes there are in seventy-two?"

Young Reilly's hand was up like a shot.

"Yes, Martin. How many do you think?" said Malachy.

"Twelve," replied Martin excitedly.

"Correct!" Malachy said and wrote it on the blackboard— 12. Then he told Martin to sit down. He tried not to look down at Webb because if he did he wouldn't be able to keep in the laughing, the stupid-looking brat sitting there with the pretend-snowflakes all over his head and his big eyes looking up why me sir I did nothing sir oh would you just shut up Webb you stupid little bollocks for that's all you are you see ha ha ha!

————————

Reclaim The Night

Meanwhile Evans carried on with her plan to destabilise the school. Which, as far as Raphael was concerned, was what she was hell bent on doing. Whether she was or not didn't matter. As far as Raphael was concerned, that was what she was doing and that was that. She had wangled her way onto the Parents' Committee for one reason and one reason alone—to manoeuvre herself into a position of power whereby she could tell people what to do and advance her own foul and dirty-minded ambitions because that was all they were, just like her, foul and dirty-minded. He hated her! How could anyone do what she did—take a little baby and murder it, kill it stone dead and then go on television and boast about it? Because that was what she had done. He saw it with his own two eyes. He had been sitting there in the parlour reading when Nessa turned on the television to watch—would you believe it—*The Terry Krash Show* for which she had lately confessed to having an affection. This depressed him but it came as no surprise. He knew the day she had insisted on his purchasing the infernal machine, that it would all come to a bad end. The programme was devoted entirely to International Women's Year, which, apparently, 1975 was.

It was only when he looked up from his book a second time that Raphael saw, to his astonishment, that one of the panellists, representing some group or other, was Evans. When he saw her, he nearly had a heart attack. The same woman who had been haunting his office since the beginning of the year with her take-over schemes and plans now spewing her dirt out on a television screen in front of the whole country. "Yes," she said, "I had an abortion. I had an abortion when I was seventeen years old and I see no reason why, as a citizen of this country, I should be vilified for that. As far as I am concerned what I do with my own body is my business."

And that wasn't all she had to say. Oh no. Mrs Evans had a lot more to say than that. She was only getting warmed up. Herself and her cronies had smuggled condoms into the Irish Republic, she said. "The Holy Catholic Irish Republic!" she said, sneering. Then she opened her bag and took out a handful of them and she threw them into the audience. Laughing. Laughing! That was only the start, she said. The next plan was to open a family planning clinic in Dublin. Any woman who wanted to would from now on be able to take control of her own body.

As he listened to her going on and on, Raphael felt sick. He hated the way her lips moved. He hated the way she waved her hands. He hated her eyes. The more he looked at her the more he got a pain in his head, directly over his right eye—throb throb

throb, thanks to her. Why did she not bother Nessa? he asked himself. Was it just him?

When he asked her, Nessa said the soul of Mrs Evans, like everyone else's, was her own responsibility. She would, please God, eventually see the error of her ways and repent, she said. The nerve over Raphael's eye started throbbing twice as much. "She won't!" he cried. "You don't know her! She won't stop! Not until she has destroyed everything! Don't you see that, Nessa! Why can't you see it?"

Far away, Terry laughed and clapped along as Evans and her buddies sang a song of solidarity. They invited all women everywhere to join them at the Reclaim The Night march against rape to be held in Dublin. Raphael had to go to the toilet. He thought he was going to vomit. But he didn't. He just stood there over the bowl with his eyes glazed.

Bombshell

Raphael's worst fears came true on what was probably the most traumatic day of his life—the twenty-fifth of November 1975. Evans had been telephoning to organise an appointment with him all week and had been so insistent that in the end he had to capitulate. When she swanned into his office swinging the bag and sat herself down with her diary and her fancy accent, to his amazement he found himself stammering. He tried to look her in the eye but again to his astonishment, found that he couldn't. Before he knew it, she was talking away nineteen to the dozen about how this could be done and that could be done. He hardly heard the half of what she said. It was as if nothing but a crackling fizz was coming out of her mouth, seemingly with no end. Every so often she'd get up and walk around with her hands in the back pockets of her blue jeans. Snippets came to him all right

—"We, the parents" and "Child-centered curriculum." But for the most part she made no sense at all. Not until the end anyway, when she dropped what might be called the bombshell.

The Parents' Committee had decided that it was no longer appropriate for the students to bring rosary beads to school. Neither did they feel it was realistic for them to be asked to wear starched white shirts and red ties. Was it, they had wondered, entirely necessary for them to line up in the military-style formation to which they had become accustomed—after all, it was 1975. What did Mr Bell think, she inquired.

What did he think? What did he think? He couldn't think. He was speechless. When she said, "I'll leave it with you," swinging her bag over her shoulder as she did so, he still hadn't replied.

He watched her stomping out the gates like she owned the world then straightaway dialled the number of the presbytery. Fortunately Father Stokes was at home. As he spoke to him, Raphael tried to disguise the tremor in his voice. At first he thought he was hearing things. Then he thought maybe he had got through to someone else. "This old thing has come up again and again," said the voice. "Sure maybe it'll be for the best, Raphael."

Raphael could feel himself going cold all over, having realised by now of course that he hadn't dialled the wrong number and that he was indeed talking to his old friend. "These people," went on Father Stokes, "sure they're desperate altogether. They know so much about their legal entitlements they'd tie you up in knots. Sure if that's what they want, let them. Anything for a quiet life, Raphael. It's changed times since you and me started out, that's all I can say. By the way, are you for the match in Croke Park Sunday?"

Raphael didn't answer the question. He had no intention of

answering it and hung up the phone at once. He didn't want to talk about football either. What would he want to talk about football for? What he wanted to know was—what was going on? Had everybody taken leave of their senses? He felt like screaming. What was wrong with Father Stokes? He thought for a minute he could hear Evans laughing.

He was on the verge of running off out the door and going up to the presbytery and tackling the priest head on. "What do you think you're doing!" he would yell at him. "Are you out of your mind?" Which he might have done had a knock not come to the door and the postman handed him an official brown Department Of Education envelope, the contents of which informed him that the inspector who had recently visited the school had been deeply disappointed by the standard he had found there, particularly with regard to the work of one teacher, in whose case it was, he felt he had to say, "appalling." It was hoped that this state of affairs would be rectified and the reputation of St Anthony's Boys' N.S., once considered among the top five Dublin schools, be restored.

O

That night, or rather that morning, in the wee small hours between four and five o'clock, a little baby came floating in the door, in through the parlour, out into the hall, all along the carpet, up the big stairs one by one into the room of Raphael Bell, Raphael Bell and his wife Nessa née Conroy the woman he loved so true, hovered about then floated away and came back again to smile at The Master, give him a great big gummy grin, a lovely slurpy babby smile that would warm the cockles of your heart and then pull its lips right back behind its ears before the blood started to pour and its legs collapsed and its fingers fell off and all the flesh went into clay as the screaming words that came out woke the poor old schoolteacher "I'm Maolseachlainn! I'm Maolseachlainn! And you're my daddy! Hello, Daddy! Hello, Daddy!" as bombs blew far away and Daddy cried because all the horses were dead and because he knew that he himself had perished in a lonely field and had gone to his grave to lie cold and alone not for Jesus not for Mary not for Evelyn not for Ireland not for Nessa not for Raphael not for the teeming unborn sons and daughters like constellations of stars that streamed into infinity but for that which young Brennan got for his sums each and every Monday morning, a great big royal duckegg, a bloated circle gawping blindly from a blackboard, a shameful zero. Nothing. Absolutely nothing at all.

Love In The Grave 2

When you're in love you think love can never end. You think the idea of love ever going into the ground is ridiculous. You say to yourself "Imagine a time when we're not together. It can't be done. When you are as much in love as we are, it can't happen. It just can't happen, my friend."

It can of course. It happens all the time. Exactly when it starts is always hard to say but once it does, before you know it, you're standing looking at a tombstone with that old familiar word on it. Funny how it happens really. It's not as if the one you love comes up to you and says "Darling, there's something I've been meaning to say to you. You remember—that love business between us?—it's all over I'm afraid." That's not the way it happens at all. It's much more banal than that. Ask Packie Dudgeon. She doesn't look at you the same way anymore. Smile when you say certain things. You tell yourself nothing's wrong, but you know there is—oh yes. You know all right. It's hard to say exactly how but you do. Just as Packie did all those years ago as he sat in the half-light of the kitchen with the shine in his eye, dreaming of a love he'd once known, now buried deep in a grave his poor stupid old son Malachy swore he'd never see again.

———————

Environmental Studies

With the nerve going tick tick tick over his eye, Raphael read the report for the seventh time:

> Environmental studies is considered to be one of the most vital components of the new curriculum. Obviously, however, not in this class as I saw very little evidence of any attention being paid to it. The nature table, for example, was practically bare. This, it would seem reasonable to argue, is hardly an indication of environmental awareness. Indeed, it might be said that it is simply another example of the general air of disorganisation which pervades the classroom as a whole.

Raphael was walking around in circles now. What was he expected to do? What was he supposed to do for God's sake! Write back a scorching letter to the inspector explaining to him just what was going on and what he had to put up with? That would look good, wouldn't it, having to admit the like of that!

> Dear inspector I am sorry to have to tell you that the teacher I employed some six months ago to take charge of Class 3 is completely and utterly hopeless and to be perfectly honest with you, if I had the choice I would not put him in charge of the school toilets.

That would look good, wouldn't it? That would really send St Anthony's reputation soaring. That would look well sitting on the divisional inspector's desk in the Department Of Education!

Raphael slammed his open hand down on the desk and the more he thought about the position Dudgeon had put him in, the fiercer his rage became. "How dare he!" he snapped. If he was to send a response the like of that into The Department, the inspector would laugh in his face. What respect would he have then? A lifetime's respect come to nothing—because of this! Because of *him*! It wasn't good enough! It simply wasn't good enough!

That was what was going through Raphael's mind which explained why he left the office looking he was about to burst a blood vessel, indeed a series of blood vessels, and stormed off down the corridor into the classroom. This time he had really had enough. This time it had gone as far as it was going to go.

Horslips Are Playing In The Stadium
It is time for art and this week in art we are doing collage, said Malachy busy as a bee talking away to himself. Now I must be extra careful because unless you know exactly what you are doing things can go wrong in art class. Very wrong indeed and we don't want that now do we we most certainly do not. Of course you can make all the preparations in the world you could be up from now to doomsday getting this ready and that ready but no matter what you do you can always be sure that in the end something will go wrong—that is one sure thing with art class. No matter what you do. *"Teacher, I got paint all over my jumper. Teacher, I did. My mammy will kill me."* Then you have to spend the morning cleaning him don't you in case little old mammy will come down

complaining to Mr Bell who of course would be on top of us like a ton of bricks. However there was going to be none of that this morning. None of it at all—Malachy couldn't believe it! He really couldn't. The class tidied up beautifully and when they were all settled he said "Now we will go on to our essay which this week is called 'Gathering Blackberries.' "

He had never seen Stephen so quiet. He was as good as gold, sitting up straight at his desk with his lips together and not so much as a sound out of him. There was a shaft of sunlight in the centre of the room and steam rising up past the window. This was a wonderful school. The best school in the world. Everything had worked out fine. Marion and him were having a few problems here and there—so what! Everyone had those from time to time for God's sake! Especially when you moved in together for the first time, not to mention both starting new jobs. Problems were only natural. If you were to get yourself into a state every time you ran into a bit of a difficulty with the person you were living with—well I mean you might as well forget it! He hadn't a thing to worry about.

The class had really good fun outlining the essay. He drew a picture on the blackboard: little stick men coming over the hill with cans of blackberries. "I'm afraid you'll have to excuse my drawings, children. I'm no Van Gogh!" he said. The kiddies laughed and carried on with their sentences. You could have heard a pin drop they were so attentive.

Then there was a knock on the door and Mr Bell came in. He was carrying a bundle of papers and his cheeks were purple. He looked at Malachy. Malachy smiled. Mr Bell didn't smile however. He crooked his index finger and beckoned him over into the corner. The class of course started to get restless straightaway. Mr Bell fumbled with the papers and handed Malachy a single sheet. He recognised his own handwriting. It was the savings club names from the previous week. A lot of the numbers had been scored out in angry red felt tip. Mr Bell had scored them out. He hitched up his spectacles and stared at Malachy. Then he said "Well?"

Malachy took the list and tried to focus on the children's names, but he couldn't because all he could hear was the sound of Mr Bell breathing and the class shifting about in their seats. If Bell stopped glaring for a second or two he might actually have been able to read the fucking thing for God's sake. But he wouldn't stop, would he? Oh no. "Do you realise I had to go through every one of those again—every single one," Bell snapped. "Do you realise that you have messed up everything? Let me tell you, for he may not want to tell you himself—Mr Keenan is furious." "I'll do them out again Mr Bell," Malachy said, lowering his head. Mr Bell removed his spectacles. "Do them again," he hissed. "Can't you see that they're done now? What do you think I've been spending my time at for the past two hours above in that office or what is wrong with you at all? Huh?"

He shone his glasses with a large white handkerchief and stuck his tongue into his cheek, frowning. Malachy could feel his face stretching like elastic. He tried to think of an answer. "I can't stop thinking about Marion. I'm afraid she's going to leave me. That's what happened." No—that wouldn't really do I'm afraid. So he said nothing. He just stood there fiddling with the piece of paper. Mr Bell went over to the teacher's desk and trawled the room. There wasn't a sound. All of a sudden he swung round and jabbed the air with his index finger.

"Hah!" he cried and sudden fear leaped in Paul Lafferty's eyes.

"Lafferty! What are you at, Lafferty!"

"Nothing, sir," replied Lafferty.

"Nothing, sir! Don't nothing sir me—I can see you! What have you got in your hand? What have you got under the desk there? Let me have it!"

Lafferty left his desk and handed over the Bugs Bunny cards. Mr Bell stuffed them into his pocket and said "Don't you worry, Mr Lafferty, sir—I have my eye on you!"

Then he glared at Malachy, "Which is more than your teacher seems to have—on you or on anything else!"

He gathered up his papers "Now get down and do your work and not another word out of you until that bell goes at three o'clock do I make myself clear?"

The class replied with one voice: "Yes, sir."

The classroom door swung shut. Malachy felt like shouting "Get back here!" after him. But he didn't shout that. He didn't shout anything. Instead a voice in his head whispered "She's going to leave you if you don't do something." He was on the verge of panic when he heard that whisper. He was on the verge of panic because he didn't know what to do.

After twenty or thirty drinks in Martin Coyningham's Bar later that night Malachy was flying. Bell? Who gave a shit about Bell! Baldy fucking bastard! Mr Bell? Anyone home? I am gonna get smashed. You got that? Smashed, asshole. By the time he left the pub he was cruising ten feet high, man! Where's that Joe Buck! Hey you peeg—breeng me zee head of Alfredo Garcia and I weel geef you one million dollar. Ha ha ha! Awright!

He was having a ball. Chuckling to himself now if you don't mind. The tinkers went up Abbey Street with a pile of junk in a pram. A metal shutter scrolled to the pavement with a jarring clang as a shopkeeper locked up. Malachy looked at his watch. It was still three o'clock according to that. Useless watch. Must have been designed by Baldy Bell. Ha ha!

When he got home there was a note from Marion saying she had gone to see The Electric Strangers.

The city was the colour of dishwater. A few papers blew around Daniel O'Connell's concrete feet. He went into an amusement arcade and played the machines for a while. The man in the glass booth ticked off horses in the *Daily Mirror* and passed out cylinders of coins one after the other. Malachy won two pounds and then lost it again. He walked as far as Grafton Street. He went into four pubs and had a whiskey in each. He was really looking forward to meeting her and these "headcase" friends as she called them. They could have a few drinks together. See that he wasn't quite the dull dickhead they thought he was, huh? Mr Frogspawn! Mr Scared-Shitless-of-Mammies-and-Baldies. I don't think so. Not anymore, ladies. Not after tonight!

They'd have a few laughs. That was what it was all about, right? They were gonna have a ball, or would have if he had managed to find anyone. He went back home to Rathmines. He bought an Indian takeaway and ate it as he walked, spilling some curry sauce on his jacket. He laughed out loud. "Hey Mr Bell! Hey Baldy! Look at this—are you gonna do something about it! You gonna do something about it, my friend?" He bounced the silver carton off a telegraph pole and laughed as it hit the ground. "You just try it, Baldy! You just try it, pal!"

Rathmines Road was full of Kentucky Fried Chicken boxes and burger wrappers rubbish blowing in the wind. There was a fight starting outside the shopping centre. A youth in half-mast jeans defied a countryman twice his size. The countryman kept repeating "I'll murder him! I'll murder the fucker!" Then the youth came flying out of nowhere and kicked him on the side of the head. The countryman came toppling down. There was blood streaming out of the wound. A woman screamed. The youth was on top of the countryman now and lashing him mercilessly with his two-tone shoes. "I'll bleedin' batter him! I'll batter him to death!" he screamed.

Malachy reckoned she just might be there waiting on him to give him a surprise. Now that would be good!

"You weren't expecting me, Malachy, were you!"

Maybe in her nightdress with her hair up or something like that.

She wasn't however.

He flicked the light on and found yet another letter from Cissie lying on the mat. There was a musty smell in the room and on the table a newspaper and the dishes from the night before. As he read the letter, he could hear the married couple arguing next door.

The wife said "All I ask you to do is to stay home one night with us. It's not much to ask, Eddie. You're down there every night of the week."

He muttered something but it was inaudible. Then she said "It was a bitter day for me the day I married you."

A train rattled across the night sky and he heard the woman whimper. Then, the husband consoling her. He said "I love you. You know I do."

She said "No you don't you don't. How could you when you're never here."

There was silence for a long time and then a slow, heavy sigh as their lovemaking came to an end.

Cissie wanted to know why he never came home, why he never wrote. She said she missed him so much and his coldness towards her broke her heart. There was a new postman in the town and Kevin Connolly's mother had sprained her ankle.

"Please write to me," she finished, "please, Malachy." He crumpled up the letter in his fist and realised his eyes were wet.

Outside the cinema opened its doors and the flushed faces streamed out. Words drifted warmly upward and melted like snowflakes. There was a ringing in his head. He dozed fitfully, waking now and then to the creak of bedsprings next door. Long groans. Oh. Oh. Then silence. He was shivering. He knew there was something very bad wrong. He had to get a good night's sleep. Once he got that, everything would be fine again.

It was after three when Marion got home. "What a night we had," she said. "You should've been there."

Then she laughed and kissed him on the forehead. She flopped into his lap and reached in her bag. "Look what I got." She held up two tickets. They were for The Stadium. Horslips were playing. "It's going to be fantastic," she said. Then she undressed and climbed in beside him, holding him close to her. "Oh, Malachy," she said, "we love each other so much. We love each other don't we?"

He thought of them sitting together in The Stadium, the crowd going wild as Eamon Carr appeared with the shamrock on his backside and Barry Devlin the bass player shouting "Hi! It's good to be here—we're The Horslips!"

Marion cheered and cheered. Everyone cheered because they were happy and he would have given anything if things could really have been that way.

Psst

The children filed in on the dot of nine and said good morning, teacher. Malachy said "Good morning, children. Now are we all ready for the prayer?" They said "Yes, teacher, we are." They all said it together. Then they all sat down and took out their books and they began *Our News*. Malachy walked up and down between the rows of desks. They had lots of news items. Each child contributed. Then he read them all out. All the little bits of news. The children performed excellently. He was delighted. He could see that everything was going to go well today. Magnificently in fact. And that was the way it would have continued if Stephen Webb hadn't started getting up to his old tricks. Malachy couldn't see exactly what it was he was passing over to Kyle Collins.

He said "What are you doing down there at the back, Stephen?"

Stephen looked up with his big innocent brown eyes as per usual. He crinkled up his nose. Malachy couldn't believe how stupid he looked. "Me?" he said.

"Yes," Malachy said, "you."

"Sir, I wasn't doing anything," Webb said.

"Oh you weren't doing anything were you not? Well what was that I saw in your hand just now?" Malachy said.

Stephen stared down at his hands. It would appear he was amazed to find them growing at the bottom of his arms. Then he shook his head.

"I wasn't doing anything," he said.

Malachy had had just about enough of this nonsense. He went straight down to him.

"Let me see what you have there please," he said. He thought it was a compass or something but as it turned out he didn't in fact have anything in his hands. Whatever it was, he must have put it back in the desk.

"Very clever, Mr Webb," Malachy said, "very clever"

Stephen gave him a big smart-aleck smile because he knew he'd got away with it.

"Oh for heaven's sake I'm worse than you to be standing

here talking to you!" he snapped and went back to the black-board. "Come on now get the rest of this news down, class," he said.

"Psst," said Webb.

Then what did he do only start smiling again. But not an ordinary smile. A cheeky, sickening smile. Before Malachy could get to him, he had his head down and was carrying on with his work. Then he put up his hand and said "Excuse me, sir—you're in the way. I can't see the blackboard."

He didn't think his teacher could ignore him. That was what he thought. But that was where he was wrong. For that was exactly what Malachy did. He could be just as much a bastard as Stephen when he wanted. That was what Webb forgot you see. Malachy smiled down at him, then spun on his heel and went over to the window. He was thinking about Marion again now. His mouth was all dry.

Even though it's cold you can still sweat. It's different sweat though. It's like scales on your skin.

Our News

8:55 A.M. and Malachy was in great form altogether. He was paring pencils. He'd been whistling for nearly ten minutes before he realised he'd been whistling at all. His chosen tune this morning was the old favourite—"Chirpy Chirpy Cheep Cheep." He grinned when it dawned on him, then grinned even more when he thought how much of a surprise a certain person might get if he arrived home with that little beauty under his arm. He could just imagine her face when he pulled it out from under his jacket. "I thought you might like this, Marion," he'd say, casual as you like. He was over the moon as he gathered up the remainder of the pencil shavings and walked over to the bin with them.

It was a great idea. It was a fantastic idea. "I thought you might like this, Marion." He couldn't wait!

Then it was time to admit the rascals. He opened the door and said hello to all the mammies. "I think that's the coldest yet," he said. They said yes indeed it is, Mr Dudgeon. Then James McCann's mammy came over and touched him gently on the forearm. She dropped her voice and whispered in his ear "James has terrible trouble with the maths." He told her they would be going over them again today and not to worry too much.

She asked him how he was doing. "Is he getting along all right Mr Dudgeon?" she said.

He said he was getting on like a house on fire.

Then Stephen Webb arrived with his mammy. She was a bit hesitant when she saw him standing there in the classroom doorway and so was Stephen. He turned towards her sullenly. She smiled weakly. Then Stephen reemerged from the bulk of her skirts. Malachy ran his fingers through the boy's tumbling blonde curls.

"And how's young Stephen this morning? All set and ready to go—hmm?"

Mrs Webb rubbed her hands and said "It's got very cold hasn't it, Mr Dudgeon?"

He said "That's just what we were saying."

One of the women said "If you ask me it's the coldest yet."

He said "Well time to put the shoulder to the wheel, eh, kids?" Then he led them all inside. Just as he closed the door he overheard the tail end of his name.

"Right, kids," he said and gave out some of the sharpened pencils. He read the roll and then wrote *"Our News"* on the blackboard. For just the briefest of seconds he thought "Oh no! It isn't going to work out! It's all going to go wrong again!"

But he needn't have worried his head. It went terrific. There was no doubt about it—he had the best kids in the school. And Webb! Not only did he give him one piece of news—but three pieces!

"Stephen come out here and read your news. Come on now —there's a good lad," he said.

So out came Stephen and stood there in his short trousers and his grey Cub Scout socks. He really was an excellent reader too, enunciating each word perfectly. He paused between each sentence and commanded everybody's attention.

This is what he read:

> I went to my Uncle Jim's house in Coolock.
> Our cat is called Marmaduke.
> My favourite is alphabetti spaghetti.

When he had finished, Malachy said he would have to give him two stars not only because he gave us three bits of news but because they were *hard* bits of news. There weren't many kids in the class who could spell alphabetti never mind spaghetti. Actually there were three altogether because he checked—Brendan Dunne, Tom Curran and Patrick Jones. So "Well done, Stephen," he said again.

Malachy didn't know where the morning went. Before he knew it he was in the middle of nature study. "Look at this little fellow," he said. "He's called a drone. Look at all these legs!"

Then the bell went.

"Phew," he said, and wiped the sweat off his forehead, "what a great little bunch you are—you really have worked hard this morning haven't you?"

— — —

He was delighted as he walked off down the corridor. Not that there was anything surprising about that. After all—everything was sorted out, wasn't it? All sorted out at last! All he had to do now was go into Grafton Street after school and get the record. He went into the staff room. There was a sectioned green frog poster wilting on the wall. Mr Keenan was practising his tin whistle. He was only learning and was finding it quite hard. He hit it off his knee.

"Damn bloody thing! I have it and then it's gone again," he said.

"It's not the easiest of instruments," Mr Boylan said.

"What is the song? Do you know—I'm nearly sure I recognise it.

"Row Row Row Your Boat," sang Mr Keenan.

Then Mr Boylan drummed on the table with his fingers and Mr Keenan hummed along with him as he bit into his sandwich. Mr Boylan sang *"Row row row your boat gently down the stream merrily merrily merrily life is but a dream!"*

"I think I'll get you to teach it to me when you have it mastered," he said. "My lot could do with a bit of music. Crowd of bloody hoboes!"

"I don't think it'd be much good me trying to knock it into mine," said Mr Keenan.

"I daresay that rascal Belton wouldn't thank you for Mozart, Mr Keenan," laughed Mr Boylan.

Mr Keenan raised his eyes to heaven. "God give me strength," he said.

Then Mr Macklin who taught first class came in and dumped a load of change on the table. "So help me God I'll be carted out of this place," he said.

"You've been doing a bit of collecting there, Mr Macklin," said Mr Keenan with his eyes twinkling.

"You might as well be talking to the wall as talking to some of them and that's not a word of a lie. I want the money for the savings club in by next Friday at the latest I says—but do you think they'd listen? Oh no! That's Finnerty's and Howard's right there—stroll in as cool as you like—I forgot! I forgot now I ask you!"

"Wasting your breath," sighed Mr Keenan. His tea geysered out of his thermos and he rubbed his hands along his thighs as he said "Well did you see it last night?"

"Fecked if I could," said Mr Boylan. "Herself had to go to the mother's and you know what it's like when that starts. It was nearly half-past eleven by the time we got out. I was fit to be tied."

"You missed it now—you missed it," teased Mr Keenan. Then he grinned and put on an American accent as he said *"Who loves ya, baby?"*

"Well man dear now it was terrific," he said. "The Mafia were running this casino you see and Kojak makes on he knows nothing about it. So one night him and Crocker go in dressed up as Mafia men themselves and there's Kojak with the lollipop . . . will you get out, Brennan! For the love and honour of St Joseph can I not even have my dinner in peace without some brat bothering me? Is that what it's come to now!"

"Sir, my ball's gone up on the roof."

"Did you hear what I said, Brennan! Are you deaf as well as stupid! I said get out. *Get out!*"

"Yes, sir," said Brennan, and left the room with his head down.

"He has my heart scalded, that fellow," said Mr Keenan, "him and that bloody ball—if I got it for him once I got it for him ten times this week."

He wiped some crumbs off his mouth with the sleeve of his

jacket and snapped "Well it can stay there. That's where it can stay! For I'm not getting it!"

That put them all in such bad humour, there didn't seem to be any point in talking about Kojak anymore. After a bit, Mr Boylan said "Well—what do you think of the latest carry-on? A school bus driver. Shot by the side of the road in front of the kiddies." Before Mr Keenan could answer, the door crashed open and in came Mr Bell jangling his keys. He was carrying a copy of *The Six Million Dollar Man Annual*. He gave it to Mr Keenan and told him to keep it in the staff room at least until Christmas. There was a bit of a quiver in his voice when he said it but no one noticed. You never thought of someone as rock solid as Mr Bell having a quiver in their voice.

Chili

Malachy licked his fingers and said "Yes indeed this chili is definitely coming on well." He let it bubble away in the saucepan. Marion loved chili. Between that and the record, she was going to get some surprise. He took "Chirpy Chirpy" out of its sleeve and put it on the turntable. It was the first record she had ever bought. That was why she loved it so much. He checked the chili one more time and then he went into the sitting room to wait for her.

The baby next door was laughing and there was a smell of frying bacon. On the radio they reported a few more murders. A politician came on and said that the people of the country would have to get it into their heads that they had been living beyond their means for the past five years. He said that an ESRI report had clearly indicated that the country was sliding deeper and deeper into recession. An economist came on and said that we had nobody to blame but ourselves what did we expect. Then another politician said that that wasn't true at all and what the economy needed was not more of these Keynesian dictators with their grey faces and sharp suits but more optimism, a reflation of the economy that's what's needed. The other politician said "Sorry, Michael, but the boom times are over we are paying for the boom times now. I know that and you know that and the Irish people are mature enough to know that and do something about it." Then there were the closing prices on the stock exchange.

All of a sudden Malachy felt exhausted. He didn't want to think any more about school. He closed his eyes so there would be nothing but there was something—Stephen Webb standing there looking at him. He was bouncing a ball and saying "Hello, teacher."

He kept on bouncing it and bouncing it until Malachy said "Stop it! Stop bouncing it!"

He said "I'm not bouncing it, sir, it's Pat Hourican."

"It was not, Webb. It's you!" Malachy cried. "No, sir, it was Pat," he said again, "wasn't it, Kyle?"

Malachy hadn't seen Kyle Collins at first but he was there all right. He hadn't a ball though. He was just standing there with his hands behind his back.

Malachy said "Get over here, Collins! How dare you tell lies! Come over here!"

"No, sir, I won't. My mammy says you're not allowed to tell me what to do."

Webb smirked and kept bouncing the ball really close to Malachy's leg to annoy him.

"My daddy says you're no good of a teacher."

"Tee hee hee," went Collins.

"Oh you're so smart, Collins, you are just so smart aren't you?"

"No, sir, he's just Kyle," chuckled Webb.

"You needn't think you're annoying me, Stephen," he said, "you can laugh all you like."

Did he really think he could annoy him? Did he really think anything he had to say was going to bother him in the slightest?

Malachy curled up in the armchair and laughed at the idea. It was preposterous! The more he thought about it the more preposterous it seemed. Which was why he laughed into the fuckhead's face. That took Webb by surprise all right. He hadn't been expecting that. Now he didn't know what to do. Malachy stared right into his eyes and said "Well—what are you going to do, Webb? You're not so sure now are you! You're not quite so sure now—hmm? Hmm?"

Webb was stunned. He didn't know what to do. He hadn't the foggiest idea. Then suddenly the phone rang.

It was Marion. She was in The Project. There was so much noise he could barely make out what she was saying. She was with The Electric Strangers and the crowd from the school. She said the party was only starting and to come on. The band were recording in the studio around the corner. Their single had made it into the lower regions of the charts in England. "They're over the moon," she said.

He said that he had a pot of chili on. "Oh fuck the chili," she said. Then all he could hear was "Hello? Hello?" The alarm was wailing again outside and he wished it would stop he just wished it would please stop.

How long he'd been sitting in the armchair he did not know. He shivered.

"Look, teacher! There's only one bar of your fire working?" said Stephen smiling. "At home we have three electric fires and they're all working." "Oh really? Have you now," Malachy said. "Well aren't you wonderful?"

"No, sir, I'm just Stephen," he said. He sucked his little white cheeks in like a girl and rolled his eyes as Kyle's shoulders heaved and he hid behind his hand.

Then Malachy said "Stephen, I have an idea." He lifted up the chair seat. "Why don't we pretend this is you, hmm?"

Webb crinkled up his nose, looking puzzled. "Me?"

"Yes, Stephen. Is that all right?"

He lowered his head. "Yes sir," he said softly.

"Very well then," Malachy said and held up the cushion. "So, let's pretend this is your face then shall we?"

Webb said yes and then Malachy sank his fist in it—*bumph!* "What do you think of that, Stephen?"

Webb said nothing.

Malachy looked at him. "How did you like that, Mr Webb? How did you like that, hmm?"

That soon shut him up. There wasn't so much cheek out of him after that. Oh but it was funny! There were tears in Malachy's eyes it was so funny as in the kitchen the record played over and over and the chili boiled away to nothing.

Eyes

He was over the moon when they met after school and headed off towards O'Connell Street. "So where will we go?" she said. "How about Good Time Charly's," he said. "Sounds good to me," she smiled.

All the way through the meal he couldn't shut up. He knew that he was talking too much and boring her but he was afraid that if he sat there like a dummy thinking about school, it would be even worse. He asked her did she want any dessert and she said no. He said, "You can have Black Forest Gateau, Lemon Meringue, Apple Pie with cream apple pie without cream. You name it, Marion, you can have it. Come on, Marion, what's it going to be?"

"I said I didn't want any, Malachy!"

He wasn't sure what to do when she said that. He just looked at her as if he'd been struck dumb.

"I've got an idea," she said. "Why don't we go and see the new Jack Nicholson movie? It's on at the Adelphi. What do you say?"

He grinned from ear to ear.

"Sure thing," he said.

She squeezed his hand.

"Oh, Malachy," she said.

"That old Joe Buck," he said.

"Yeah—do you remember that?" She smiled.

When he went up to pay he kept looking back at her. He just wanted to look at her and the way she had her hair combed back and the freckles around her eyes. He knew he shouldn't have been staring like that. Then maybe he mightn't have dropped the money. But he did. He dropped it all over the place.

When they got outside Marion said "Sometimes I just wish you wouldn't do that, Malachy. I get so embarrassed."

"Do what?" He asked and she said "You know—you *know*!"

He said, "What, Marion? I don't know what you mean."

"Looking at me the way you were doing in there—what do you think I'm going to do? Do you think I'm going to get up and run off out of the restaurant or something?"

His tongue went all sandy when she said that and he felt like a bollocks. Not that it helped things very much when he started blabbing on again instead of shutting his mouth and leaving it alone. "Marion, I'm sorry," he said. "I won't do it again, I didn't realise I was doing it, Marion," and so on. Which was disastrous because it was just the kind of thing you don't want to say when you know you are creeping towards the edge of the grave.

But it didn't bother Malachy. Oh no! He knew they had been together far too long to let a little thing like that bother them. They sure had! Off they went up Abbey Street to the Adelphi like the old days when they had gone to *Midnight Cowboy* and *The Graduate* in the very same cinema! "Hey—where's that Joe Buck! Excuse me—can you tell me the way to the Statue Of Liberty? Yeah—it's up in Central Park taking a leak. If you hurry you might be in time to catch the supper show!" Ha! Boy did Malachy laugh when he thought of that.

Right now Marion had her head stuck in a big box of popcorn. Next thing you know Roman Polanski comes tearing at Jack Nicholson with the knife. The hoods held Jack fast and the blade went right up his nose. Roman said that he didn't like snoopers. He did not like them at all. He poked the knife up a bit further. "Here, Kitty Kitty," he said as he took a slice out of it and sent blood skiting all over the place. So that was the end of his nose for Mr Jack Nicholson or should I say J. J. Gittes private eye. After that, he spent the rest of a movie with a big plaster stuck on it. He wasn't too pleased about that. When Faye Dunaway said something fresh to him, he got her up against the wall and said "I like my nose, Mrs Mulwray. I like breathing through it. You got that?" She sure had. When you were dealing with Jack Nicholson you made sure you had. You didn't fuck around with Jack. Other people maybe. But not Jack. On the way out, Malachy was still saying it, his adenoids on overdrive: "I like my nose, Mrs Mulwray. I like breathing through it."

"You do him really well," Marion said, "you really do."

She hugged his arm as they turned into O'Connell Street. He put his arm around her and kissed her on the cheek. Man, it was just like the old days! "Let's go up to Stephen's Green," she said, and so off they headed.

Everything was OK now as they sat watching the ducks. The bad times were over at last. They sat there together as happy as they had ever been looking at the old ducks swimming away. "They love their bread," said an old woman in a rain hood as she chucked half a loaf onto the water. "They go mad without their bread."

"They do," said Marion as she blushed a bit then laughed.

"They do," said Malachy.

"I never seen anything like ducks for bread," said the woman.

All of him wanted to cry out "Please, Marion!"

The late afternoon sky was the colour of lead.

Broken Alarm

He loved the way she ate yogurt. She licked it off her fingers and made sure to get any of it that slid around underneath the spoon. She always ate yogurt when she was watching TV. She brought her knees up to her chest and puckered up her nose at the best parts of the programme. Tonight she was watching *Coronation Street* and he was sitting beside her but he was no more interested in *Coronation Street* than the man in the moon. He was too busy thinking about *Chinatown* and the day they'd just spent together. A few times he stroked her hair without thinking and she said "Oh please—I can't concentrate!"

He knew what she meant. It can be irritating trying to watch something when someone is distracting you. So he went into the kitchen and sat down in the armchair to read for a while, but suddenly he wanted to go back into the sitting room and ask Marion if she still loved him. He was on the verge of it but then he said to himself "No—don't!" When she came in he was just standing there staring into space. He didn't even realise he had just stood to attention. Who did he think she was—Mr Bell? "What are you doing, Malachy?" she said breezily. "You look like you're going to go for a crap in your trousers or something."

He gave her a big grin.

"Oh you know!" he said. Whatever that was supposed to mean.

"Is there any pickle left?" she asked. "I really fancy a sandwich." She hummed to herself as she opened the fridge door and it was just then that he wanted to hold her and say "Please help me, Marion, I think there's something wrong," but all he said was "Yes, Marion there is." Meaning the pickle, of course.

But it didn't matter because when he looked again she was gone.

What time it was when he woke up he didn't know. His eyelids shot open like sprung trapdoors. The broken alarm was going hell for leather outside. He was all sweaty again. He wanted to take his vest off but he was afraid to get out of the bed. He was afraid if he didn't get back to sleep he would start thinking about Stephen Webb. In the end that didn't matter, really, because when he rubbed his eyes again Stephen was standing there beside him with his hand up and a smirk on his face. "Excuse me, sir," he said. Malachy swung round so that his face was level with Webb's. "What do you want?"

Stephen's eyes twinkled and he smiled. "The lead on my pencil is broken, sir. It's broken, sir. It's broken, sir. It's broken, sir. It's broken, sir. It's broken, sir. It's broken, sir. It's broken, sir. It's broken, sir. . . ."

The moon shone on Marion's locket as her chest rose and fell.

Malachy had to admit that it took him a long time to pick up the courage but in the end he did and when he turned over he saw that yes she was awake too, just lying there in the dark with her eyes open, not eyes that were happy at last because the bad times were all over, but eyes that were glistening and wet with tears thinking about the way it had once been between them.

Surprises

And it would be that way again, for he would see to it. So what if they had had an argument before he went off to school that morning? A fucking argument wasn't the end of the world. It wasn't as if other people didn't have them. No, he was right on top of it now, after tonight there was going to be nothing to worry about, nothing to worry about at all. From now on he was going to wise up. To hell with Bell and his fucking school. Why should he be stuck in a poxy flat night after night worrying himself sick over nothing, almost losing everything he had in the process? Just as well he had come to his senses in time. Marion was going to get some surprise when she saw him.

He was standing in the rain across the road from The Project Arts Centre. Marion and her mates went there most weekend nights. The latenight gigs they were running had become a huge success. The rain was really pouring down now but that didn't matter. The rain could pour down all it liked for all he cared. The only thing he was going to care about from now on was Marion. She'd be out any minute. He could hardly contain himself. What a surprise it was going to be! No more frogspawn,

Marion, he'd say. Tonight or any night. And would she be glad to hear that! At last, she'd say—at long last.

Another half-hour went by. He was beginning to have second thoughts about his carefully thought-out surprise plan when the punters began to file out through the opened doors. His heart leaped when he saw her. Laughter rippled out into the night. She was laughing at something Paddy Meehan was saying. He pushed his curly mane back from his face as they came down the steps. Paddy flicked a cigarette away in a tail of sparks and she laughed as he put his arm around her. You dread something and it's a sort of relief when it happens. When he looked again he couldn't see Marion because Paddy was in the way.

You think you know how someone feels but until it happens to you you really don't know anything at all and it was only at that moment Malachy realised once and for all just how Packie had felt. When he looked again they were standing by a white sports car and she was smoothing back her hair from her eyes. Paddy helped her into the car and then climbed in after her. For a long time afterwards Malachy just stood there in the pouring rain, frozen. By the time he started to walk, the place was deserted and The Project Arts Centre locked and shuttered.

Marion!

So that wasn't very nice was it, no indeed it wasn't, no one was saying it was and of course obviously it would be hard to know quite what to do about it but there must have been a better way —attacking her was not the thing as I suppose he knew. But knowing made no difference. After a good eight whiskeys in Martin Coyningham's Bar he went right ahead and did it. One word borrowed another and soon they were at it hammer and tongs. "What do you want me to be?" he snapped at her.

"A fucking rock star? Would you like me better then, would you?" He was trembling as he stood there in the kitchen facing her.

Her voice was shaking too.

"Leave him out of it. You have no right to bring him into it. He's just a friend!"

"A friend. Some fucking friend. You think I'm stupid—wrapped round him outside The Project like some fucking tramp—"

As soon as he had said it, he knew it was wrong. Very wrong. She went pale.

"What did you say?"

He wanted to take it back. He would have given anything to be able to take it back. But he couldn't. It was too late.

"I asked you a question, Malachy," she said. "What did you say?"

"Nothing," he said. "It doesn't matter."

"You followed us, didn't you? That's what you did—you followed us!"

"I didn't have to follow anyone! I'm not blind, Marion! I'm not fucking blind!"

"I can't believe it. I can't believe you'd do that. How could you do a thing like that, Malachy?"

"I told you—I didn't follow you! I didn't have to fucking follow you! You were open enough about it!"

"Jesus Christ! Will you stop it! Shut up, Malachy!"

"What the fuck do you expect me to do? What am I supposed to think? How long has this been going on? How long have you been deceiving me? How could you do it, Marion? How could you do it on me!"

All of a sudden, she looked away and said "I'm sorry, Malachy."

The way she said it, you could have knocked him over with a feather. He just stood there staring at her with his mouth open. "Marion!" was all he could manage to say.

"I never wanted to deceive you. I swear to God I never wanted to do that," she said, and it all came out. He didn't want her to. He didn't want her to tell him these things that he was terrified he'd hear. That ever since they'd started working, things hadn't been the same. Maybe they'd been a bit hasty in moving in together, she said.

His head was buzzing and he knew that if he didn't do something now, he was finished. But he didn't know what it was he could do.

She went into the bathroom to get a towel for her eyes. When she came back Malachy was still standing exactly where she'd left him. Still trying to get some words to come to his lips. But they wouldn't come. Why would they not come when there were so many things he had to say? He wanted to ask her if it wasn't too late could they try again? He would forget about the school and Bell and everything else. It would be all OK then, just like it had always been. They could put all that behind them and start again. He knew they could. You didn't love one another the way they did then stand back and watch what you had being destroyed like this in front of you. You couldn't. As if it mattered, for in the end, the only word he could manage to get out was "Marion!" and it was so faint and weak and pathetic you could barely hear it.

Not that it made any difference because she'd left the room and all you could hear was the sound of her sobbing in the bedroom and outside the whole world going on about its business.

The Abortionist Walks

Evans was put in charge of playground supervision the day the rumors started on the radio about getting rid of *The Walton Programme* once and for all. It was a good old programme but was no longer relevant surely. "So I'm afraid it's good luck *Walton Programme* very soon," they said.

As he sat there in his office, Raphael's cheek jerked a little. "Ah well," he sighed, "that's that. No more *Walton Programme*. No more Leo Maguire and no more Tommy Dando with his Lowry organ. Sure what would you want him for? He's too silly. Nobody wants silly men with silly organs. Not nowadays. What you want now is Evans. Mrs Evans. Or should I say *Ms*. Evans as she calls herself. Well excuse me! *Ms*. Evans, chairperson of St Anthony's Management Board. *Ms*. Evans, Bachelor of Abortion. There she is now walking around the playground with a big smile on her, laughing and joking with the kiddies—the ones she didn't abort, that is. They are very nice clothes she is wearing, aren't they? Very appropriate I would have thought. Red bell bottom jeans and beads if you don't mind. Red bell bottom trousers and beads, walking around the playground. Hello, children —my name is Evans. I am an abortionist. Perhaps you have heard of me? I've come to kill your school. Yes indeed I have, that's all I came here for and you must admit I am doing a very good job. Look—here comes Father Stokes! He's my friend now. He's a priest but he doesn't care that I kill babies. He thinks it's good. He smiles and laughs and jokes with me. That's because he is my friend. We're all friends here now. All except old Baldy over there in the office and sure who cares about him? The days when he had it all his own way are long gone. Did you hear the news? They're going to take off the stupid old *Walton Programme*. Well thanks be to God for that! Goodbye and good riddance, that's what I say to you, Mr Walton, and your bog-trotting dirges and bogs and stone ditches into the bargain. I suggest now you might start playing some decent songs for a change—such as 'Babies In The Fire' and suchlike. That would be more like it now, I think. Hello there, little Paul. Working hard at your sums? Hello, John. Hello, Michael."

Raphael didn't realize his hands were all chalk. He just went on turning the stick round and round in his hands as he stared out the office window across the playground.

Waterworld

The last straw came when Evans overruled him on the school journey. Every year Raphael took the boys to Kilmainham Jail to honour the dead who had fallen in the 1916 rebellion. Where they could read the letters written by the insurgents the night before the executions. Where they could see the bloodstained vest of James Connolly who had been tied to a chair and shot to death by the British. But this now was not to be, apparently. The Parents' Committee had deemed it "inappropriate."

Evans swung her bag and crossed her legs as she sat before him. "We really think the boys would have a much better time at Waterworld." Great fun, by all accounts, this Waterworld. Slides and skating rinks and fountains and adventures and fun-packed excitement of all kinds. It had only just been opened and every child in Dublin was mad to get going there. The way she spoke about it you would be forgiven for thinking she was eight years old herself. "It's fantastic!" she said, beaming at him. Raphael said nothing for a long time and then: "They're going to Kilmainham Jail where they always go."

When he said that, Evans' mood changed dramatically. She went sort of grey and her lips tightened. "I don't think so, Mr Bell," she said and stood up. Raphael stood up too. He could not believe how much he loathed the woman. In that instant he thought of Maolseachlainn, his poor dead boy and all the infant corpses she had thrown into the fire. She laced her fingers as she spoke again.

"What you don't seem to realise," she went on, "is that Father Stokes has already agreed to this."

Raphael paled. "Then he has exceeded his authority," he said quietly.

"Ah, Raphael, we don't want to get on the wrong side of them. You know what parents are like these days. It's not like it used to be. You step on their toes and you have the whole lot of them down on top of you. And a lot of them do good work for the school now, it has to be said. Sure we'll let them go, just this once. What harm can it do?"

Raphael did not show it but was deeply disappointed as he listened to the priest. It saddened him to think that his old friend would turn around and do this. "She's trying to kill my school. She's trying to ruin everything we've worked for."

"Ah now, Raphael, not at all. Sure she's not the worst of them."

"She has had an abortion."

Father Stokes went white.

"For the love of God, Raphael!"

"She has! And she's in my school!"

"Keep your voice down, man! Do you want to land us in court?"

"I don't care where I land us! She is interfering in the running of my school and you are supporting her. My boys are going to Kilmainham—do you hear me? My boys are going to

Kilmainham and I want you to tell her so. Do I make myself clear?"

Father Stokes lowered his head and when he looked again, Raphael was gone.

The school journey date was set for the twelfth of February 1976. As they arrived with their packed lunches that morning, the boys were as giddy as could be with all the excitement. Especially since this year, they were going to Waterworld instead of boring old Kilmainham Jail. Not only because of that but because lots of the mammies and daddies were going with them! Mrs Evans clapped her hands as they all piled onto the bus.

"Come on, you guys!" she cried. "Shake a leg!" She was great fun. She was wearing a T-shirt with Goofy on it. As the bus pulled out of the gates, she went up to the front and before you knew it, had everyone singing. This was going to be the best school journey ever.

Raphael Bell wouldn't be going however, so he wouldn't know that. He was too busy lowering whiskeys in The Harcourt Hotel on this, the first day, outside of sickness, that he had taken off school in forty-three years.

That night, he fell in the door, muttering and mumbling the whole story about Evans and Father Stokes with a smell of whiskey off him that would knock a dog. Nessa had never seen him like this before and she was livid. When he started muttering again, about what he was going to do to Father Stokes, and Evans too, when the time came, she told him to catch himself on and could not believe her ears when she heard him swear at her. Nor believe her eyes when he caught ahold of her arm and squeezed it, asking her whose side was she on? She had never seen him like this before in her life. His face was bloodred and his eyes were wild. He squeezed her arm again, even harder, and bellowed "Do you hear me? Listen to me when I am talking to you! Whose side are you on? Whose side are you on, Nessa Conroy?"

He was hoarse as he shrieked "Tell me! Tell me!" She cried out and pulled away from him, burying her face in her hands as she ran from the room.

That night in a drunken dream, a little boy came to Raphael, came floating up the stairs to smile and then went floating back down again as Evelyn Bell in a field of golden corn reached out to her son and whispered softly "It's going to be all right, Raphael. Raphael, son, I promise you it's going to be all right," and it made him feel so good, made him feel just so peaceful except that when the words "Will it, Mammy? Will it?" escaped his lips she didn't answer him because she was gone.

Old Friends

Another little surprise for Malachy around this time was the mysterious return of our old friends Alec and the lads. Just standing by the harbour grinning away, as if they hadn't moved in years. Not quite real, of course, but not exactly unreal either, like a lot of other things lately. But they were in good form. As soon as they saw Malachy, they were all smiles. "Ah hello there, young Dudgeon," said Alec. "We were just wondering when you'd come along. It's about time you'd show your face." When he said that, all the lads started to laugh. Alec flicked his cigarette away and hooked his thumbs into his belt. "We only heard the news a while ago. Isn't it daft the way things turn out—first Packie and now you. Man, but aren't youse the pair of bollockses!" Then he turned to the boys and said "I say, boys—aren't they the right pair of fucking bollockses all the same!"

There was great laughing for a while and then Alec decided it was all a wee bit more serious. He smiled as he stroked Malachy's cheek, ever so slowly as he whispered "You've really fucked it up now, haven't you, Dudgeon? Not that it's any big surprise or anything. But by Jesus you've really gone and done a good job on it—I have to hand it to you. Can't even handle a bunch of kids and now look what's happened. She's going to leave you. She's going to do a Cissie on you and there's not a thing you can do about it! Do you hear me, you stupid dumb fuck? Do you hear what I'm saying? She's going to leave you—can't you see that! What happened, son of Packie? Couldn't cut the mustard, could you not? Was that it? Tell us the truth—tell us the truth now! It all got on top of you and you couldn't cut it anymore! You weren't able for it, were you not? Couldn't give her the baldy fellow anymore! Oho boy but you're a son of your father's and no mistake! He'd have been proud of you! Proud, boy!" All he could hear was Alec's voice, rising until it became a shriek. "Come on now—tell us! You can tell me and the boys! We're your old friends!" he cried and you could tell that he was prepared to go on and on until Malachy went mad.

Which, by the look of things, would be sooner rather than later. The doctor gave him Librium and Tryptasol for anxiety and depression and said they would do the trick. Most likely they would have, if he hadn't had naughty boys to teach, who pointed at him and said "Psst! Psst! Dudgy's falling asleep at the desk!" or if he didn't have to remain on full alert in case a baldy headmaster who seemed to have gone crazy lately would decide to launch one of his lightning raids and catch him on the hop.

So between all that and Marion wanting out, which she did,

as was becoming more evident every day, it was hard to see how things could get much worse. But then, that was before he went and organised his stupid walk in the park, wasn't it?

A Walk In The Park

Well good morning, children, and how are you today? All feeling well, are we? Very good. Right now what I want you to do is sit up straight in your seats and listen very carefully because I'm going to tell you a little story. It's called "A Walk In The Park" and although it is just a teeny little bit sad I still think you should all hear it because as we all know, sadness is part of life too isn't it?

Our story begins one beautiful spring afternoon when everything was covered in a soft white blanket of snow. The children were so excited they didn't know what to do with themselves. They were excited because they were going on a nature walk. Yes—off to the park to gather up some leaves and conkers and little bits of sticks and all sorts of knickknacks for their nature table. They just could not wait until it was time to go. "We're going to the park! We're going to the park and it's snowing! Hooray!! We are going to make snowmen! We are going to make lots and lots of snowmen!"

They all had to make sure and wear their Welly boots and duffel coats. They made sure to do that because they knew if they didn't take precautions they might catch cold. That was what Kyle Collins had said to his friends Stephen Webb and Pat Hourican as they walked across the playground that morning. He said "My mammy says I can play in the snow as much as I like so long as I have my gloves and my Welly boots and my woolly hat on."

Stephen smiled and said that that was what his mammy had

said too. "And she said I could make snowballs and snowmen if I wanted to. She said I could make as many as I liked." Kyle and Pat smiled when he said that. They smiled because they were looking forward to making them with him. Pat could hardly contain himself he was looking forward to it all so much. Stephen and Kyle had been his best friends for as long as he could remember. Right back as far as their first day at school. Stephen and Kyle and Pat liked school. Sometimes they were a little bit afraid of Mr Bell because if he saw you he might shout at you. If he saw you running he would definitely shout. He would call you back and make you stand outside his door with your hands down by your sides. Then he would say to you "Would you mind telling me what you were doing? Would you mind telling me what you were doing just now, boy?"

It was very hard to know what the correct answer to that question was. If you said "Nothing, sir," his spectacles would steam up and his cheeks would go red and he would say "So you have nothing to do have you not? You have nothing to do except barrel along the corridors like some kind of wild animal, is that it? Very well then. Perhaps you'll come inside now to my office and we'll see if we can find you something to do. Do you think that might be a good idea, Mr 'Nothing Sir'?"

When he talked to you like that you had to hang your head and play with your fingers while your cheeks burned. But that didn't mean you didn't like Mr Bell. It didn't mean that at all. That was one thing about him. Even if he scolded you sometimes you still liked him. It was only teachers like Dudgy you didn't like because they weren't really like teachers. They weren't really like teachers because it was so easy to annoy them. If you wanted to annoy them all you had to do was keep putting up your hand and ask questions over and over again, especially if you didn't want to know the answers.

Kyle and Stephen and Pat liked doing that. They liked it when they made Mr Dudgeon lose his voice. They sort of smiled when he lost it. It was funny when they did that because it made him lose it even more. Which would then of course lead to another of Mr Bell's investigations. Mr Bell didn't like that, having to lead the investigations. He said he had other things to do. He asked the class did they think he had nothing better to do than run in and out. "Is that what you think?" he said. "That I have nothing better to do than run in and out?" Also of course it often proved quite difficult to find out exactly what it was that had happened. For instance if a ruler had been broken one boy would claim that he had done it. And would appear quite convincing. But then another boy would put up his hand and say "No, teacher. *I* saw what happened. *I'll* tell you." Then Mr Bell, quite relieved, would say "Very well then—tell me." But almost as soon as he had said that yet another boy would say "No—he didn't see it, teacher. *I* saw it. I can tell you exactly what happened."

And so it would proceed like that until the veins in Mr Bell's face showed up more than ever and he asked the class what was wrong with them. "What is wrong with this class?" he would cry hoarsely. "What is wrong with it?"

Which was a silly question to put to the class because it was quite clear what was wrong. It was a rubbish class—that was what was wrong. It was plain to see. Even the juniors in the playground were aware of that. Had been in fact for some time, consequently they did not pay a lot of attention to what Mr Dudgeon said. If he told them not to do something they would simply go ahead and do it. Even some of the pupils who were normally quite mannerly, even shy, found themselves becoming giddy and ill-at-ease in his presence. It was only really when Pat Hourican got it into his head that he was a bit of a comedian that the situation began to deteriorate rather seriously. He liked pulling funny faces to amuse all the other boys. Particularly Stephen and Kyle. They thought he was hilarious. Whenever they got the chance they rolled up pieces of paper into balls and played hand-tennis with them across the room.

So between that and a few other things, the class slowly but surely turned to rubbish. Which it most definitely was the day Kyle Collins looked up from his work to see Stephen Webb pointing to the top of the class. Kyle was on the point of telling his friend to leave him be as he was busy but Stephen's pointing only became more frantic and Kyle found himself quite interested after all. At first he could not really believe it when he saw Dudgy crying. It was simply impossible to believe because you just did not see teachers crying. Crying! Hee! Hee! Kyle chortled behind his hands and tried to catch Pat's attention. He was afraid Dudgy might see him but he needn't have worried because he didn't. He was too busy blubbering like a baba. Like your little baby brother. Stephen rolled up a paper ball and threw it at Pat. "Look!" he whispered as Pat turned around.

But anyway, that is all by the by. What we are talking about now is the park, and the class's visit to it on this beautiful spring afternoon. The children formed a crocodile and followed Mr Dudgeon. Mr Dudgeon did not anticipate any trouble because he had warned the class. Pat Hourican in particular. He had told them if they misbehaved in the park and spoiled it for everyone else he would see that they did not have another playtime for the remainder of the term. He was pretty sure that they had got the message this time.

The park looked quite beautiful in the snow. A high wall ran around it and there was a row of bare trees which Mr Dudgeon had asked some of the class to sketch. A man in a lumberjack shirt sat on a bench eating a sandwich and reading a newspaper.

An old lady with a shopping basket stopped to smile and say "Off on your travels, boys?"

Mr Dudgeon had done quite a lot of preparation for this lesson. Each child had a special notebook and a pencil. The class was divided up into groups. Mr Dudgeon warned them to stay in the groups to which they were assigned. "I want no boy to break away from the general body," he said firmly. Then each group set about its particular task.

Everything was going swimmingly until a boy came over to him and said "Teacher, Stephen Webb isn't here." When he heard those words Mr Dudgeon went white. "What?" he snapped, and the boy repeated what he had said. It was just then that he happened to see two figures at the far end of the park which he realised were Stephen Webb and Kyle Collins. They were trying to climb a tree. Climbing a tree if you don't mind! "Right, this is it," he said to himself and ran as fast as he could across the park. When he got to them he was speechless with rage. Stephen and Kyle had never seen him so furious. Stephen even found himself crying a little bit as his teacher snapped at him. Mr Dudgeon told him he had done it now. He had done it for good this time. He gave Kyle a little push and said "Get over there as fast as your legs will carry you, Collins! Do you hear me talking to you!"

The funny thing was that after he had said that, Mr Dudgeon felt great. He felt like he was capable of anything. He could not believe it! It was a wonderful feeling. The most wonderful feeling in the world. And he was just beginning to enjoy it when he looked up and saw one of the boys waving and calling Pat's name. What was he calling that for? As far as he was concerned he could call it a hundred times. A thousand if he wanted. He wasn't going to be rushed by some upstart of an eight year old. He had dealt with Collins, hadn't he? He had dealt with Webb.

And he would deal with Hourican too in his own good time. Except that it was only when he approached the line of yew trees that he realised what was going on. The children hadn't listened to him at all, had they? They hadn't listened to a word he'd been saying. By God there would be trouble when they got back to school. Look! They were all over the place! Oh for God's sake! Now what was wrong? What did she want? Yes! Yes! I'll be with you in a minute, just as soon as I've dealt with these brats!

The old lady was in hysterics. Her shopping bag was lying beside her on the snow. The man in the lumberjack shirt came running over. He did his best to calm her down but it was no good. Mr Dudgeon went cold all over and started to run. But it was no use. It was too late for him to do anything. By the time he reached the pond, it was all more or less over and he just stood there like a simpleton, staring at Pat's black head bobbing about sporadically on the surface.

Which was very sad of course, and not helped by the fact that it also turned out to be the day Marion had chosen to move out, as the note she left explained.

Burgerland

At night when you go into Burgerland, the light and the colours come racing at you all together to bludgeon your eyes with yellow and lime-green fists. Not that this discouraged Malachy or dissuaded him in any way from making his customary choice. As soon as his order arrived he seated himself by the window as usual, staring out at the beautiful city streets he was coming to know so well this past few weeks as he rambled aimlessly through them, mourning the loss of the one he loved and waiting to get kicked out of his job.

A cardboard cheeseburger man waved at him and told him

that he could get one cheeseburger free if he collected enough "Free Cheeseburger Offer" coupons. Outside, everyone was having fun. They were spilling out of the pubs onto the pavement with their glasses of beer, singing songs about all the trouble in Northern Ireland. One of the songs had a message. It said that northmen and southmen from Dublin to Belfast to Donegal could all be friends and there would be no more killing or bombing. When the chorus came the girls swooned back into their boyfriends' arms. Their boyfriends' sweaters were knotted around their waists. They were having great fun. They sang that we were all on the one road and even if it was the wrong road who cared as long as we were together. When the song was over they all cheered. There was another song playing too, just over Malachy's head in fact, coming from the wall speaker. He knew it well. The song was called "Have You Seen Her?" and what a sad song it was. The words would bring tears to your eyes. They were all about a poor man whose girlfriend did a very bad thing. She upped and left him. One day he came home and she was gone and that was the last he ever saw of her. Which was a pity because all he ever thought about after that was her. He couldn't get her out of his mind. The poor man could not sleep because he was thinking so much about her. Then he would go for walks in the park hoping that he might see her. Catch a glimpse of her. Even that would do. But it was no good. It didn't happen. He kept asking the same question: *"Why oh why did she have to leave and go away?"* But there was no answer. He just kept asking the same question—why did she have to go away? When the song ended the tape went right back to the beginning and began all over again. What Malachy was wondering was—was it ever going to stop? Please let it stop.

He bit into his cheeseburger. There is one slight problem with the food they serve in Burgerland. You really have to be careful when you are biting into your burger. You have to be extra careful because if your mind is not on what you are doing in all likelihood the ketchup will spill on you. It will spill all over your jacket or coat or whatever. Which is what happened to Malachy. A gout of it went plop. "How could I have been so silly —so stupid!" he said to himself. But then he thought "On the other hand—what would you expect me to do? Hardly likely I was going to be able to eat a burger all on my own without fucking up in some small little way now was it?" Oh no. He wiped the ketchup stain and cleaned his coat as best he could.

By the way, there is another slight drawback with Burger- land, for anyone who might be thinking of going there on a regular basis or even on a one-off visit. Skinheads occasionally drop by to eat after their nightly rave-up in whatever cider- swilling den it is they frequent. Malachy was crumpling up the tissue when the door swung open and they came in, shouting and jostling each other and so on. He couldn't say exactly how many of them there were. Six, seven maybe. They were talking about some women they had met and what they were going to do to them. They said they were going to "shag" them. "Shag" them and "Pull the gee out of them." By all accounts this was what they had in mind. One skinhead was bigger than the others. Both physically and in the mouth region. That was why Malachy chose him. He smiled as he walked over and said "Hey you— fuckhead. Yes—you!" For a moment everything was quiet. It was as if nothing at all had been said. It was only when Malachy mimed "fuckhead" again with his lips that the skinhead did any- thing. There were quite a lot of people screaming. "He's going to kill him! He's going to kill him!"

In actual fact, Malachy could feel very little. Even when he was lying on the tiles and they were booting the hell out of him. Not that he doubted for a moment that they would have killed him if it had been at all possible. However shortly afterwards the police came along. A considerable crowd had gathered across the road. They were watching as he was put into the ambulance. They didn't keep him overnight. The doctor told him he was lucky. How he came to that conclusion Malachy really couldn't say.

The Plan

Mr. Extremely Bruised Bubblehead had spent over a week devising his master plan, and now at last came the time to put it into action. So here he was outside the famous Baggot Inn where Paddy Meehan and The Electric Strangers were playing. DUBLIN'S NEXT BIG THING! said the poster. Well well well. Right on in he went, Jack Nicholson style. Fuck you, pal—know what I'm saying? There was of course absolutely no hurry so the first thing he did was to go to the bar and order a drink. Meehan was enjoying himself on stage. His guitar was screeching. So was Meehan. "*I'm on fire! I'm on fire for you!*" was all you could hear.

The sweat was running down Malachy's face. Once more he went over the plan in his mind. He had rehearsed the words he was going to use many times over but he wanted to be sure. The last thing he wanted to do was blow it! He went over what he was going to say once more. "You look pale, Marion. Surprised to see me, are you? Just thought I'd drop by to see the band. Just to see how they are getting on, y'know? So tell me, Marion. How's Paddy? Cut the mustard, can he? Keeping you happy in that department, I hope. Hey, Marion—you there? Maybe you didn't hear me or something. Could it be that maybe you didn't hear me or something like that? You know, Marion, this is pretty crazy. All of a sudden you seem to be struck fucking dumb or something. I mean how can you be? So this is it, Marion—you've gone deaf. You've gone fucking deaf on me, huh? I mean can you believe that—Marion with nothing to say for herself? That's a change for sure! Huh, Marion? A change? A change don't you think?

If she cried, she cried. That was a risk he would have to take. Big deal. Who gave a shit?

Just then he saw her. Sitting in a corner on her own. She smoothed a strawberry blonde hairstrand back behind her ear and smiled up at Paddy who hit his guitar a windmill swipe to impress her. That was enough for Malachy. He took a step forward, then turned right around and walked out of the pub.

The Pembroke Inn is a very popular bar. He liked it. It was just unfortunate that he couldn't be left in peace. Some women's group or other was getting ready for a meeting upstairs. He didn't mind what they did as long as they left him alone. They couldn't, however. They couldn't even do that. There were two of them, practically sitting on top of him. One of them had spiky hair and was rolling a cigarette as she nodded every time Leather-Jacket opened her mouth. This was what she said: "The education of men by the movement is not the issue. As far as I am concerned men are now out of the picture. We need to devote all our energies to women and the political education of women. Particularly working class women."

He stared straight at Cigarette—but she ignored him of course. What she didn't realise was that she had picked the wrong night. He stood over them but they had to show how tough they were by refusing to look up, didn't they? "OK," he said, "OK." He cleared his throat and said "Who do you people think you are? I mean just who the fuck do you think you are?"

So at last she had decided she would do him the honour of looking up, had she? "I'm sorry," she said, "but we're having a private conversation. Please leave us alone to have our drink in peace."

He said "Isn't it a strange sort of private conversation when you're broadcasting it all over the pub? I mean that's a strange kind of private conversation wouldn't you say?"

They said nothing. No doubt they thought he would leave it at that. Go and scuttle off back to his hole. Big mistake, friend. "You know something about you people?" he said. "You make me laugh. You make me laugh, you really do."

He stared straight at them. Right at them, man. "You want to know something about you people? You're living in a fucking dream world! A dream world, lady!"

How he managed to fall across the table he did not know. Unfortunately however, that is exactly what he did, taking five or six glasses with him. The barman had been watching everything and this was the last straw. "Get the fuck out!" he snarled.

Malachy tumbled off into the night and was still laughing when he reached the Grand Canal.

Patrick Kavanagh

Patrick Kavanagh was a poet. He wrote about nature. One of his poems was: *"If ever you go to Dublin town fol-dol-de-di-do."* Or something like that. He wrote a lot of his poems along the banks of the Grand Canal, right where Malachy found himself sitting. When he died, Patrick wanted to be commemorated where there was water. That was why they built the concrete seat for him. They erected it along the banks of the canal where he had spent so many happy hours composing his poems. Malachy found all this very difficult to understand. He found it difficult to understand how anyone could bear to sit by the canal at all much less write poetry about it. For Patrick, however, there were no such difficulties. Any chance he got, he was back along those old banks scribbling away. He wrote about its waters tumbling like Niagara, and about the sun glinting off its surface on a summer's day. Admittedly it wasn't summer right now but it still required an extraordinary leap of the imagination to understand how poetry could be written about it. There was a foul green scum floating on the top of the water. Little islands of green scum. Blobs of slurpy scum. Awkwardly jammed in the lock gates was a rusted iron bedstead. There was also the corpse of a dog, half-rotted away. He wouldn't have thought it the place where one would be inspired to write poetry. He would not have thought so. But then of course, he was probably wrong about that too.

It was quite foggy now. You wouldn't have been able to write poetry even if you wanted to because the fact was you could barely see your hand in front of your face. All he could see of the woman was her white shoes. As she came up close to him he saw that she had long lank blonde hair which was darkened at the roots. She was wearing a red imitation leather coat. Between her fingers she held an unlit cigarette. Her voice was cracked and hoarse as she asked him for a light. When he handed her the matches; she hesitated for a moment then sat down beside him. She looked at the cigarette and said "It would be twenty pound." There was nothing he could think to say. On the far side of the canal a chimney stack belched smoke. A half-drunk man went by behind them, supporting himself against a tree until his drink-fumed coughing spasm passed. She repeated "That's what it would be. Or maybe for you—fifteen."

Malachy was only barely aware he had spoken to her at all. He looked at her when he said it. He didn't turn away. It was all quite low-key. I mean he wasn't crying or anything. In fact, his voice was quite emotionless. What he said to her was: "I let a young boy die."

She didn't say anything. She just lowered her head. He felt her move closer to him. She squeezed his arm gently. Then she said "I'd let you do anything you want. For fifteen, I'd let you do anything you want. Just you." She opened her coat and he could see the pale white flesh of her neck and upper bosom. "Anything?" he asked and she nodded. She was nice, he thought. She had a kind face. Sad that that wasn't what he wanted. He knew it was wrong, even to think of asking her but his hand was already in his pocket. He took out the two Wilkinson Sword blades wrapped in white tissue paper. He stroked her hair and whispered softly into her ear. When he looked again she was standing facing him. "You don't understand, mister," she pleaded. "I have a girl. Gráinne. Mister, she's only three. Please don't hurt me. That's all I ask. Please don't hurt me. Don't cut my face. That's all I ask."

Behind her the grey smoke continued to billow from the chimneys. He looked at her pale, drained face and felt saddened by it all. She thought *he* wanted to hurt *her*. That was the last thing he wanted to do, to anyone. He closed his hand around the wrapped blades and replaced them in his pocket. Far off in the city a window smashed and there was a cry. Followed by the scream of a police siren. When he looked again she was gone. A plastic bag flapped idly, poetry trapped in the locked gates.

Boot

A few weeks later, they gave him the boot as he expected. Dear Mr Dudgeon—here is the money we owe you—please get out of Irish education and don't bother coming back. He wrote to Cissie and explained what had happened as best he could. She begged him to come home and in a way it would have been good if he could have but when love's gone into the grave, there's not much you can do, is there? In the end he just wrote her a short note to say goodbye and left for London the following day.

When Raphael heard of the department's decision, he ought to have been overjoyed. By right there ought to have been cheering and dancing in Madeira Gardens for weeks on end. I mean it was his dream come true, wasn't it—at last getting rid of Dudgeon who had caused him nothing but trouble from the day he walked in the door. Unfortunately however, that wasn't the way it was, it most definitely was not—and in Madeira Gardens especially, for as far as trouble was concerned, poor old Raphael had seen nothing yet.

Little Dominic

Pat Hourican fell in the pond and drowned. His little coffin rested on trestles in the cold gloom of the chapel. His mother in her mantilla clutched the coffin. She asked why did her boy have to die. No one could answer her because they didn't know. Her screeching tore at everybody's heart. Especially Raphael Bell's.

Some time after the funeral he had a dream. This was the first time he'd had it but one thing he could be sure of, it wouldn't be the last. A dream of an old story he had told to his class so many years before: the story of Dominic the little Christian boy. He was a holy boy, the holiest boy in the world. All the boys should try and be like him, their master told them. "Always try and be like little Dominic in every way you can," he said. The master loved telling that story. He loved telling it because he knew all the boys liked listening to it. You could hear a pin drop as he stood by the window staring out at the chestnut tree with the sun in its leaves, his voice lowered as he began:

It was a dark time for the Christians. The city of Rome was

full of spies. Shadows scuttled. The sky was overcast. No one knew what was going to happen next. Deep in the catacombs the hunted Christians huddled together, their murmured prayers echoing in the cold stillness. Late that night the message came through. A poor Christian man was dying on the far side of the city. It was imperative that the Holy Eucharist be brought to him before he breathed his last. But how was this to be done? No Christian was safe. To venture out would have been folly in the extreme. This was when Little Dominic stepped forward to eagerly volunteer. The assembled followers of Christ listened in admiration and awe as this little follower proudly declared "I will go. I will take the Body Of Christ to the poor sick man." His round fresh face shone with youthfulness and trust.

There was much debate among the elders. Eventually however they decided they had little option. They would accept the boy's gallant offer to carry the Eucharist, that he ought indeed to be the Messenger of Christ. Before his departure they asked of him "What will you do if you are confronted by the enemies of Christ?" He thrust out his chest and proudly said "I will never deny the Lord Jesus the son of God because He is Our Lord and Master."

With not a little sadness in their hearts the elders watched as he slipped out silently into the rainwashed streets of Rome. To the north, angry clouds glowered in the sky and his little heart was pounding as he made his way across the city. He felt the cold silver of the Pyx, the sacred box in which the Son Of God was secure against his skin.

Only minutes from his destination, he looked up to see a centurion flanked by militia. They challenged him and he ran until he found himself in a blind alley. A phalanx of men appeared as if out of nowhere, their hands hovering just over the hilts of their short flat swords. The shadow of the centurion fell across him. What was it about the centurion he felt he knew? The answer eluded him although it skirted tantalisingly about the recesses of his mind. "What have you beneath your cloak, boy?" boomed the centurion's voice. "Nothing, sir," he replied and felt nothing then until he realised a short flat sword had been drawn and thrust into his stomach, not once but three times. As he swayed across the muddied cobblestone, he saw the glint of the rolling silver box, trapped finally beneath a sandalled foot. The words in his mind seemed so sad yet so reasonable. "Why does it have to be like this?" As he lay there, blood streaming from the gaping wound in his stomach, the centurion stood above him fingering the silver box. Little Dominic looked up and tried to say "Centurion, why did you kill me?" but when his eyes met the soldier's and he saw that they were those of Raphael Bell, he could not help but weep.

As did the headmaster when he awoke in the night, the only sound that of his heaving chest and the whole world outside the window in darkness deep as the darkest well, whispering his name softly again and again.

About a month after the sad death of little Pat Hourican, Father Stokes looked out the window of the presbytery and saw Nessa Bell climbing the steps, in tears.

Setanta

Making his wife cry wasn't the only bad thing Raphael did around that time. Once he put their cat Setanta halfway across the room with a kick. Almost as soon as he had done it he said he was sorry. Indeed he tried to catch the cat to apologise, but the terrified animal went away under the table and he couldn't get at it. Then Raphael tried to soft soap Nessa but she just screamed at him to go away. The sad thing is that he really was sorry because he loved Setanta, or at least he had until recently.

Raphael didn't know what to think as he sat there by the dying fire rubbing his eyes and taking swigs out of the small bottle of whiskey he now brought home with him every night after visiting The Harcourt Hotel. If he said it once he said it a dozen times—"I'm sorry, Setanta. I'm sorry, Setanta." He was especially sorry because he was thinking of the days when he would never in a million years have done such a thing, of the day when he first got the little cat, as frisky a wee kitten as ever you clapped eyes on. No sooner was he out of his wicker basket than he was off tumbling across the grass and making wild swings at midges and insects to beat the band. What a laugh Raphael and Mrs McCaffrey had at that.

Mrs McCaffrey was a lovely woman. Her son Joseph was a great little footballer in his day. It was him who had told Raphael about the litter. When he heard that Master Bell was on the lookout for a pet he was nearly wet himself and his hand shot into the air as he cried "Teacher! Teacher! My mammy has kittens!"

Which was exactly how it all happened. He smiled as he thought of Joseph, and Mrs McCaffrey standing there on the lawn with her arms folded saying "I wonder what we'll call him, Master Bell?"

"With energy the like of that," said Raphael, "there's only one thing we can call him—Setanta!"

The boy beamed because he knew exactly what Raphael was talking about. But Mrs McCaffrey looked puzzled. "Setanta, Master Bell? Now there's a funny name!"

Raphael shook his head and briefly rested a gentle hand on her shoulder. He removed his wire-framed spectacles and shone them with his starched white handkerchief. Then he coughed lightly and, drumming with his fingers on the lapels of his silver tweed sports jacket, he continued:

"This little fellow here will tell you—won't you, Joseph? What we've been doing all week in history class. Back in ancient times in Ireland, Mrs McCaffrey, there was as fine a band of men who roamed the hills and dales and they went by the name of The Red Branch Knights. Now around that time there was a youth who went by the name of Setanta and his prowess both in the sporting arena and on the battlefield were legendary. Mrs McCaffrey, he could hit a hurley ball so hard into the sky that it would travel a hundred miles and do you know what he would do then?"

Mrs McCaffrey shook her head, deeply impressed by the breadth of the master's knowledge.

Raphael paused and contemplated the toes of his shoes. He drew a deep breath: "What would he do, Joseph?"

"Catch it coming down, Master."

"Now there's the scholar for you!" beamed Raphael.

Mrs McCaffrey's eyes moistened. The kitten continued to leap and bound through the air. Then, putting her arm around her son's shoulders, she said "I know he'll be happy with you, Master Bell. I know he'll be happy with you—little Setanta."

Raphael extended his hand and she clasped it warmly. "It's a present, Master. For all you've done for our Joseph. You're a credit to the school. All the mammies and daddies say it. You have made St Anthony's what it is today."

Raphael lowered his head and thanked her for her kind comments. "We do our best, Mrs McCaffrey. It's all any of us can do."

Mrs McCaffrey looked into his eyes, and as if reaching for words which were beyond her grasp, she said "God bless you,

Master Bell." Then she and Joseph made their way to the main road where her husband was sitting in the car waiting for them.

Raphael glowed with the happiness occasioned by her kindness, thinking about those private little triumphs which made the profession of teaching such a rewarding one: the expression of wonder on a child's face as a complex, impenetrable problem suddenly reveals itself as if by magic, the trusting clasp of a child's hand in the playground, the warm affection and appreciation which often grew up between parent and teacher, as had happened in this instance. And of which little Setanta was the living proof. Raphael smiled to himself as he watched the squealing ball of fur spin in the air. Then, unable to contain himself any longer, he found himself laughing aloud as he strode briskly across the playground and, breaking into a trot, cried "Setanta! Setanta! Pish-wish! Pish-wish! Come here to me now like a good boy!"

But what a little devil Setanta was! Could he lay his hands on him? Not on your life! Just when he thought he had him cornered, the scallywag would be away in between his legs and off like a bullet again. But at last the headmaster managed to pen him in between the septic tank and the wall and with one leap, had him bundled under his coat. He was as warm as toast in there, mewing away like nobody's business. And the wriggles of him! Raphael was afraid those claws would stick into him and he'd be caught off guard and the last thing he wanted was to have to start the same thing all over again. So he tapped the outline of the animal gently but firmly and said "Now no more of your nonsense, Setanta. We're going home now to get you a warm bowl of milk. If you're good that is! There won't be very much milk if you don't mind your manners—do you hear me?"

But by that stage they had already reached the car so the master climbed in and depositing the new addition to the family safely in the backseat, he began to whistle "My Grandfather's Clock" and turning the key in the dash, chugged off towards home, barely able to contain the excitement he felt at the prospect of his wife's reaction to the arrival of the surprise guest.

Which, it has to be said, was a lot better than a kick in the face, and an awful lot better than being left to rot away and die and be eaten by maggots in The Dead School which was exactly what was in store for little frisky Pish-Wish although of course he didn't know that yet—how could he?

When Nessa came down the following morning she found her husband still in the chair with the empty bottle in his hand, snoring away like a pig.

Whispers

Around that time the whispering campaign started. It wasn't enough for Evans to come along and kill his school stone dead. Perhaps in the beginning that might have been enough for her, but the death of Pat Hourican had whetted her appetite and now nothing only Raphael's complete banishment would satisfy her. You could see it in her eyes. And that smirk. Of course when he put it to Stokes, he denied everything and said that he was only imagining things. But then, what else could he say when he had been in league with them from the start? Actually, the first time Raphael had heard the words, he thought himself that he had imagined them. He was pulling out the school gates when he heard Mrs McCaffrey, the very woman who had given him Setanta, now thick as thieves with Evans, whispering behind her hand "Whose fault is it then, Pat was killed? It's *his* school." He passed no remarks on that until one day he was buying cigarettes in the shop around the corner when, beyond all shadow of doubt, he heard a woman saying "If it was anyone else, he'd have lost his job."

He didn't sleep a wink that night or the next night either. When, at 4:00 A.M., Nessa followed him to the kitchen and asked him what was wrong, he looked up at her with bloodshot eyes and winced a little. Outside the city slept. She asked him again. "Oh there's nothing wrong with me," he replied as he blew the skin off his cocoa.

No Nothing

Things didn't go really bad however until Thompson started. Raphael might have known. After all—you couldn't expect much else from the Thompsons, could you? Three of them had been through the school already and, not to put too fine a point on it, they were as thick as two short planks. No major problem to map out their destiny—the street corner or the high stool, and that was more or less it. But insolence—in all fairness that had never been a characteristic you could attribute to them. No, that most certainly had come as a surprise. So much of a surprise in fact that he could not believe it when he came upon the Thompson boy playing with a game of some sort in a corner of the playground. This, despite a notice clearly displayed for all to see in the corridors and on the front door of the school: ALL TOYS PROHIBITED IN THE SCHOOL BUILDING AND PLAYGROUND. What he simply could not believe was the boy being so engrossed in the infernal game that he did not hear him. He actually had to repeat "Do you hear me, boy?" before the insolent whelp looked up with the drooping eyes and gormless expression of all his brothers before him. "What is it you have there?" the teacher asked. "It's a game," the boy replied. Mr Bell pushed his index finger into his collar and said "I am perfectly aware that it is a game! What sort of game?"

"The Six Million Dollar Man," the boy said.

Mr Bell lowered his head until his face was level with the boy's. He spoke calmly and firmly.

"Don't ever bring it in here again," he said.

The boy did not reply. He just stared at him with lifeless, stone-dead eyes.

What happened next was practically impossible to believe. The following day what did he do—he brought it in again. And there he was standing in exactly the same place playing it. Raphael was beginning to wonder was he hallucinating. He half-expected that when he touched the boy on the shoulder that he would simply turn to dust and vanish or something. He didn't however. "Oh no" Raphael said, smiling to himself, "we couldn't have a Thompson boy doing that now could we? That would be showing too much intelligence."

Raphael decided to remain perfectly calm about the situation. Drumming a silent little tune on the lapel of his jacket, he cleared his throat. "What did I tell you yesterday?" he snapped. "Don't know," the boy replied and stuck his tongue into his cheek. Raphael smiled. "You don't know?" The boy shook his head. "No."

Suddenly Raphael felt his cheeks burn. Not that he cared what burned. If Thompson thought he was going to somehow make him lose his temper, then he was sorely mistaken. Oh yes. He knew only too well that there were certain people who would be more than delighted to witness such a spectacle. Yes, a little display of temper would go down well with that lot. With a certain Evans for example. Oh ho, she would like that all right. That would be just what she was waiting for. But she wouldn't get it, you see. No sir. I'm afraid you'll be waiting a long time for that, friends.

He smiled down at the boy. "No—what?" he said.

Thompson tugged at the belt of his trousers and, unbelievably, looked him in the eye as he replied "No nothing."

Which was a very good answer. A wonderful answer. Or so Thompson thought. No doubt because it started all the little juniors laughing as they gathered around. "Did you hear what the boy said to the headmaster?" one of them whispered. No wonder Thompson was pleased with himself. Grinning away. It probably came as quite a surprise to him when he saw that Mr Bell was grinning too. He didn't expect that, any more than he expected the flat of the headmaster's hand to catch him across the face—not once, not twice, but three times. Then he began to bawl like one of the infants in Mrs Corry's class. Which he continued doing all the way across the playground to the office. As far as Raphael was concerned, this was a lesson which had been coming to Thompson for a long time. He was going to see to it that the likes of this never happened again. He gave him the hiding of a lifetime. Thompson pleaded and pleaded, but he was wasting his time. Raphael had been teaching much too long to be manipulated by these pitiful pleas. He had embarked upon a certain course and was going to see it through. It would be quite a long time before Mr Thompson attempted any of his insubordination again. "Give me the game! Give it to me!" Raphael snapped as the boy sobbed in the chair.

With a trembling hand, Thompson proffered the game. Raphael stared impassively at the bionic man leaping into the air on the plastic bagatelle. He sucked his teeth distastefully, then placed it on his desk, and raising a heavy marble paperweight he brought it down and broke the toy into a thousand pieces. The once-insolent Thompson now began to howl pathetically. The headmaster folded his arms. He was content. It would be quite some time before Mr Thompson said "No nothing" to him again.

The Flower-Seller

He thought the whispering would stop. That sooner or later they would see sense and stop listening to the likes of Evans. That they would remember all he had done for them in the past and put the death of Pat Hourican, the one thing that had gone wrong in over forty years, out of their minds and start afresh.

But they wouldn't. It even got to the stage where the flower-sellers in Grafton Street were talking about him. He was going past the woman who sold the roses outside the news-agent's one day and heard her saying "That's him—that's Bell. He let a young boy die." This saddened him. Of course it did. But he understood. He didn't blame her, or any of the other women who were talking about him. He knew they would have stood by him if Stokes had shown some leadership.

"By Christ she wouldn't have tried that carry-on with the pair of us in the old days, Father, I can tell you!" he said to himself one night as he pulled off his socks. "We'd have been more than a match for the likes of her!"

Last Breath

Raphael was delighted with himself. This time she had gone too far. This time he would shut her up once and for all. What did she think he was—mad? That he would allow her to get away with the like of this!

As soon as he heard about it, he summoned Father Stokes to the office. He paced the floor with his hands behind his back and tried his best to remain calm. Then he turned to the priest "What I have to say I will keep brief and to the point. There will be no change in school policy. The children will continue to attend Friday evening sodality as they have always done. Rosaries and prayer books as before. I reiterate—there will be no change." He coughed politely and looked away as he said softly "I take it I can rely on your support, Father."

Father Stokes ran his countryman's weathered fingers through his shock of white hair and screwed up his face as if in pain. He faltered as he spoke, then began anew. "It may be unnecessary in this day and age," he said. "The children don't have the same interest now, I mean. In any case, a majority on the Parents' Committee have voted against it, so in all honesty, Raphael, there isn't really an awful lot we could do even if we wanted to. I see your point of course, and I'm all for it—but sometimes maybe it's better to just let sleeping dogs lie. And after all, the Parents' Committee have done an awful lot for the school. . . ."

Raphael stared at the face of his old friend and in the silence that ensued thought of the Phoenix Park on that day when a million people fell to their knees, of a summer garden where a young priest laughed with a scone in his hand and as the words came to his lips, knew in his heart in that instant that this was the last effort he was ever going to make. "Please, Father . . ." he pleaded:

"I'm sorry," replied the elderly clergyman as he lowered his head.

If you can single out a specific day upon which the school Raphael loved so much, and to which he had devoted most of the forty-three years of his teaching career, drew its last breath, then it was indeed this particular day in May 1976, exactly two months after the death of Pat Hourican, as he knew now only too well, his hand trembling on the wheel as he drove all the way across the city to The Harcourt Hotel to spend the day with the barman who was a former pupil, drinking himself once more into a giddy, explosive stupor.

Early Retirement

Not that there's anything wrong with drink, mind you, for there is no better way of enjoying oneself than having a few glasses of an evening but it can't be denied that overindulgence does have its drawbacks, particularly if you are prone to hearing the odd whisper, because what it tends to do is make them louder. And louder. It does nothing for your ability to judge a situation either, as was the case with Raphael one day when he was on his way home to Madeira Gardens and happened to catch a glimpse of Father Stokes leaving by the back door. Thanks to the cumulative effect of God knows how many whiskeys over God knows how long, he went and got it into his head that the purpose of the clergyman's visit had been to talk about him, indeed not only that but to plot and scheme about him with his wife Nessa. Once something like that starts, it doesn't take long for it to gather steam, and by the time he had turned the key in the door, he was more than convinced that they too were both in league against him. The more he thought about it, the more he came to realise just how bad his predicament now was.

Only a couple of days earlier, Stokes had called to the school and started stuttering and stammering about the Thompson boy, going on about his parents being up in arms and how they had to take him to the hospital. Raphael had felt like laughing in his face there and then. He felt like laughing and saying to him "What—his parents are up in arms, are they? I'm afraid you must be mistaken, Father! The parents in this school would never cause a fuss! Oh no! Not in a million years! It must be someplace else you're thinking of!" Indeed, he was on the verge of saying this, or something very similar, when would you believe it, Stokes started to mutter something behind his hand.

At first, Raphael didn't know what he was saying and to be honest with you, cared less, but then he heard it all right. Stokes was mumbling about "early retirement." At the age of sixty-three, Raphael was due to retire in two years anyway and here was this idiot of a priest blathering on about "early retirement"! Was he mad in the head or what? Did he really think he would agree to that? He couldn't even begin to think what it would be like to be retired, much less two years before your time! The more he thought about it, the more infuriated he became. The cheek of him to even dare suggest such a thing. Because of the likes of Thompson! Tick tick tick went the right eye nerve. "Get out!" snapped Raphael. He slapped his open hand down on the desk. "Get out of my office!" Stokes was nearly bent double as he crept out of the office! You should have seen the look on his face!

But sneaking out of the house behind his back—that was a much more serious development. He couldn't believe that he would stoop to this level. Trying to turn a man's wife against him —it was unbelievable!

What was even more unbelievable however was that he appeared to have succeeded because when he confronted Nessa she denied everything. She was not in league with Stokes, she said. She didn't know what he was talking about. She was just worried, she said. That was all—worried. Raphael looked at her and for a split second wondered who she was. "You're telling lies," he said, through thin lips. When she began to cry, he was on the verge of melting when it dawned on him that what he was witnessing was another ploy. He had seen such behavior in the classroom hundreds of times. To think he had almost fallen for it! "It will be a long time before you or any of your duplicitous colleagues ever force me to do anything against my will!" he said tersely. Before he left the room to go to his study, he turned and said "I deeply regret what you have done here today, Nessa. I want you to know that."

Not that he cared. He hadn't done anything wrong. He could face his maker with a clear conscience—which was more than most of them could do. Isn't that right, Stokes? Do you hear me, Evans? Isn't that right—mm? Oh but it is, you see! Early retirement! Oh Stokes, you fool! You silly silly fool!"

———————

White Punks On Dope

Which in all honesty now is not the best of behaviour for a man who is supposed to be guiding little children through life but bad as it was, it was nothing to what old Bubblehead was getting up to, sitting on his big backside in a busted armchair in Shepherd's Bush, London, and sucking huge drags out of a telegraph pole of a joint. Of course it's hard to believe, but let me tell you this, if it's hard for us it was twice as hard for him! I mean, one minute there you are, Mr Bollocks-Face Frogspawn Wouldn't-Say-Boo-To-A-Goose-Couldn't-Keep-His-Girlfriend Dudgeon, off every morning with your head down to St Anthony's School for crazy baldy bastards and the next there you are in a squat full of loopers and headbangers who wouldn't know a day's work if it kicked them in the goolies. There was "Chico The Head" and "Mad Peter" from Kerry with his head nodding like a cloth donkey in the back of a car. In the fire, half the furniture, and over the mantelpiece a great big painted eye with the words YOU ARE THE YOU, whatever the fuck that was supposed to mean. Not that

Bubblehead cared, he was too busy puffing and shouting "Fuck frogspawn!"

Thanks to his old buddy Kevin Connolly he had wound up here. "It's a cool place," he had said, "They'll look after you there."

And, man, could you say that again as off they went, cruising the tube all the way to Piccadilly where they were going to get out of their heads, man, out of their brains and that's a fact because Chico's just gotten lucky, waving thirty quid in the air and shouting "OK you assholes so what are we gonna do lie around here blowing this shit I mean you call this dope this is bullshit, man, we're gonna get ourselves something that's worth smoking so come on you guys get your ass in gear and move it cos you know why by tonight we are going to be gone, man, and I mean fucking gone!" And were they, or what? Chico and Malachy and The Prince Of Tangier all the way from Cork, heating Red Leb in a chillum pipe as the beer went streaming down and Philip Lynott blasted "The Boys Are Back In Town." Yeah they were back in town all right and that was where Malachy Dudgeon was going to stay forever, man, right here in London Town, smelling of patchouli with his bomber jacket zippered up and his hair so wild and curly bouncing on his shoulders. Already Dublin seemed like a million years ago, since The Prince stood in the doorway and stuck out his hand then dragged him in. "They call me The Prince," he said. "I'm The Prince of Tangier, man, I know things. You wanna know some things, friend of Kevin Connolly's? The Irish pipers, man, way back. You know what they used to do? Like what I'm saying is, they used to bind their pipes with hemp and like when they're playing, when they're playing, right, they're taking in all these fumes, man, so they're playing, right, and half the time they're out of their fucking heads! Out of their heads, man—it's true! Hey,

Malachy, you want to know something? You're okay. You used to be a teacher, right? They fuck up your head. Their heads are so fucked up, they want to fuck up yours, right?" "Right," says Malachy, "you got it." "I know I got it, man, I'm The Prince," says The Prince, "The Prince—you hear me? They busted me there you know—tried to do my head in. But it's their own heads they're doing in. They don't know that but it is. Oh yeah. Their own heads, man."

On the wall, a naked girl on a Harley-Davidson rode off into the smoke. As the beercans tumbled and the record sleeves flew all about him, Chico in an afghan danced crazy on the floor, screaming into his air-microphone *White Punks On Dope! White Punks On Dope!* And The Tubes gave it all they'd got. "It's not fucking loud enough!" he shouted as he fell across the turntable with the tears running down his face. "It's their own heads, you see," said The Prince. "You gotta remember that. If you remember that, you're OK." Red-eyed strangers came and went. Malachy looked up and saw an arse in the air. It was Chico's. "Jesus, man, I'm so stoned," he said to the girl. "Oh baby," she groaned. Malachy took another blast of a joint and started laughing when he saw The Prince looking up at him with melting eyes, saying "Teacher, can I go to the toilet?" and then collapsed in a fit of hysterics. Malachy stumbled across the floor with a pain in his head from laughing. "Oh Christ!" moaned Chico. "Oh Jesus and his mother Mary!"

"Teacher!" shrieked The Prince. "Teacher! Teacher! Me wanna go toilet!"

Malachy handed him the joint. "Here, man!" he said, "Come on!"

"Teacher—don't slap me!" yelped The Prince.

Then Malachy went and dropped the joint and had to go looking for it in case it set the place on fire. As he crawled around on his hands and knees he said to himself "I wonder what she'd think of this? So what do you think of this Marion babe, out of my head looking for a joint in Shepherd's Bush. I mean can you believe it Frogspawn Dudgeon out of his head in England. What do you think of that?" Electric Strangers hey Paddy remember me yoo hoo oh fuck me Prince I can't find it we're all going to die we're going to be burnt alive hee hee. No, don't worry man it's going to be all right it's all in your head as long as you believe that's all you got to do oh man I've got to have some rice I've got to have Ambrosia creamed rice I've got to have some hey Malachy look—look at his ass up in the air look at his fucking ass hey ass what are you looking at shut the fuck up Prince oh Chico you don't love me anymore Malachy he doesn't love me no more shut up and change the record *White Punks On Dope White Punks On Dope!*

"You wanna know something?" The Prince said before he hit the sack. "You wanna know something I can't remember what it is." He folded again and Malachy had to hold him up as tears of laughter came down his face making Malachy just as bad as him every time he thought of it, lying there in the camp bed with The Tubes far away and a snapshot of Marion in his hand as he tried not to think of that day in the park.

And so the weeks went by while every night they cruised the tube, falling down Shaftesbury Avenue after scoring in The George or Trafalgar Square. When Chico got the munchies it was supermarket time, lots and lots of niceys. The Prince fecked a pair of Ray Bans and climbed the stage in The Wellington shouting "We're talking Joey Ramone here!" before they all got fucked out. Back in the squat, Malachy took the stage on the beer-soaked floor and shouted into the broom handle "Goodnight, London! This is Philip Lynott and Thin Lizzy loving you and leaving you with 'The Boys Are Back In Town!' Aw right!"

"Thaggew!" screamed The Prince and cupped the joint in his hands.

What her name was, Malachy never did find out. She just appeared after a party and all Malachy knew was that she was there beside him in the bed. She stroked his cheek and said soft things in his ear, her breasts warm against his skin. When she asked "What's wrong?" he didn't know what to say. He could see her face in the dark and she looked sad. She pushed her hair back from her eyes and moved in closer to him. "What is it?" she asked. "You're so tense. Don't you like me?"

"It's not you," he said. "You're beautiful."

She kissed him on the eyes. "Then why don't you like me?"

"I want someone else" wouldn't have been the right thing to say. It wouldn't have done anyone any good. He just looked away, and when he looked again a long time afterwards, she was asleep.

It was a pity things had to be like that. When he woke up in the morning she was gone and he never saw her again.

The months went by in a blur of The New York Dolls, The Ramones, Thin Lizzy and Rory Gallagher. The parties went on long into the night and Malachy and The Prince and Chico rode the tube for Leb and Paki Black and anything else that was going. Sometimes Malachy would start the chuckling and wonder how The Electric Strangers would like this shit! He slammed a chord on Chico's three string guitar and shouted Bob Marley down, "You better watch it, Paddy! You'd better watch your baby, man!" he cried, then went and knocked over the table with The Prince's beer on it. "You asshole," screamed The Prince. "My beer! You've spilt my fucking beer! It's OK, beer. It's OK. It's gonna be OK," he said as he lapped it up with his tongue. Bob Marley chugged on as Malachy smiled to himself, because he knew you see, he *knew* when Paddy and Marion and him met again, this time it was gonna be a whole lot different—a whole new story, man!

That night the boys were back in town big time. All Malachy remembered was standing in Shepherd's Bush Green in his army coat shouting "Come on now! Back up! Make way for the slot machine! Come on—show a little bit of consideration there!"

When he opened his eyes the next morning, he saw Chico and The Prince and the plainclothes cop standing at the bottom of the bed. What could he do only laugh, The Prince with the big mournful face on him and Chico shivering in his jocks. It was wild!

So what does the cop want, wants to know what they've done with the fruit machine, for fuck's sake! "What slot machine," says Malachy and the cop loses it then—"That slot machine, that fruit machine," he says, *that* bloody fruit machine!" And Malachy looks up to see it beside the fucking bed decked out in his fucking army coat and Chico's knitted Commando cap.

So what were you supposed to do? I mean just what were you supposed to do except dance round the kitchen, waving the fucking joints and singing "White Punks On Dope" while The Prince howled in the corner because he missed his dog Buster back in Ireland.

———————

Dust

How long exactly Nessa and his so-called colleague had been plotting against him, Raphael could not say for sure. He had to admit that he was deeply saddened by the way it had all turned out. Oh he was, there was no denying that. Over time, however, he began to come to terms with it. He had had plenty of knocks in his time oh yes he had and he was damned if he was going to let this one get the better of him. The worst thing was that it wasn't just any ordinary old betrayal you see. It was a lot more serious than that—a lot more serious, I'm afraid. Because what it meant of course was that all the precious moments they had shared together down the years—well they weren't really anything at all now, were they? You certainly couldn't call them precious moments, that was for sure! A better name for them might be something like this: Dust. Because when you examined them that was more or less what they turned out to be. They were what you would call a big useless pile of dust, of absolutely no use to anybody. A dinner in The Dolphin Hotel after the most exciting All-Ireland Final of all time: Dust. A play they had attended in the Abbey Theatre, a Saturday afternoon listening to *The Walton Programme:* Dust. A journey to the Ring of Kerry one glorious week in August: A journey to dust. That was what it was. Oh my head, thought Raphael. I have a pain in my head. Why am I always getting pains in my head? It's not fair. Stokes doesn't get them—why does he not get them? Is there anything worse than dust? Yes. Worse than any dust is lies. How could the most beautiful woman who had ever lived tell him lies? How could she have gone and done it?"

He drove into town and sat in his usual spot. He drank half a bottle of whiskey and that put him in good humour. The barman wiped the table and said "You seem to be in good form, Mr Bell. Laughing away there!" "Am I laughing?" Raphael replied. The barman said "You're an awful man! Don't you know well you are!" and Raphael told to him to have a whiskey. "Ah sure I will," said the barman. And it wasn't long before the pair of them were laughing away just like Raphael had been earlier on, even if he didn't realise it.

The following day, when he was buying the paper, he heard

the flower-seller at her mouthing again, only this time worse than ever. "There he goes," she whispered to the woman beside her, "the child-killer. Young Hourican wasn't enough for him of course. He had to go and batter young Thompson to a pulp. All I can say is the Department of Education must be stuck, missus. That's all I can say. Get your roses here! Lovely fresh roses."

Dust and the way things turn to it was still on his mind when he got home from The Harcourt a few nights later. Nessa was sitting in the parlour waiting up for him. She said his dinner was still warm if he wanted it. But it didn't matter to him if his dinner was warm or not. He didn't care. All he cared about was getting at the truth, which was why he caught her by the wrists and looked deep into her eyes and said "Please tell me the truth. That is all I ask. Nessa my love that is all I ask." Now Nessa was crying. She started to answer, then stopped and started again. "Please tell me!" cried Raphael. "Tell me—can't you! Tell me, Nessa! Tell me!" "Father Des was worried about you, Raphael" she blurted out finally. "That was why he was here. He was worried about you—can't you see? You're overwrought! Since that dreadful accident you're not yourself! Can't you see that? Please, Raphael—can't you see that!"

There were tears in her eyes as she reached out to him but he recoiled. "Don't touch me!" he cried. "Don't touch me, liar! For that's all you are!"

Then he pulled away and ran off out of the room and up-stairs.

Resignation

If Raphael had slipped a lump hammer out from under his jacket and hit Father Stokes a few times across the face with it, the effect could not have been better. He thought Raphael was play-

ing some kind of joke on him. At least, that's what he thought in
the beginning. But when the headmaster's face didn't move a
muscle, he soon realised that it was far from being a joke. He
started to stutter and fumble around for something to say. But "I
don't understand, Raphael," was all he could manage. Raphael
didn't bother to reply. His words had been perfectly clear. As
well they ought to have been, considering he had been up most
of the night preparing them, the most important words of his
life, and he wanted to get them right. He wanted to show Evans
and Stokes and all the rest of the turncoats once and for all. He
wanted to show them once and for all! He wanted to assemble
them all in the school playground and shout the words out right
across the city: "You want me to slip quietly out the back of the
school to which I've given my entire life! You want to put me out
to grass like an old horse—is that what you want? I'm an embarrassment to you all am I? I'm an embarrassment to Evans! That's
it isn't it? You're afraid of her! You're afraid of her and her
takeover friends! It will be all right once you get rid of me won't
it no more trouble no more Thompson but I'm not doing it—
that's where you've all got it wrong! I'm just not doing it and
now you see I've gone and spoiled your little plot haven't I? Oh
yes, you had it all worked out. Mr Bell isn't with us anymore.
He's taken early retirement. But I haven't you see! And I won't! I
won't—because I'm resigning! Go on—take my beloved school!
Destroy it! Murder it! Kill it like all the little babies you've
burnt! Kill it, Evans! Throttle it until it dies at your feet for
that's all you're good for! And you, Father! You help her! Go
ahead—help her! Hold its head under the water. But not with
me! Not with me, my old friend!"

That was the image and those were the words floating
around in his mind as he entered the presbytery reception room

to make his speech to the blanched priest. He read from the sheet of vellum paper:

> "Rev Fr. I have considered your suggestion re early retirement. I regret very deeply that you feel it is necessary to make such a suggestion. In the light of this I have given the matter much thought. Consequently, I feel it is incumbent upon me to tender my resignation. May I take this opportunity to thank you for all the kindness and consideration you have shown toward me in the past. Yours respectfully, Raphael Bell N.T."

When he had finished, he folded the letter and replaced it in the envelope. That was really all he had to say so before Stokes could open his mouth to say aye or no, he turned on his heel and walked out the door. As he strode across the school playground, the blood was still crashing in his head and it was only after the little fellow had said it three times that he realised he was asking could he go to the toilet. "Yes yes of course," Raphael replied as he curled the toes of his right foot inside his shoe, to help keep him on the ground like an anchor because he really did feel like he was about to lift off and go sailing away right over the school.

A Baldy Old Scarecrow
When Nessa heard the news, of course she tried to dissuade him, saying that it wasn't what he really wanted to do and that it was all because of Pat's death and all the other business that had happened after it with young Thompson and so on and what was the point of falling out with everyone, he could retire early and everyone would be happy and he could do this and he could do that and they could forget all that had happened. "Oh could we?" he said. "Yes we could," she said. And when she said that,

that was enough. "Shut up," he said, "would you mind please shutting up." He wanted her to shut up because if she had all these things to say, why didn't she say them before Stokes started coming to the house to help her say them. Why couldn't she say them then? He looked at her to see if she had an answer. She hadn't of course so he said "If you'll excuse me I have business to do." Harcourt Hotel business in other words, with himself and the barman laughing away to their heart's content. "Will you ever forget the time McGinley broke all the ink bottles in the corridor?" says the barman. "Oh now," says Raphael, "will I ever forget it?"

"An awful character," says the barman.

"Oh now—who are you telling!" says Raphael.

Then home to find Nessa sobbing in bed, not that he cared what she did, after what she'd done on him. Her and Stokes and company, for God knows who else she had had in the house, plotting behind his back. "To hell with them!" he roared as he fell across the bedside cupboard. "I fixed Lally in the handball alley and I'll fix them! My father died for Ireland! Stand up when I'm talking to you! Where's your rosary beads, boy! Open your books at page sixteen!"

Then he'd fall on the floor or into an armchair and sleep there for the night.

He did that every day after school now and was going to go on doing it until he left for good. Why shouldn't he? He didn't care. He didn't care if he looked like a baldy old scarecrow in front of his boys. Why should he? They weren't his boys.

Not anymore.

Flowers For Nessa

They could say what they liked to him. They could say absolutely anything. Raphael didn't care. He had trumped them all—Evans, McCaffrey and the whole whispering tribe of them. The flower-seller in Grafton Street wasn't so smart now, was she? It wasn't quite the same thing saying "There's Mr Bell. He made a fool of Father Stokes" as "There's Mr Bell. He made a boy drown."

Which was why he turned to her with a triumphant smirk on his face. Not so much as a murmur out of her. And why? Because he had had the last laugh, that's why. Nobody had been expecting Raphael to go to the bad so they hadn't the foggiest notion what to do about it when it happened. There were meetings and suggestions and all sorts of things but they came to nothing. For a while Father Stokes called to the house to see Nessa but it got so nerve-racking wondering would Raphael be in or out that the visits became less and less frequent and after a while began to peter out altogether.

Of course Raphael was distressed at the way she was behaving. What did she expect of him? Had she not considered the effect her actions might have had?

He simply ignored her and went up to his room. He felt sad of course that their once-spotless home was becoming little more than a midden now that she had evidently decided to suspend her domestic duties, for some reason best known to herself. Some form of protest, perhaps. As if it mattered now. The sheets in their bed were flea-ridden. Stinking dishes piled up in the sink. He didn't care. Why should he? He ate his dinner in The Harcourt Hotel. It might, indeed most likely would have, gone on like that indefinitely had it not been for the barman. On hearing the whole sad story from start to finish, he had scratched his neck and said "Ah God, Master—you wouldn't do that on her? You wouldn't treat the poor woman like that!" It was the gentle way that he said it, and because he was such a good old stick that it occurred to Raphael for the first time that he had been, after all, a trifle harsh. "Would you not think of going a wee bit easier on her—would you not, Master?" As he stared at the barman's kind face, all of a sudden a little thought came to him and he found himself smiling. "Yes!" he said to the barman. "I will! After all—she's not the worst of them!"

"Now you're talking!" said the barman as he poured him another Jameson.

No doubt the flower-seller was more puzzled than ever when he bought the big bunch of flowers. But then, that just went to prove it, didn't it—they would have to get up early in the morning before they would begin to understand Raphael Bell! He smiled at her as he took his change. She didn't know what to say as he went on beaming at her. He was feeling tremendous now, he had to admit. It was just a pity the barman hadn't made his suggestion sooner. But no matter. Better late than never.

And so, having paid the taximan, off he strode up the avenue and into the house calling his wife's name, not exactly saying darling but feeling for some strange inexplicable reason like doing so, not that it made an awful lot of difference what he felt because she didn't hear a word.

Of course, like any human being, when he saw her sitting there with her mouth open, the furthest thing from Raphael's mind was that she was dead. Indeed it wasn't until he touched her on the forehead which turned out to be as cold as ice that he realised what in fact he'd done was make one of the biggest mistakes of his life, one of those mistakes which would unfortunately, no matter what he did, be with him until the day he died.

The Dead School Opens

The Dead School was first opened on July 21, 1976, the day they blew up the British Ambassador. Raphael walked into Pat Mc-Nulty's hardware shop in Clontarf and said "Could I have two dozen black bin liners please?" As Pat was taking down the bin liners from the top shelf he said "Wasn't that terrible about the British Ambassador, Mr Bell? What the hell is wrong with these people? What do they hope to achieve?" He shook his head then went "Tsk tsk" as he put the bin liners into a big brown paper bag. "What do I care about the British Ambassador?" Raphael said. Then what did he do, without another word, paid for the bin liners and walked off out into the street. Pat McNulty looked after him and felt his cheeks redden. "I wonder what the hell's eating him?" he said to himself.

That was the day after they buried Nessa.

Raphael was standing outside the cemetery repeating to himself "Nessa's gone. She's gone, you see," when Father Stokes came over to him and laid a leather-gloved hand on his shoulder. "Let me take you home, Raphael. And maybe we can stop for a bite to eat on the way. What do you say to that?"

Raphael looked blankly at him. Then, before the clergyman could say anything, he pushed past him and started walking off down the road in the direction of Dublin City.

Some people reckoned it was the hottest day for fifty years. T-shirts and shorts and sunshades were everywhere. Lawn mowers whirring away to beat the band. Cars whizzed along the coast road with the kids all yelping "We're going to the seaside! We're going to the seaside!" Which indeed they all were, with the result that Madeira Gardens was practically empty. A warm suburban ghost town. Except of course for Raphael who was busy as a beaver in his shirtsleeves, tacking up his bin liners. He had all the back windows done and now he was starting on the front ones. He dumped all the curtains in the bin. When he had that done, he gathered up all Nessa's clothes, her lovely womanny perfumey clothes, and packed them all into a trunk and dragged it upstairs. Then he locked it in a storeroom. So that was the end of that.

Now what was there to do? "I have a hundred and one things to do here in The Dead School," he laughed. Then he sat down and said "Ah to hell with it, I'll have a rest!" He opened a bottle of whiskey and took a swig out of it. Once he heard a fellow in the pub saying "He was as black as the riding boots of the Earl Of Hell!" Raphael thought that was a good one. It certainly was a good way of describing what had once been the parlour of 53 Madeira Gardens! But anyway, that was enough of that! He couldn't sit there all day drinking whiskey—there was work to be done!

He opened his briefcase and took out his books. *A New English Primer. Catechism For Boys And Girls.* Hall And Knight's Algebra. J. C. Beckett's *History Of Ireland. My Friend Our Lady.* A pamphlet called *May I Keep Company?* Lots and lots of books. Homework books. Sums copies. Jotters. Books by the hundred. And pens. And bottles of ink. What a lot of things Raphael had in his briefcase! He flicked on the table lamp and started to read what J. C. Beckett had to say about Mr Parnell and his carry-on with Mrs O'Shea the dirty trollop. "Now where are we? Parnell is off to visit her at her home for the weekend. Is he now," said Raphael "well you needn't think I'm going to waste my time reading rubbish the like of that no I think I'll skip back here to the eleventh century and see how Brian Boru is getting on at the Battle Of Clontarf." But he couldn't see how Brian was getting on because the words started floating in front of his eyes, swimming off here there and everywhere so that he couldn't read anything. Not a stitch! Off they went into the air like big spidery insects. He tried to stop them but they wouldn't listen to him. "Stop it!" he cried. "Get into your lines at once!" Fortunately this time they listened to him and kicked their heels as they got back into line. "At last!" said Raphael. "You're showing a bit of manners!" He didn't mind so much now after the way it had all worked out. But unfortunately just as he was about to start reading again the words went and swooshed away off the page and round the room like wordy tornadoes curling all about him and trying to tease and make a cod of him. He tried to get ahold of them, shake some sense into them but it was like trying to wrestle smoke and anyway there was no point because the more he tried the more they tickled him and laughed at him and called him names, singing "Belly can't catch the words! Belly can't catch the words!"

It was at times like that Raphael didn't want to be in The Dead School. He didn't want to be anywhere near it. He wished it would collapse and fall to bits. He wished it would burn down. He felt like crying out to the statue of Our Lady looking over at him from the mantelpiece: "Why can't you help me like you used to do, Our Lady? Why can't you help me like you used to do when I was small and me and mammy and daddy used to be so happy? Why do you just stand there and look at me with no feeling in your eyes?"

But he didn't do that. He didn't because he was too tired and that was why he just let the book fall out of his hands and onto the floor and felt his lips and his eyes go dry as he saw them again, standing waving to him in a field of golden corn, his mammy and his daddy who were so proud of him and had been ever since the day he was born sixty-three years before.

Days

Sometimes now he thought of days and would they ever come back to him. He stood before his boys and, hiding the quiver in his voice as best he could, asked them "Will I boys please tell me will you. Days that once could never end all of them now dead. Why boys? Why are they?" He tried to steady his hand as he wrote on his makeshift blackboard: Today we are doing: DAYS. He wiped away the thin watery mucus under his nose with the sleeve of his jacket. He had done that so often now, the whole sleeve was almost silver. Anyway, he licked the chalk and wrote:

1. The day I won the prize for best altar boy 1921.
2. My first day at St. Martin's Diocesan College aged 12, Sept 1925.
3. Special commendation from the principal of St Patrick's Training College Drumcondra 1931.
4. My first day's teaching Sept 1931.
5. Eucharistic Congress April 1932.
6. Marriage to my darling Nessa August 7 1933 Clarence Hotel Dub

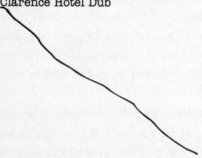

He stared at the chalk on the floor. "Why did you fall, chalk? Why did you have to?" he wanted to cry to it. But he couldn't. He was too tired. The pain in his head was starting up again and there was someone talking at the back of the room that was why he could write no more why would they not stop talking didn't they know their baby died? He knew they did he knew and that was why he shouted. That was why! "Stop it!" he cried. "Will you for the last time stop it! Our little boy died! Do you hear me! Do you hear me Rogers do you hear me talking to you do you want me to go down to you by God if I go down to you you'll be the sorry boy I can tell you what are you doing Mulhern do you hear me Mulhern you brat you! Listen to me—put that pencil down!" He waited to see what Mulhern would do but then all of a sudden it didn't matter anymore he just went down on his hunkers, trying not to let any more tears come into his eyes in front of the boys.

Two Naked People

Raphael was doing the nine counties of Ulster when he heard the noise. "Now come on lads," he said, "put your thinking caps on. Which one of you can stand up there and name the nine counties of Ulster for me. What about yourself, young McQuillan? You look like you might be able for them. Come on now—I'll give you a hand. Donegal, Derry, Antrim, Down . . . up you get now like a good lad!" But young McQuillan never got a chance, did he, because the noise came then. If you could call it a noise— more a grunt, like a pig would make. Raphael went cold all over. "Don't move, boys!" he cried. "Don't move now till I get back!"

He came running down the stairs and by the time he got to the back door he was out of breath. He couldn't turn the key why couldn't he turn the key? "Turn key—turn!" he cried. He pulled the door open and shouted at them: "You needn't think you'll do that in here! You'll get away with it everywhere else! But not in my place—do you hear me? Not in my place!"

His voice was shaking when he said it. He expected them to turn on him and abuse him, that was what you would expect that was what they all did nowadays. But they didn't in fact and when he looked again they were gone. There was no writhing white flesh, no gleaming sweat. The lights of a car rose up along the coast road, then dipped again and were gone. Then a dog barked in a distant garden. But apart from that—nothing. Raphael clasped his head in his hands because he really did think it was going to crack in two. Then he went inside and sat in the dark, shivering.

———————

Security Man

Meanwhile back in Bubble-Land, after half a dozen ounces of Lebanese Red and a few thousand or so cans of McEwan's Export, Malachy was now beginning to give some thought to the notion of securing regular employment. The Prince handed him a number and said "Give them a call. You'll walk right in there, man. No problem at all. All you gotta do is say you know me. Say you know The Prince—got that?" Malachy had it all right and off he went with the hair flying behind him. The building site was in South London and would you believe it, all he had to do was sit there in this gammy uniform, keeping an eye out for any bastard who might be inclined to do a bit of robbing. It was a breeze. An absolute breeze, man. Or would have been until the Head Asshole came round and started asking questions. "Were you smoking drugs on duty here last night?" he says. "I had a report that you were smoking cannabis. I don't want any bullshit now—OK? Just tell me—is it true or is it not?"

Malachy didn't know where to look. He had just had a joint

five minutes before and he was afraid he'd burst out laughing in the asshole's face right there on the spot!

"Well—were you?" he says, and was he pissed off or what. "Yes—I was as a matter of fact," says Malachy—and man did fuckhead like that!

"Oh, babe—if only you'd been there! If only you'd been there, Marion!" he said to himself as he came cruising down the road with a big fat jay in his hand. "It was unbelievable—fucking unbelievable, man!"

As indeed it was of course—but it put an end to Malachy Dudgeon's burgeoning career in the high glittering world of nighttime security, I'm afraid!

Still Room Assistant

Malachy was a proud man. And why wouldn't he be? He had just been appointed head of the still room! It was a very important position in a very important gentlemen's club in Central London. They had given him an apron and everything. His job was to make French toast, ordinary toast and Melba toast. But he didn't make any toast. He just stood there eating it or else letting it burn. The headwaiter wasn't pleased. He said if things didn't improve, Malachy would be fired. Malachy pleaded. "Please give me one last chance," he said. "OK then," said the headwaiter, "just one. You stop your daydreaming and letting toast burn, I'll give you a last chance. How's that?" "That's fine," said Malachy and let more toast burn. He didn't mean to do it of course. He just kept daydreaming, that's all, thanks to all these drugs he was taking. The headwaiter said "OK one last chance—you do the sandwiches." That was the best job of the lot. You had to go and get the ham or the tongue out of the kitchen and put it in the sandwiches. What you didn't do was get the munchies and eat it all on the way back to the still room. Because if you did, then a gouty colonel with a handlebar moustache would come storming in with two bits of bread, shouting "Who's the comedian!" and get you fired.

"What is the meaning of this?" the waiter bawled at Malachy. Colonel Blimp looked like every blood vessel in his face was about to burst. Malachy looked at him. "Huh?" he said, hoping that there weren't too many ham or tongue crumbs around his mouth.

High Dudgeon

All in all, Malachy had twenty-seven jobs but in the end he decided that he would have to give them all up. This was because Chico had offered him a better position as assistant sales manager with his company Lebanese Red Incorporated. Like he said, "Ten bob a week and all the draw you can smoke." Not that they were an international organisation or anything. "We serve mostly local retail outlets," said Chico as he chopped up the dope into little nuggets and put them in cellophane bags. "How about free gifts? Beach balls maybe?" asked The Prince from the armchair. "No," said Chico, "no gimmicks." Then it was off to the hostelries of North London with any amount of five pound and ten pound deals for the needy. They were happy days in London town with the sun burning down and pigeons flapping in Trafalgar Square and Malachy Bubblehead, the dopiest doped-out hippy in town, off down the street in his army surplus coat and the hair halfway down his back.

And so on it went—a hard day's work and then home to the squat to blow what was left and listen to the latest albums. "I wonder what Marion and Paddy are listening to right now," said Malachy out of the blue as he took the joint off Chico.

"Paddy and Marion who?" said Chico and they both burst out laughing, flying high somewhere over Shepherd's Bush Green.

Picnic

We like picnics don't we children oh yes we do we like them the best of all because you get boiled eggs and cakes and sweets and buns and lots of yummy orange and you can sit out in the field with the bees buzzing and the birds singing and the farmer doesn't say get off my land because at picnics everybody is happy. At least they are supposed to be and who knows, maybe if Malachy hadn't gone and freaked out, they would have been. Still, you can't blame him—how was he to know it was going to happen. As far as he was concerned, dropping three—not one, not two, but *three* tabs of acid was the best idea ever. And for a while it was. All the way down to Wales, all you could hear out of him was "We like yummy orange!" and then, big snorts of laughter. Chico got something into his head about being "in charge of the picnic" and fell off his seat with the tears running down his face. The Prince said he didn't care who was in charge. "As long as I get my cut of the boiled egg suss, that's OK by me," he said. In all seriousness, it was the very last thing you would have expected to turn out bad. If anyone had mentioned boatsheds or Mrs McAdoo or Bell or Pat Hourican or your father throwing himself in the water or any of that stuff, you would have laughed at them. You would have said "I'm sorry, man, but it's just not that kind of a day. You've got your facts wrong!" Which wouldn't be true either because it's always that kind of day, whether you know it or not. As Malachy discovered when he went away off climbing hills on his own. He could hear Chico shouting after him but he just laughed. He had had it with the picnic, he said. He was off into the mountains where the warm wind stroked your face with long silky fingers. He could see them all down below. They looked like little blobs of paint. "Hello there, blobs of paint. Can you hear me? Having a good picnic, blobs?" he cried. He waited a while for them to answer but then he forgot all about them.

His whole body was a crackle of tingles. All the tingles in the world were having a meeting in him. The Annual General Meeting of the Tingle Association. He was Mr Tingle. "Hello I'd like to introduce you to Malachy Tingle." "How do you do?" "I'm fine, thank you. Tingling a little bit but fine apart from that. Ha ha. And you? Who are you anyway?" Stomp stomp stomp up the mountainside in your seven league boots full of tingle feet. You could go on stomping forever in these boots if for some reason out of nowhere the word "Marion" hadn't come into your head. Well maybe that wouldn't have been so bad but followed by the words "I can't love you" in Marion's voice—well that was very bad. Very bad indeed, I'm afraid. Because that's the trouble with acid, although Malachy didn't know it. All it takes is one thing to go wrong and then—well everything else decides to follow suit I'm afraid. Mr Sun, who a minute before was saying "Hello! I'm Mr Sun! I'm your friend on this happy picnic day!" is opening up a big sunny mouth full of razor teeth. Then, just when you're getting used to that, a great big tear comes rolling out of Mr Sun's eye for no reason. It gets to the stage where you don't know where you are at all. There is probably some way you can say to yourself "Oh this is a lot of nonsense! Suns with tears coming out of their eyes and teeth that look like razors—oh for heaven's sake it's a lot of old rubbish, that's what it is!" In fact, just when everything was starting to go wrong, Malachy tried that particular strategy. But if it worked for other people, it didn't work for him. The sun just laughed at him. So did the grass. It sounds ridiculous I know—grass laughing. But the grass did. It laughed right into his face. Not only that in fact—it talked to him. It said "You poor stupid bollocks! You've really fucked it now!" He hadn't however. Not yet. The big fuckup was yet to come. The big fuckup came when he thought of Pat.

He shouldn't have done that. He shouldn't have thought of Pat at all. Thinking about Pat was a bad thing to do, because then he thought about Collins and Webb. And not just Collins and Webb but bad, awful Collins and Webb. With voices that said "You let Pat fall in the water. You did. We saw you." Then he did an even worse thing. He tried to reason with them. That was a really fucking stupid thing to do. I mean, you don't reason with the likes of Collins and Webb. They'll only laugh at you and worse, they'll start singing *Pat fell in the water Pat fell in the water* and you won't like that will you? No, that will drive you mad.

But bad and all as it was, it was nothing compared to the wasp. What the hell did it have to come along for? Going bzz. "Go away, wasp," Malachy said. But it hadn't the slightest intention of going away. At least, not before it had done what it came to do in the first place which was sting Malachy. Now that's something which is not very nice on an acid trip—a big ugly wasp sting going into you like a hot wire. And Malachy knew that. Go away wasp, he pleaded, but it wouldn't. It gave a great big waspy grin. A grin that said "Me sting you! Me sting you!"

"No! Please!" was what Malachy said back.

"No yes! Me sting you!"

In went its big wiry sting as far as it could go. Then what did he do but start running. He was running all over the place. Up, down and around the mountain. But fortunately, he ran into someone just up ahead. Oops! It was Mrs McAdoo. "Look—my face is all worms." That was all she said and so it was. Then who pulled up in an accordion-pleated Morris but the bold Father Pat with blood streaks all over his face. "There youse are," he said as he chucked the brake and pulled up beside him. "Hop in!" But Malachy didn't hear him because he was transfixed by the face of his father in the back window. He looked so sad. "I loved your mother," was all he said. "Don't ever think I didn't. She just didn't love me, that's all." It might have been all right if Marion hadn't decided to get in on the action. Well it wouldn't have been all right but it mightn't have been as bad as it was. She was standing by the frozen river with her back to him, with the snow all about her as she clutched her folder to her chest and stared at something far away. He had been watching her for a long time before she turned to him and smoothed her hair back behind her ears as her lips slowly parted. She was going to say it. He begged her not to say it. Marion please oh please don't say those words. "I love you," she said and that was really the end. It was like his head caving in, a tent collapsing ever so silently and after that he didn't care anymore, which was why he was in such a state when Chico and The Prince found him, gibbering away to himself, raving all kinds of rubbish nobody could understand.

They managed to get him to the cops who took him to the nearest general hospital. Three days later he arrived at Friern Barnet Mental Hospital. Not that it made much difference for as far as Malachy was concerned, he might as well have been on the moon.

The Dummy

Through the haze came The Dummy smiling. His voice was soft and soothing. "Don't worry, Malachy," he said, "I'll look after you. Put your trust in me and I'll tell you all about it."

"It's been so long since I've seen you, Dummy," Malachy

said. "Tell me what has happened. Why am I in this place where everything is a fog around me? Please tell me what has happened to me." "Of course I will," said The Dummy, "you know I will. The Dummy is always there when you need him—isn't that right, Malachy?"

And Malachy knew it was. The Dummy was the happiest man in town and always had been for as far back as anyone could remember. Whenever his name came up, someone was always sure to say "I met The Dummy this morning coming across the square and do you know what, I don't think there's a happier man alive in this town." To which the response was likely to be "Or any town." And how true it was, as Malachy knew so well. No matter what hour of the day or night you happened to meet him, he would have a grin on his face the like of which you wouldn't see on someone unless perhaps they had won the sweepstakes maybe. The wonderful thing about it all was the fact that The Dummy's not speaking didn't seem to bother him in the slightest. Everyone found this very impressive because they felt that if, God forbid, they themselves were suddenly struck dumb through some dreadful accident or something, that far from going about the place with a great big happy smile it would be much more likely they would be found sitting inside in the hotel bar drinking a bottle of whiskey a day if not more, looking at everybody with dead eyes and a sad face that said "Do you see me? I can't speak. I used to be able to but not anymore. Why should things be like that? It's not fair. Everyone else is able to speak and I'm not. I have been struck dumb. Dumb for the rest of my days! What do you think about that? I will tell you what you think. You don't care. You don't care just so long as it's not you. Of course you are going to deny it. Well deny it all you like, my friend, but it's true! You're glad aren't you? You're glad that you can talk and I can't. And never will again until they shovel me into the ground! To hell with you! Damn you! Damn you for not caring!"

They knew perfectly well that was probably what they would do. Which was why they were so impressed by The Dummy and never let an opportunity go by without praising him. There he would be, smiling and laughing away with all the kiddies who loved to play with the broken pump, a giant umbrella of water skitting all over the place. Sometimes it got all over The Dummy and dripped down his face and onto his clothes. Any other adult would have said "You stupid children! Look what you've gone and done—my good clothes are ruined!" The children might even have got a clip on the ear for themselves into the bargain. But not on this occasion. Not from good old Dummy. In fact what he did was laugh his head off. If you could call it laughing. Laughing without any sound perhaps. Whatever you called it, he was having the time of his life with the kiddies dancing rings around him and the water dribbling down his cheeks and making a big puddle at his feet. As people went by they said "There you are, Dummy. Good man yourself!" and he touched his forelock and away off with him then into another bout of no-sound laughing.

Another thing about The Dummy was that he never seemed to sleep. By all accounts he didn't need to. Whenever he did he did so in an old hayloft in a farmyard. But most times he didn't bother. He was too busy going off around the streets laughing and joking and being the happiest man in town. Rarely a day went past but Malachy would meet him up the street and say to him "There you are, Dummy! That's not a bad day now" and would receive in return an enormous melon-slice grin. What cheered Malachy up was that at least there was someone happy about the place. It certainly beat Nobby Caslin and his baby counts and body counts and all the rest of it. As far as Malachy was concerned it knocked all that into a cocked hat. Which was exactly what he was feeling the day he met The Dummy after he left the church. Not that it had been bad in the church, for indeed it hadn't. In fact it had been quite nice in there. The organist played away and Father Pat and the sacristan were dickeying up the altar with the most beautiful flowers Malachy had ever seen. There was a beautiful smell. It took Malachy off to a distant land of shining suns and mysterious perfumes. Then Father Pat came down and started chatting to him. He wanted to tell him about the goal he had scored in the last minute of a needle match in 1949. No, he didn't, he just wanted to chat to him about his mother and his poor poor dead father. When that particular part of the conversation was over, Father Pat went on to talk about the christening, which of course was due to take place that afternoon, hence the riot of blooms. "Yes!" said Father Pat. "Another little baba comes into the world! And a lovely little fellow he is too. Do you know the Cunninghams at all, young Dudgeon?" Malachy nodded and said yes he did. The priest squeezed his shoulder and said "Mammy Cunningham is the proud woman this day!" The organ swelled as Malachy thought of the little crying baby and all the women in headscarves going through boxes of Kleenex. After which they would all go off down to the hotel and have the party of a lifetime and say we are the best family in the world and we all get on together don't we, we love each other yes we do. Which, Malachy thought, was probably true but then he really wouldn't be the one to ask as all he knew about that was what he had picked up in a certain boatshed one sunny day. But as he sat there with the sun streaming in through the stainglassed windows and the organist soaring away off like there was no tomorrow with "Jesu, Joy Of Man's Desiring," he had to admit that there wasn't very much wrong with the world. At least for that moment or so it was beginning to look like a pretty good place indeed.

As he was leaving, Father Pat gave him a wave and a big wink and out he stepped into a town steeped in sun. Everything was cruising along fine. The breadman had arrived at the corner shop and as he strode across the street with a tray of hot pan loaves he said to a woman with a shopping basket "That's one of the best days yet" and she said "Yes it is we could be doing with a few more like that." The petrol pumps were humming away outside the garage and in the sky the clouds sat still. Everyone was going about their business but they weren't in any hurry going about it and he thought that was just fine because he wasn't in any hurry to go about his either. It was just then that he met The Dummy, coming past the cinema. His mouth was shaped like an O which of course meant that he was whistling. No-whistle whistling of course but nevertheless merrily whistling along. When he saw Malachy his face lit up with a big grin and he made the shape of his name with his lips. They stood there together for a while and it was good. It was good standing there beside The Dummy with his eyes twinkling and the sun shining all over the quiet happy busy town. A man went by and saluted. "That's a powerful day, Dummy," he said, then added "And young Dudgeon! Couldn't forget you, young Dudgeon! Ha! Ha! Ha!" They hung about some more, chatting and talking about this and that, at least Malachy did, with The Dummy nodding and lighting up and practically foaming at the mouth with excitement every time Malachy mentioned the slightest little incident about the town. Then Malachy thought he had better be off about his business and he said to The Dummy "And so where are you off to now, Dummy? Off on your travels I expect!" The Dummy grinned again, even more this time, if such were possible, then stuck a stiff index finger into the air like a mime artist you might see on the television. What he put on then was more or less what you would call a little play. Malachy of course had seen him at these little plays before so it didn't take him too long to work out what he was trying to tell him.

It was clear that The Dummy was off to spend the day at the lake. Malachy said that that would be good. He said that there would be great fun out there. He asked The Dummy was he going for a swim. He said "Is that why you're going out to the lake?" But The Dummy said no and shook his head. He was most emphatic in fact. He wanted Malachy to know that that was not the reason he was going out there. That wasn't the reason at all. To tell the truth, Malachy got a bit confused then, but The Dummy didn't mind that. He was well used to people getting mixed up and frustrated when he was trying to tell them something. He was never at a loss in such situations. His contingency arrangements were always taken care of, namely an old scrap of paper torn from a child's copybook in which, with a stump of a pencil, he now scribbled the words *To get some peace*.

Whether he liked to admit it or not, on this occasion Malachy could not make head nor tail of what he was on about, which was why he thought the safest course of action was to laugh away with him and to see the pair of them standing there in the street, and what with The Dummy chewing the stumpy pencil and laughing away at the same time, you would have been hard pressed not to sign the pair of them up for the circus. In fact by the time they had finished laughing Malachy thought to himself that he had never laughed so much before in his life. Actually he was almost sick from laughing. His cheeks were flushed and he had a pain in his head. As he was crossing the square, he thought to himself "I think I could be doing without all that giddy carry-on for a while, I can tell you."

On which count he needn't have worried because only the

day after, it dawned on him what The Dummy had been talking about. The whole town was on about it, of course. Everyone had seen him just before he did it. Nobby Caslin was running up and down the street like a blue-arsed fly. Of course, as always, there were a few liars who claimed to have seen it coming. In the hotel bar, they said they had always known there was something odd about him. "It was only a matter of time," they said. But of course everyone knew this was what you might charitably describe as "shite-talk" and in the end they made the right decision and at long last shut their mouths. They said no more about it after that. The laugh of it was that they had found his clothes neatly folded behind a bush on the shore of the lake, and it looked more like his intention had been to pay a visit to the laundry.

They were out on the lake for two or three days but in the end they found him. From that day on the lake became known as "The Dummy's Water" and everyone agreed that that was good, because every time you passed it now you wouldn't be able to think of anything but the poor old Dummy and his great big happy face. You would stand there listening to the grasshoppers clacking and the birdies singing to their little baby fledglings and as you stared across the flat expanse of the still blue lake, you would think of him deep down there in the silent blackness, tumbling like an astronaut with his eyes staring and his long limbs floating, with two words struggling to clamber from his mouth but never of course succeeding: *Help me. Help me. Help me.*

Which were no longer the words he was using to Malachy as he stood before him now after all these years, any more than it was The Dummy he had once known. For now the smile on his face was bitter and twisted and as he repeated the sentence, Malachy wept and begged him not to but it was no use, again the soft words came: "Your father did it after me because he thought it would bring him peace. He thought the waters would close over him and there would be no more pain." Malachy was close to weeping as he went on. He was going to go on forever. "But there is!" snarled what had once been The Dummy "There is and there always will be! As he knows now! At the bottom of that lake he knows it now! Go and join him if you don't believe me! Because it's true! For all eternity he will rot there in pain—as I did! And now you! You too! Do you hear me? Do you hear me, Dudgeon! Throw yourself into the water if you don't believe me! Then you'll know! Then you'll know once and for all! Go on Dudgeon—do it! Swim into the darkness where you belong! Swim until you die! Do you hear me? Do you hear me! Die, fucker, die!"

The sweat was streaming off Malachy as the orderlies held him down. For days after he remembered nothing. They told him he had been screaming. A woman's name by all accounts. Marie or Mary. Marianne maybe.

For the first month he couldn't stop shivering. He was terrified to sleep. He was afraid The Dummy would come again. "You're afraid of a Dummy," laughed Stephen Webb. "Kyle—he's afraid of a silly Dummy!"

"Tee hee hee," laughed Kyle.

Thus, in overheated rooms and infinite corridors, the days went by.

Bray Head

The whole of Dublin city must have decided to go out to Bray Head that day. As they lay together on the grass, close by the hush of the sea, he brushed her closed eyelids with the petals of a daisy. She smiled, then rolled over on her stomach and tried to push him away as she cried "Don't! Don't do that!" He kissed her on the ear. "We've got to go back, Malachy," she said. "I have to finish my essay for Ed. Psych." He put his arm around her waist and she turned her face to his, then put her arms around his neck and he kissed her on the lips.

Fever

She had been up half the night. "I don't know what's wrong with me, Malachy," she said. "One minute I'm all shivery and the next I'm sweating all over. I must be coming down with something." Her face was flushed and her brow shone with sweat. "Get back into bed and I'll go down to the chemist's," he said. He didn't go into work that day. He rang in and said he was sick. He knew Bell didn't believe him but for that one time in his life he didn't care. On the way back from the chemists he bought a bag of coal and lugged it all the way up Rathmines Road. The snow was coming down thick and fast and by the time he got home, the hands were about to fall off him. "Is that you—is that you, Malachy?" said Marion in this shaky voice. "Don't worry— it's me all right," he said, "Dudgeon the coalman." "Oh Malachy," she said, half in this world and half out of it.

He built up a huge fire and in no time the room was flicker-ing with warm shadows. Then he made a pot of hot broth and fed it to her from a spoon. She touched the back of his hand and said "I love you, Malachy. You're so good to me." He smiled and said "Come on now, ma'am—eat up. We've got to get this fever out of you." After that, she slept and he sat there reading and watching her as she turned over in her dreams. Outside, the snowswept city was a thousand miles away and in that room of warm shadows, they were the only two people in the world and it really did seem back in those first few weeks they spent living together as if that was how it was going to be forevermore.

Bell's History Lesson

Man did she laugh as he sucked the match between his teeth and spun the chamber. "I'm sorry, honey," he said. "There's nothing you can do or say." He was wearing his Jack Nicholson shades. He flicked the match away. "I've gotta take the motherfucker out." He knocked on the door and out came the man himself. "What can I do for you?" he said. Malachy sighed and shook his head. Then he took off his shades and repeated "What can I do for you—well how about that!" He was still laughing when he stuck the gun in Baldy's back, gave him a kick on the arse and told him to get the fuck inside. "You can't do this to me! You can't do this to me!" was all you could hear.

He gave him another kick up the hole and then got down to business. "Shout, I am a bollocks!" he said to him and gave him a poke with the gun. For a minute it looked like he wasn't going to do it. "No I won't!" he shouted. A few jabs more with the pistol put an end to that bullshit however and before long he was hopping about the place like nobody's business, shouting "I am a bollocks! I am a bollocks!" for all he was worth.

After that he made them tea.

"This tea is too weak," Malachy said. "Make more."

"Yes, sir," says Bell and off he goes.

By the time they were finished, there wasn't a peep out of him.

"I hope you've learned your lesson, asshole!" snorted Malachy as he stuck the shooter in his belt. "Otherwise—you're history! You got that?"

"Yes, sir," says Bell and hung his baldy head.

"Let's go, girl," he said and laughed as he squeezed her hand and they headed off up Grafton Street to Stephen's Green.

Head In A Box

Another favourite after a belt of the afternoon medication when you were feeling nice and woozy and smiling at nothing out the window was Marion and yourself driving around in a beatup truck with a head in a vegetable crate in the back, except that this time it wasn't Alfredo Garcia's, it was poor old Bell's. Boy was he getting a hard time these days! Malachy shifted gears and shouted "Hey, Meester Bell—how you like eet back there? You theenk ees nice being in a box, no?"

"Let me out! Let me out!" shouted Bell. "You can't do this to me!"

"Maybe you should have thought a leetle beet about that before you fuck around with me in your school, no?"

Man, what a laugh that was! Cruising in the dust and the head just going crazy in the heat. Especially when they stopped at a roadside diner and all it could see through the bars of the crate was Marion and Malachy sipping an ice-cold beer as they called "So how you feeling now, Mr Bell? You feeling OK in there?" and gave each other a kiss to drive him twice as mad. It was crazy. It was a crazy dream.

Rathole

Raphael and Malachy had both retired from society in or around the same time, and now, as the minutes turned into hours and the hours turned into days and the days turned into months and the first year came and went, it was hard to say which of the pair of them was the worst. I suppose to Malachy's credit, if he did shuffle about the place with a big fat mopey head on him, at least he didn't keep his room like a rathole, which was all you could call No. 53 Madeira Gardens these days. Yes, it was a right old dump now and no mistake. Damp streaks on the walls, cobwebs on Our Lady's eyes, rotten fruit and stale bread in the kitchen, not to mention the hundreds of empty bottles that were lying about the place. A sorry-looking tip now and no mistake. Not that its owner was any better. A right-looking candidate now to be running any school, private or public or dead or alive or any other kind.

Maths Lesson

You don't use a stick or a pointer in The Dead School. Instead you use big old-fashioned iron tongs. That soon puts manners on the boys. Raphael stood at the blackboard and roared. He slammed the heavy tongs-pointer down on the desk again and again. "No! No! No! there are *not* five sevens in forty-two!" He wiped the gleaming beads of sweat off his forehead with the flat of his hand and shook his head in exasperation. There was a bubbly froth on his mouth as he looked up and yelled "What are you doing, Connolly, for the last time do you hear me—put that pencil down! You needn't think you'll come in here with any of your lip for by God I'll put the smirk on the other side of your face and don't think I won't! You won't do it here, indeed by

God you won't! You'll not get away with anything you want here, my friend—if that's what you want go on down to Evans. She'll let you do whatever you like! Divorce—of course you can, young Connolly! Drugs—would you like some? Of course! I happen to have some right here in my handbag. Is that what you want, Connolly? Is that the way you want to behave? Well you won't! Not here. Not in my school, my friend!"

The tongs came sweeping down again in a huge arc and nearly broke the table in half.

Break Time

When he wasn't beating algebra and the history of Ireland into his charges, Raphael would wander about the house in a half-daze. He'd sit there in the kitchen chuckling to himself, thinking what a fool he had been all those years ago to believe that he was important. He knew now how important he was. Just about as important as one of the spots on the heel of mildewed bread he was eating for his lunch, as John McCormack sang his heart out on the old gramophone the way he had done that day when *Glorificamus* was beamed into the sky and one million people sank to their knees, uttering those words which Raphael had whispered to the young woman he had loved so much—

> *Macushla! Macushla! Your sweet voice is calling,*
> *Calling me softly again and again,*
> *Macushla! Macushla! I hear its dear pleading*
> *My blue-eyed Macushla, I hear it in vain.*

and she had turned to him and held him close, his own dear Nessa. Now dead. In the grave. Yes. Her face eaten away. Not Nessa anymore.

The record played all day long. That was why it was in bits. There were so many scrapes and scratches on it you couldn't hear half the words. Not that Raphael cared. From her wooden plinth, Our Lady looked down upon him with pitying eyes. "What are you looking at?" he said and started chuckling again. They thought they were going to break him completely. They thought they were going to wreck this school too, didn't they? But they weren't, you see—that was where they were wrong. He laughed. "Oho no!" he said. "Your wrecking days are over, my friends! Well and truly over—make no mistake about that! Do you hear me?" he barked and then, when he was satisfied, threw the rest of the bread away and went back to class.

Army Surplus Greatcoat

To tell you the God's honest truth, Malachy would have been just as happy to stay in the hospital for the next ten years, for by now he was well into the swing of things and there was nothing he liked better than smoking his rollups and listening to his records, then off for a walk around the grounds and back in to watch telly or just sit by the window and dream away. But the doc was having none of it and said that eighteen months was more than enough for anyone to be stuck in a place like this so once again it was the boot for Mr Dudgeon and down the avenue of Friern Barnet Mental Hospital he went, off on his travels once more. They got him a flat in Stoke Newington and a job in a pub in Camden Town. The job was good for a while but then one day he let a heap of crates fall and they told him to get the fuck out he had nearly killed the barman. But he didn't mind. "Fuck you too, man!" he said back to them. What did he care? This was

London town for Christ's sake! Jobs were ten a penny. You could leave one and walk into another the same day for Christ's sake.

But he didn't stay in the next one very long either. He was supposed to pack hamburgers into boxes, and for a while it was OK. Then one day he just didn't bother going to work. In the end he got fed up altogether going looking for jobs. He knew he could exist on the dole and the allowance they gave him for the flat so fuck it he said to himself and just spent the day smoking and listening to his records. He listened to them all day long. Horslips and Mott The Hoople. Mott The Hoople sang the songs of summer's end, when you drifted through the college grounds with your sweater knotted and your folder under your arm and you didn't give a fuck about anything in the wide world.

Outside London heaved as Malachy tried to steady the rollup in his hand.

Hey, Malachy!
The day he met Chico coming out of Piccadilly Circus tube, he couldn't believe it. It was only when he heard him speak that he believed it was him at all. "Hey, Malachy—how are you doing for fuck's sake!" Chico said. They went to a pub and Chico told him they'd all long since left the squat. The Prince, believe it or not, was back studying at university. Chico himself was working for Lloyd's as an insurance underwriter. "The suit, man!" said Malachy. "I can't believe it. You look like me in my fucking teaching days!"

"I guess," laughed Chico as he downed a lager. Then he patted his briefcase and said "Well, I gotta go. It was great to see you, Malachy. You mind yourself now—you hear?"

The sun was streaming in the plate glass window as Chico vanished into the crowd. Punk music blared from the jukebox and all about Malachy orange-haired youths in tartan struck poses and snarled at nothing. Malachy felt the warm, comforting arms of four pints around him and smiled as he looked at himself in the mirror. His long, lank greasy hair was way past his shoulders. Sure it was crazy to be wearing a green army surplus greatcoat on a blazing hot summer's day. But who cared? Who cared what was crazy to wear on a hot summer's day, blazing or otherwise, as he ordered another pint and said to the punk beside him "The Clash, that's not music, man. Horslips—now there's a band, there's a fucking band, man!

Oceans Of The World

Inside the cinema, Malachy was half-asleep. Beside him an old man snored with his head tilted back on the seat. Coming from the screen, in the distance he heard the sound of a ship's horn and through bleary eyes that had not closed the night before he watched the grey fog drift over the lapping water. There was something out there, just floating along with all the time in the world. At first it seemed to be a dolphin or a seal, bobbing with an easy, leisured rhythm. Then, the stranger standing along the wharf just staring out to sea saw that it was the body of a young girl slowly drifting toward him. She was so pale. Hardly more than a child. Her white body nudged the cold stone as the stranger perplexedly stroked her bloodless cheek. The pale tremor of the ship's horn sounded again and in the silence broken only by the occasional creak of the rigging and the swaying hawsers, the stranger whispered abstractedly to the torch-bearing patrolman: "Who do you think she was?"

For a long time nothing passed between them and then, frantic, the stranger gripped his lapels and pleaded with him "Please—who do you think she was?"

The patrolman gently eased him away and as he knelt by the inert, eyeglazed body, he tipped back his cap. "Christ knows, mate," he sighed. "We pull at least one of these out of the river every week."

The oily water licked her fingers. The stranger could not hold back the tear that moistened his eye. The patrolman said something to him but he did not hear it. He was searching for some impossible word or words that would somehow make her live, smile again. But he could not find them. When he raised his head to look again, the patrolman was gone. The echo of his footsteps lingered. The girl's lips were frozen blue. He would have given all he had to know what her last words might have been, if they told of the vast grey oceans of the world where even now so many like her drifted unnamed, each coming slowly into port like empty vessels after wasted voyages, fetched up without a sound in the vast, unknowing silence.

Our Lady

Our Lady looked down at Raphael and said she was sad because he hadn't bothered to bury Setanta. He just laughed at her however. He said if she was so sad about all these things, why hadn't she done something about them, like she was supposed to? It wasn't much good coming along when all the damage was done. Anyway, when he had first noticed that Setanta wasn't moving and was probably dead, it had occurred to him to bury the animal. But then he went and forgot all about it and by the time he did remember, it was already too late, for what had once been a grand old cat growing old gracefully was nothing so much as a pile of mucky goo and moving maggots lying beneath the kitchen window. Of course it was sad but there was nothing he could do about it now was there, no matter how much she whinged and looked at him.

Raphael opened another bottle of Jameson and switched on the radio. Leo Maguire's merry voice floated out of the wireless into the warm summer air: "This is *The Walton Programme*, brought to you by your weekly reminders of the grace and beauty that lie in our heritage of Irish song—the songs our fathers loved!" Of course Leo Maguire came floating out—who else would you expect? Except that he didn't. He did in his hat, because he was dead. Like everything else.

But Terry wasn't dead. He most certainly was not! "Hi!" he said. "This is Terry Krash with the sixty-second quiz! Have you all got your pencils and paper ready?" He wanted to know what country Delhi was the capital of. Raphael snorted as he slugged his whiskey. "Are you all ready, boys?" he scoffed. "Have you all got your pencils and paper ready? I mean—it's such a hard question!" "Norway," replied the caller and Raphael spluttered the whiskey all over himself. Next, says Terry, can you tell me what Hitler's first name was. "Heil," the caller answered. Yes indeed, a lot of bright people on *The Terry Krash Show* today. But then, Terry was a very clever man himself wasn't he? Of course he was! He was one of the first to interview Evans wasn't he? He was clever enough to see that she was going places. Running for election now, as a matter of fact! It wasn't enough for her to wreck schools you see—oh no. That was just to start her off. When she had achieved that, she would move on to bigger and better things. Which indeed she did. Now you couldn't open a paper but there she was—give your vote to Marie Evans! A big rosette and a happy smiling face. She said Ireland was moving forward with her. Of course it was! She was *Ms.* Evans wasn't she!

Raphael chucked the bottle at the wall and it broke into

pieces. He howled until tears came into his eyes. If you didn't know better, you'd have thought there was a wolf living in Madeira Gardens. Then he went one better and knocked things off sideboards and pictures off walls. As if the place, after almost two years as his own private educational establishment, wasn't bad enough. But this time he really excelled himself. When he was finished, the place was a complete and utter wreck. There was even jam on the wall where he had fired the jar at it. "That's it, Evans!" he bawled. "Forward with Evans! Rob the poor! Fiddle the taxes! Divorce your wives! Blow up your neighbours! Melt babies' eyes! Torture animals! Laugh at your teachers! Go on— do it, Evans! Laugh at me! Go on!"

By the time he had finished all that, he thought his head was going to crack in two like a coconut. He wasn't able for any more. He wasn't able for a little baby who came floating down the stairs with a face as pale as flour, who pulled his cheeks right back over his ears to bare a gummy grin and whispered "I'm Maolseachlainn" and floated off back up the stairs again. He wasn't able for the woman whose gentle hand brushed his stomach in a boardinghouse in the long ago. He wasn't able for the happy freckled face of Paschal O'Dowd as he stood under a laburnum tree in the grounds of St Patrick's Training College or the words he spoke: "Will we ever meet again, Raphael?" And he wasn't able for the sight of his father broken in a summer field with gushes of blood pouring from his mouth as a Black and Tan soldier with a smoking revolver stood over him triumphantly as his pitiful screams scattered the crows from the treetops.

No, he wasn't able for any of it and that was why he sank to his knees and began to chuckle because when something is so sad that you will never have the tears to do it justice, what else can you do? And that was what he did, just knelt there with his whole body heaving, tears of laughter rolling down his cheeks as Terry cried "OK, folks! We'd like to continue now with a little number from Racey called 'Some Girls'! Yes—some will and some won't but right here on *The Terry Krash Show*—everybody does! Here we go!"

Behind Raphael, the disembodied plaster head of Our Lady stared impassively at the ceiling. Beside her in the cracked glass of a framed photo, Nessa Bell, née Conroy, with a belted suitcase at her knee, smiled towards the future.

———————

Cop

Which, as it happens, was exactly what Malachy was doing the night he came home and to his amazement found a cop standing on his doorstep. Yes, smiling towards the future he was, for he had decided once and for all to get himself together and stop all this fucking around. So, what was he going to do—dope the rest of his life away? Rot in fucking Stoke Newington with days turning into weeks and weeks into months and before you knew where you were you were an old fucking man! Was he going to go on like that forever? "I don't think so!" he said. "No fucking way, man!" He was on top of the situation. This time he was right on top of it. Which explained why he came on so cocky and officious to his visitor. "And may I ask what I can do for you, Officer?" Yeah, this was the new Malachy Dudgeon, the 1979 model. He felt like a million dollars. At least until the cop said "Are you Malachy Dudgeon?" and then "I'm afraid your mother is dying."

After that, there wasn't quite so much cool coming-on. He just stood there staring at the cop like an imbecile. He looked like he was about to say "You're joking!" to the cop, who wasn't joking at all. Anyway, it didn't matter now. The cop was gone.

Out of nowhere her face came to Malachy and he started to laugh. "Well how about that! Cissie's gone and screwed it up again! I hope you've got your boathouse story ready because they're going to be asking you a lot of questions, Cissie baby!" By the time he was finished, he felt great. He was on top of the world. So Cissie was dying. Big deal. Who gave a shit? That's her problem, man. "Whee hoo!" he cried as he strolled off into the neon-lit night.

Like fuck he did, standing there shaking like a leaf. That was the way he had always thought it was going to be. But then —you think a lot of things, don't you?

———————

School Of Rubbish

"Good morning, boys. I am sorry to have to tell you this school is a load of rubbish." Now that is the last thing you would expect your headmaster to say when he comes in in the morning, isn't it? That's just not the way headmasters go on. If the parents heard about it, there would be war. They would come down and say "Just what is going on in this so-called school! My Nicholas says that you're coming in in the morning telling them it's a load of rubbish. Is this true?" They would expect Raphael to go all pale in the face and start stuttering and apologise and say no no no and all this. But that wouldn't be what he'd say at all. What he'd say would be "Yes! That's right!" and look at them with big eyes the size of plums. Then, God knows what he'd do. He might start shouting "Rubbish! Rubbish!" again, or push them or start laughing into their faces or hit them over the head with a Jameson bottle. You just didn't know what he'd do anymore. Sometimes, after a few shots, he'd jump up in front of the boys and go "Don't move, boy! I see you!" and then make a joke of it all, saying "Do what you like! Do what you like! I don't mind! No rules in the School Of Rubbish, I'm afraid!"

The radio played all day long now too. He simply couldn't be bothered turning it off. Sure why should he—Terry was getting better and better! "I'll tell you what's wrong with divorce," says one old fellow, "it's a mortal sin, that's what's wrong with it and anyone who practises it will go to hell." "Oh really," says another fellow, "oh really, well I'm sorry to disappoint you but I don't believe in hell so it would be very hard for me to go somewhere that doesn't exist, don't you think?" "So it doesn't exist," says your man, "it doesn't exist, well all I can say is I wonder will you be saying that when you're lying on your deathbed roaring for the priest with the bedpost in your mouth." "Ha ha," laughs Terry, "I haven't heard that one for a long time, roaring for the priest with the bedpost in your mouth! Well now, that's a good one!" It is indeed, and everyone laughs away. Raphael as well. He's laughing the loudest of all. Roaring for a priest! He slams the tongs down on the desk and takes a good big swig. "What do you think of that, Mahoney!" he barks. "It's good, sir," says Mahoney. Raphael grins. "Do you think I'll be got roaring for a priest with the bedpost in my mouth?" he asks him.

"Oh no, sir," says Mahoney.

"Oh no, sir," says Raphael, "and why might that be, sir?"

"Because you are our teacher, sir."

Raphael laughed. He laughed and laughed and laughed.

"Well man dear but you're the lug, Mahoney! You're worse than your brother. I'm not your teacher! I *USED* to be your teacher. Say that. I *USED* to be your teacher."

Mahoney lowered his head. "You used to be our teacher, sir," he said.

Raphael gave the air a poke. "That's right, Mahoney," he said. "Do you all hear that, boys? Do you all hear that?"

"Yes, sir," the class answered as one.

"I used to be your teacher. But I'm not anymore. And you all know why that is. You know why that is, class?"

"No, sir."

"You don't?"

"No, sir."

"Say: No, sir, we don't, sir."

"No sir we don't sir."

"Well I'll tell you. Because you know what this school is? It's a rubbish school. It's even worse than a rubbish school. And you know why that is? Because it's not a real school. It's a good for nothing school! I want my old school back! I don't want any rubbish schools—do you hear me? Lafferty—are you listening?"

"Yes, sir!" cried Lafferty, wheyfaced.

"Say: I don't want any rubbish schools!"

"I don't want any rubbish schools!"

"Say it again!"

The class complied.

"Again!" he cried.

He made them repeat it until they were blue in the face. Then he opened another bottle and grinned at them. His eyes widened.

"So why shouldn't I close it down? It's mine! I can do what I like with it! Say: I can do what I like with it!"

"You can do what you like with it!"

"I know," he chuckled. "And do you know what I'm going to do?"

The boys didn't answer. Raphael wiped his Jameson-speckled lips with the sleeve of his dirty white shirt and went over to them. Then he got down on his hunkers and, making sure there was nobody around only himself and the lads, said in a dead whisper "I'm going to kill the headmaster."

Sweetbriar Lawns

And so, boys and girls, after two and a half happy years in Stoke Newington, it was time for Mr Bubblehead to say goodbye to the prostitutes and the druggies and the community care man next door and the tramp who slept on the stairs and all the little doggies who kept roaming in and out. So he pulled on his army coat and put on his shades. He put the record "Chirpy Chirpy Cheep Cheep" into its sleeve and, taking one last sad look at his beautiful little home with its camp bed and its rows and rows of sour milk cartons and empty bean cans, set off down the road to the travel agent's to buy a ticket for the big aeroplane home.

Of course it's sad when you have to go back home because someone close to you is ill, especially when it's your mother, but then you have to remember there's always the possibility they'll get well again, isn't there? And that's what Malachy was thinking at about 35,000 feet above the Irish Sea. "Maybe she's not so bad," he was thinking. "Maybe she'll get well again." He felt good thinking that. But, in retrospect, maybe it wasn't such a good thing, because the problem with such happy hopeful thoughts is that they lead you on to think of even happier, more hopeful thoughts. Such as looking up your old girlfriend when you get to Dublin, for example. Not that this didn't seem like a good idea all the same. At 35,000 feet, it seemed like just about the best idea he could ever think of. Him standing there with his shades on, going "I like my nose, Mrs Mulwray. I like breathing through it," and Marion laughing away. "So—how've you been?" she'd say. "Oh fine, you know," he'd say. "You know how it is. Hanging in there." Then when she saw he had kept the record after all this time—that was really going to be something!

But to hell with the past. What had herself and Paddy been up to? After a bit of a rap, maybe they could head out on the town. Paddy of course probably knew half the fucking city, so they could leave it up to him. "Where'll we head, Paddy?" he'd say. He didn't care where they went. Any of the clubs would be fine by him. All he knew was that it was gonna be great to see them again. After all the stupid shit of the old days and everything. That was all long gone. That was history, man. This time around they were friends and that was the way they were going to stay.

The first thing Malachy did when he landed was hit Grafton Street. The city was looking fantastic. He went into a shop to get some Rizla rollup papers. "I thought the hippies were all dead," snorted a turquoise punk in the doorway as he went in. Malachy didn't give a shit—he just laughed. He checked to make sure he still had the record in the pocket of his greatcoat. "You must be warm with that coat on you," the assistant said but he didn't hear her because he was gone, off on the trail of Marion and Paddy Meehan.

It wasn't hard to find her. Her mother gave him the address over the phone. Maybe he should have asked for a bit more information than that but he was so excited at the prospect of seeing her that he just hung up and away off out the door of the telephone booth to get the bus. All the way out there, he kept checking to see if he had the record and trying out the different things he was going to say.

"So—how have you been, Marion?" "How are the band doing, Paddy? Things working out OK?" "So what do you say we head out for a beer?"

By the time they got to 47 Sweetbriar Lawns, he had it all sorted out. "Hi there, Marion. Good to see you again." That would do it. That was all he needed to say. No need for any overelaborate shit. Whatever they had to say, they would get around to it in their own good time. I like my nose, Mrs Mulwray. I like breathing through it. Man, it was crazy.

Of course, as soon as the door opened, he didn't say that at all. He just stood there with his mouth open, half-ready to tear off down the avenue and never be seen again. But that was understandable, because the last thing he had been expecting was a harassed-looking woman in a powder-pink tracksuit saying "I'm sorry—I was in the middle of something." By the time he got himself together, he was flustered and fiddling about with the piece of paper trying to explain how he'd somehow got the wrong address when a strand of strawberry blonde hair fell down over her eyes and as she pushed it back she said "Malachy?" When she said that, he went white and he knew it. "Please. Please come in, Malachy," she said. He didn't know what to say. He hadn't the faintest idea. It wasn't him but someone outside him who went inside. And who, for at least ten minutes, was nothing so much as a complete stranger sitting in his place in the armchair. Marion kept talking at ninety miles an hour. She picked things up and put them down again and then the baby started crying in the Moses basket. She lifted it up, softly stroking the back of its head. "It's going to be all right, baba. It's going to be all right now. Ssh. Ssh now." The television was flickering away in the corner. Bosco the puppet was on. Pat Hourican liked him. "I like Bosco," he used to say. "He's my favourite." "I don't like him," Stephen would say. "He's rubbish." Bosco laughed away as he clapped his cloth hands. He said he was going to open the magic door. He did. He opened the magic door and went inside.

When she had the baby tucked in, Marion said "I'll get us a coffee. Would you like a coffee, Malachy?" He said he would.

He didn't say "Marion." He couldn't bring himself to say her name.

He could feel all these pinheads of sweat breaking out on his forehead and kept wondering could she see them. When she called "Malachy—do you take sugar?" from the kitchen, for no reason at all what did he do only stand up. "Yes," he called, "two please," and sat back down again.

Bosco was pointing at an elephant he had discovered behind the magic door. "Look, Gráinne!" he squeaked. "It's a elephant! I love elephants!" Gráinne smiled and said "Gosh, Bosco! It's a big elephant—isn't it!"

When Marion came back with the coffee, she asked him what he had been up to in London. How it all started he did not know, but once he began he couldn't stop himself. He was working with this band and that band, sure he was, roadie for this outfit, and roadie for that outfit. You might have heard of them, Marion, they've got a really good sound. By the time he was finished he must have named every band in London. Then he wiped his forehead with his sleeve and said "So—how's Paddy? His outfit still doing well?"

When he said that she curled her hand around the cup and looked at him. "Paddy?" she said. "Paddy Meehan? God, Malachy—it must be nearly three years since I saw him."

She had only just said that when the key turned in the door and he looked up. "Malachy," Marion said, "this is Eamonn. He teaches in St Michael's in Lucan. Eamonn—do you know St Anthony's? Malachy used to teach there. Before he went to London. We used to know each other at college."

Malachy shook his hand and Eamonn smiled warmly. "Malachy's in the music business now," Marion went on. "He got sense and gave up the teaching."

"A wise man, Malachy," Eamonn said, as he went over to

the Moses basket. "I swear to God there's time's I'd swing for some of those fellows in my class. They had my heart scalded today, Marion, and that's a fact." He picked up the baby and cooed to it.

"It's well for you, that's all I can say," he continued. "If we could afford it, we'd be out of it in a shot wouldn't we, Marion?"

"Oh now," she said, "you can say that again."

"But sure someone has to pay the bills. Isn't that right? Hmm? Isn't that right, baba?"

They talked a little bit more after that but it was too hard for Malachy and he wanted to go. For a split second, their eyes met and he had to look away. Being there was too much for him and he knew that if he stayed any longer he would make a fool of himself.

Standing together in the hallway was probably the hardest of all. She was so close to him. He could see now that she looked no different, and that even though her hair was shorter and she looked a bit tired, she was the same Marion all right, the same Marion she had always been and he wanted to say "I've got something for you Marion do you remember this—look! 'Chirpy Chirpy Cheep Cheep'—do you remember?" He wanted to say that more than anything but he didn't and when the moment passed, it was too late.

She smiled as they said goodbye. "It was so good of you to call, Malachy. If you're ever back in Dublin—you'll call, won't you?" He nodded and then walked away.

He wanted to cry out "Marion!" and run back to the house and hammer on the door until she came out to him. That would look swell, wouldn't it? So he didn't. He just kept walking until he could walk no more. Then he sat down on a park bench and took out the tattered record. He stared at it, not knowing whether to laugh or cry, wondering what it would have been like

if he had been able to give it to her, and wondering just how big
a bollocks you can be as he dropped it into a litter bin and
headed off into the city to catch the bus that would take him
home to Cissie.

Goo Goo

As he was going past the harbour, Malachy half-expected a wallop of a prawn on the back of the neck or Alec and the trawl-
ermen to let rip with a few choice nuggets such as "Hey!
Dudgeon! Just where do you think you're going? Get over here
the fuck out of that till we talk to you! Where have you been
hiding yourself, you cheeky little bubblefaced cunt! Off without
as much as a word to anyone! Are you looking to get yourself a
row of arseholes up your back—is that it? Well—come on!
Where were you? Out with it!" But of course he didn't get a
wallop of any prawn or a tirade of abuse either for Alec and his
fishy buddies were nowhere to be seen. They were all long since
married or dead or fucked off to other towns to annoy somebody
else and no more cared about old Puffy-Head in his bargain bin
shades than they did about the man in the moon. Or Cissie
either for that matter, for the sunny Sunday mornings when she
said her prayers to Jemmy Brady's baldy lad were about as important now as a dog having a shite on the street. Yes indeed,
there would be no more Jane Russell impersonations for her I'm
afraid, and one look at her would tell you that, with not a tooth
left in her head and her face sunken in now like an old rotten
apple you'd find on the dump. In fact Malachy had to walk up
and down the ward five or six times before he even recognised
her. She wasn't up to much in the head department either.
When he stood by the bed, she looked at him all right but that,

as he soon realised, was about as good as it was going to get. All he could manage to get out of her was "Goo goo."

When he mentioned this to the nurse, she said it was a miracle she could speak at all, considering she'd been left lying for three days on a cold kitchen floor before anyone came near her. It wasn't as if the nurse was trying to blame him or anything. She was just stating a fact.

He had been sitting there for about an hour when the hairdresser came along. She said she was in charge of all the girls' hair. "My name is Vera," she said. "Have hair-dryer, will travel!" She leaned in and tweaked Cissie's cheek. "Isn't that right, Cissie? Isn't that right, you old divil you!"

Cissie looked up at her and said "Goo goo."

Vera scrunched up her face and tweaked her again. "I'll goo goo you!" she said. "I'll goo goo you now, Mrs Dudgeon, you and your goo goo!" She chuckled as she squeezed Malachy's arm. "Do you hear her, Mr Dudgeon!" she said. "Oh now—the laughs we have with her!"

"Goo goo," said Cissie again as the hairdresser swung a bag off her shoulder and got to work on her.

"A wee bit of pink here to perk you up, missus—what do you think of that? Now doesn't that look better! It does surely! God but you're a picture!" She scooped out a handful of face cream and said to Malachy "I like to put a bit of makeup on them too. Sure it works wonders. Especially on her nibs here. Isn't that right, Cissie? H'ho but I'd say she was the right wee rascal when she was young—were you, Cissie? Indeed and you were surely. Had all the boys' hearts broke! Man but you're the divil! You needn't think you'll fool me! Come on now—sit up out of that. By the time I'm finished with you, you'll be raring to go. Oh, they think some of the lassies in here, butter wouldn't melt in their mouths but that's where they've got youse all fooled! Am I right, Cissie? Would you look at her! Do you see her laughing! Lord but you're a terror! She knows what I'm on about all right! I see you! I see you, Cissie! Quit your old tricks now! Quit that, I'm telling you! You're the girl has the eye for the men and don't think I don't know it! You'd be off to the dance in a shot if you were let! Wouldn't you, Cissie? Wouldn't you? Go on—tell the truth! You can tell Vera!"

"Goo goo," Cissie said.

Vera hit her thigh a slap.

"Do you hear her!" she yelped. "God but she's a ticket!"

By the looks of things, the party was only starting in St Dympna's Women's Ward. The patient in the next bed was having herself a great laugh. Her name was Nan and her poor old relatives were out of their minds with worry about her. Not that there was any point in them worrying for anyone could see there was nothing they could do with her, worry or no worry. "Fuck off!" was all she would say. "Fuck off!" and "Ba!" Every time her daughter tried to get her to say her prayers, she took the rosary beads off her and fired them across the ward. Then she laughed again and croaked "Fuck off!" and "Ba!" The daughter looked over at Malachy and fiddled with her fingers. "She used to be the holiest woman in the town before this came on her," she said absently, her eyes moistening. For a while after she said nothing and then, "What are we going to do?" The husband spoke then, although he himself seemed unaware of it. He wanted to know who was going to win the big game on Sunday—Dublin or Cork? Malachy said he reckoned Dublin. "I'd say Dublin too," the husband said. You could see he was on the verge of tears as well. That broke Nan's heart. Of course it did. Which was why she was sticking her fingers down her throat to make herself sick. "Get a cloth! Get a cloth!" cried her daughter hysterically. Nan thought that was the best yet. She chuckled away as she rubbed the sick into her bodice. Then an alarm went off and an army of nurses went tearing down the corridor.

Finally Vera finished up. "Would you look at that!" she cried. "Elizabeth Taylor wouldn't be in it, Mr Dudgeon—I'm telling you! Cissie, you're a picture!"

Cissie stared straight ahead with glass eyes as Vera put the final touches to her face mask and crinkle-cut coiffure. She wiped a smudge off one of her rouge spots with her thumb and stood back beaming, hands on her hips. "Now! There's not a bother on you!" she declared as she started gathering up her bits and bobs. Grinning, she swung the bag over her shoulder and shook Malachy's hand. "Well—I'll be off! No rest for the wicked as they say! You be good now, Cissie Dudgeon! You be good now, you little divil you! Ha ha! God but she's a character!" Then off she went, singing.

"Please pray with us," pleaded Nan's daughter. "Pray with us like you used to long ago." But Nan had no intention of praying. Instead she hit her daughter a slap across the face. Then she tried to get the rosary off her again. That was too much and the daughter just lost it and broke down. As her body shuddered and the tears rolled down her cheeks, her husband comforted her as best he could. Cissie looked over at Malachy and said "Goo goo." "Goo goo," she said again, "goo goo."

Before he left, Malachy got a message that the consultant wanted to see him. He told him at first they had thought his mother would be dead in a matter of weeks. Now, he said, things didn't look quite so bad, although it was more than likely Cissie Dudgeon would be in a wheelchair for the rest of her life.

Options

Now the big question for Raphael in so far as killing the head-master went was not so much when as how. I mean the last thing you wanted were the lads going hysterical and shouting and screaming "Our Master's dead! Our Master's dead!" or going mad running off out into the street or any of that. Indeed he didn't want to make it too hard on himself either. "After all—I'm an old man, lads," he said to the boys as he wiped a tear from his eye. He thought of his options and wrote them all down on the blackboard under the heading VARIOUS OPTIONS.

    1. Poison—weed killer.
    2. Wrists.
    3. Carbon monoxide—car.
    4. House—petrol.
    5. Rope.
    6. Drowning.

Drowning was supposed to be the best of the lot, but you couldn't believe that. That might be another lie. He thought about it so much he started to shake. He pulled himself together. The best thing to do was go out and get more Jameson, then come back and think about it again. He put his coat on and asked the boys would they be all right until he got back. They said they would. He was proud of his boys. sad that soon everything would be all over and they would never see each other again. "Ah but sure there you are," he said to himself as he hunched up into his coat and went off out the door.

Wee Hughie

This time he made sure to get a couple of bottles of sherry as well, which he got stuck into straightaway as soon as he came back. Of course it was a little bit extravagant but sure what odds —it wasn't every day you closed The Dead School. "Isn't that right, boys?" he said, and put the bottle of Amicardo to his lips. "Have one on me!" called Paschal O'Dowd. "I will to be sure, Paschal!" The Master cried. To start the ball rolling, Raphael himself got up and performed a recitation. He stood up on his desk and cleared his throat and then launched into the poem he had recited for his mammy and daddy all those years ago in the little cottage in Cork, with his Uncle Joe watching, puffing his pipe as proud as punch of the best young nephew in the whole wide world. "Good man yourself!" he said. "I'll be giving you a go on my horses on account of this—you need have no fear of that!" And would Raphael blush!

But now, it was full steam ahead as his boys looked adoringly on and he stuck out his chin and he stuck out his chest, declaiming with great gusto:

> He's gone to school, Wee Hughie,
> And him not four
> Sure I saw the fright was in him
> When he left the door
> But he took a hand o' Denny
> And he took a hand o' Dan
> Wi' Joe's auld coat upon him
> Och, the poor wee man!

Everything was going great guns altogether until he forgot the fourth verse and then would you believe for the love of God was it any wonder the boys laughed—he went and tumbled off the desk with the sherry and the whole lot round him and lay there with his legs in the air like an eejit going "Wait a minute— I think I have it now! I'm nearly sure I have it now, boys!"

Maybe he had, in his own mind. But what the boys would have heard, if they had been there, wouldn't have been anything remotely like "Wee Hughie." What it sounded like to normal ears was "Blub blub blub blub" as the famous master-raconteur struggled to get to his feet and went crash back down on the seat of his threadbare cavalry twills again.

Disco of Dreams

Oh yes, Malachy took it bad. I'm afraid he took it very bad indeed about Cissie, which might explain why he is raving now, out of his mind on the demon drink! Oh but he is, kiddies, drunk as a lord in Dublin city and there is no getting away from it. Lying against the smokestained wallpaper and laughing away if you don't mind. So what do you reckon he says to nobody in particular "You think maybe I should take a walk down Burgerland way and see if I can find myself some skinheads? Ha ha. Well you just go right on thinking that my friend but you see that is where you are wrong, that is one thing I am not gonna do no sir and you know why? Because them days are gone, friend. Long gone. You hear what I'm saying? I hope you do. I hope you are listening, you guys out there, you and anyone else who wants to know what's going down. Excuse me but do you know my name? My name's Malachy Dudgeon. Yes, that's correct—Malachy Dudgeon whose father fell off the fishing stand. No—I'm not from Dublin. I only came here after I saw my mother. Perhaps you know her do you? My mother I mean. Cissie is her name. She's quite a girl. She's had the last laugh on all of us hasn't she? Ladies and gentlemen! *Night Of The Living Dead*! It's funny isn't it? Of course it is. But then everything about me is funny. I'm a funny fellow. I'm a funny little fellow. I am a funny-little-fellow! Funny funny funny. If you want to have yourself a laugh you can always rely on old Bubblehead. Look—here he comes! Hello, Bubblehead! Hello, Son Of Stallion! Hello, Malachy son of Cissie who fucked the cowman crooked!"

Yes, the night is young in Martin Coyningham's Bar where the strobelights swirl and the soft bodies squeeze and the music hits your head over and over with a huge big hammer: "Ain't Gonna Bump No More No Big Fat Woman." Malachy is having the time of his life. Having the time of his life in the Disco Of Dreams. He is chatting up the girls. He knows how to handle the women, our Malachy. "Hi, gals—the name's Mal. Like me to do a J. J. Gittes impression, maybe?" They marvel as he lays it on the line. He is so cool—so assured. He lets them know just what it is he is gonna do to a certain person. To a motherfucker who has had it coming for a long time. "No, sir," he says, because he has nothing to lose anymore. "That's why I'm gonna do it," he says. "I am gonna make him crawl!" And the girls laugh. They say they have never met anyone like him before. "You're from London, aren't you?" one of them says. "You better believe it, lady!" he says. "Ask for me any night in The George Bar, Stoke Newington—awright?"

As he reels past the blurred Rathmines moon, his fist defies the inky sky and he cries *Did you hear me, Bell? Are you listening to me? I'm coming for you! I'm coming for you, motherfucker!*

Tonight's Story

And so, lads and lassies, tonight's story is called "Falling Across Dublin City Because You Are Out Of Your Mind On Drink." It is quite a nice night for a story. Everyone is out having some fun —particularly Malachy. He is off on his travels. Making his way through the happy, nighttime streets to see his old friend Mr Bell once more. "Mr Bell—it's been quite a long time, hasn't it?" "It certainly has, Mr Dudgeon. Do you know something—I almost wouldn't recognise you." "Is that a fact, Mr Bell? Is that because I have long hair now and an old tattered army coat a tramp wouldn't be caught dead wearing?" "No—I don't think it's so much that, Mr Dudgeon, I think it's more those mad eyes of yours. They are like something you'd see on a drug addict." "Oh those? Don't mind those old eyes of mine, Mr Bell—every psycho has eyes like that." "What? You're telling me you're a psycho now are you, Mr Dudgeon? Well well well I've heard a lot of jokes in my time but that just has to be the best yet. Sure we all know you wouldn't say boo to a goose. You used to shite yourself every time I came near your classroom." "Oh yes that might be true, Mr Bell, but that was a long time ago. It's not today or yesterday, oh no. And while I might not have been a psycho then, I certainly am now. That is why I am going to make you pay. Mr Bell—you're a motherfucker. Did you know that? Well in case you didn't, I'm telling you now—that's what you are. Mr Bell—do you know what I'm going to do tonight? I'm going to make you sorry. Of course you can laugh. You can laugh until the cows come home. But I'm still going to make you pay. Make no mistake about it."

Malachy stood on O'Connell Bridge outside The Film Centre. That had been a favourite haunt of his too in the long-ago days of his wide-eyed Dublin ramblings. Showing tonight: *The Female Bunch* and *Sex In The Classroom*. Malachy would have liked nothing better right now than to go inside and sit alone in the urine-smelling dark watching Sergio losing his virginity to his mother-in-law or the lesbian boss of the outlaw women sticking a pitchfork in the groin of the little Mehico farmer just because he is a man. It would be just like old times, stumbling off home then to Rathmines, stopping for barbecued spare ribs and sauce to smear all over his face before he fell asleep in the fireplace, the happiest man in Dublin.

city," says Mr Policeman. Oh yes. Of course they have. "Look—
it's me! Yoo hoo! Die, motherfucker!"

The lights of the taxi swung back onto the coast road as
Malachy fell through the gate of No. 53 Madeira Gardens with
his vodka bottle stuck in his pocket.

"Whee-hoo!" he shouted as he pounded on the door.
"Open up! Open the door, man—it's The Night Stalker!" he
shouted as he swigged the vodka. "Open it up or you're history!"

A Knock At The Door

John McCormack was singing away at the top of his voice and it
was a wonder Raphael heard the hammering at all. He was trying
to get the boys to make up their minds which it was going to be
once and for all, hanging or carbon monoxide, when he heard it.
Yes he definitely heard it. Someone battering the front door. He
froze, considering this was his first visitor in almost three years,
apart from the nosey-parker neighbours, who wouldn't be calling
at this hour anyway. He put his finger to his lips and whispered
"Ciúnas, a bhuachaillí! Ná bí ag caint anois. Carry on with your
work and don't make a sound!"

He winced as he heard it again. Muffled by the music but
definitely there. Then—nothing. He was about to relax and tell
the boys that it was all over when he heard the clatter of the bin
around the back. Every muscle in his body tightened. He
grabbed the tongs, turned the gramophone up even louder and
told the boys not to move. Then he left the classroom and went
out into the kitchen, standing in the doorway with his breath
caught in his chest and the nerve ticking over his eye.

The shadow moved across the window and his knuckles
whitened around the tongs.

Maggots

Malachy couldn't see what the fuck he was doing. First he went flying over a dustbin full of potato skins and the next thing a yowling cat appeared out of nowhere. "Fuck you!" he shouted. "Fuck you!" But there was no going back now. He managed to put his elbow through a pane of glass and pulled himself through but then he went and stuck his foot in a pile of gooey muck beneath the window. What was that but poor old Setanta, or what was left of him, now a sticky mess on the bottom of The Night Stalker's shoe as he hopped around on one leg with the sweat rolling off him and the maggots all over his hand, which was bad enough without looking up and seeing a pair of eyes glaring out of the darkness. And not just an ordinary pair of eyes either but the eyes of Raphael Bell who was running at him with the tongs, flailing them like a madman. *"You! After all you've done you come back here to my house! You come back here to my house!"* he screamed. *"I'll kill you! I'll destroy you like you destroyed me!"* which he did his best to do as he sent poor Malachy flying across the room with a belt of the heavy iron tongs and brought them down on top of him again and again. *"You made me lose my wife!"* he screamed. *"You made me lose her and you ruined my life! You cur! You imbecile! Do you hear me! Do you hear me, cur!"*

"No! No, you fucker. You ruined mine!" were the words that Malachy wanted to utter, but as another blow thudded into his ribs, they left him and there was nothing but silence and the giant shape that swayed above him far away.

Happy Birthday, Thomas!
And far away he too was bound, to an old familiar place where Nobby Caslin was standing by the garden gate puffing away on his trusty pipe. There wasn't so much as a hint of a breeze and inside the little brown bowl a glow began to pulse straightaway. The sun was shining in the cloudless sky. The fledglings were huddled close together in their nests with their eager mouths wide open. Their mothers were close by them singing. Then came the sound of voices. It was Alec and the lads. "Hello there, Nobby," they said as they passed. They said they were on their way out to the boatshed to see what was going on. Then they burst out laughing and said that they were only fooling around. Or "Acting the jinnet," as Packie used to say. "Not at all, Nobby," they said. "That's all over and done with. The boatshed? Sure we haven't been out there for years!"

"Well there you are," said Nobby as a cloud of sweet-smelling blue smoke floated past his face. "All over now at last." When Malachy looked again, they were gone, swallowed up by the blue sky. He walked up the garden path to where Mrs McAdoo and her little son Thomas were sitting at a picnic table, before a bright beautiful birthday cake. Thomas was beside himself with excitement because of course it was his birthday. He could not wait to get blowing out the candles. His mother was as excited as he was but every time he ballooned his cheeks and got ready to blow she laid her hand gently on his arm and said "Now now, little Thomas—it isn't time yet!" and he blushed and she laughed. The windows of the town were thrown open and through them the ecstatic bleat of Michael O'Hehir carried up and out and into the faraway clouds. *"Yes and a fine sunny day it is here in Dublin. The Artane Boys Band is now leaving the field and what excitement there is here today for this match, what must surely be termed a meeting of the giants!"* Nobby waved to the boys on their way back to the boats. "Who are you for, men?" he cried. "Armagh!" they called and he laughed. "Armagh every time" he said. They laughed too, dragging on their Woodbine cigarettes. Mrs McAdoo tweaked Thomas's cheek. She said to him "Who's my little man? Who's my little chubbies?" Thomas got all embarrassed. But he soon forgot all about it when he looked up and saw Father Pat and The Canon coming chugging along in the old black Morris. The Canon rolled down the window and said "Have youse forgot all about The Dummy? Or what the hell is wrong with youse? Jesus Mary and Joseph only youse have me to look after youse I think you'd forget to put your trousers on in the morning."

As soon as he heard that, Nobby started to fall over himself with apologies. "God forgive us, Canon, do you know what it is we were having such a good time yarning here and having ourselves a bit of a laugh that we clean went and forgot all about our old friend The Dummy."

The Canon shook his head and chuckled. "Ah never mind —I'm only acting the jinnet. Look—stay where you are and don't be worrying your head and let me look after The Dummy. I'll go on out to the lake and get him and I'll be back in two shakes of a lamb's tail. How's that?"

As far as Nobby was concerned that just simply could not have been better.

"Do you know what it is, Canon?" he said. "That's topping. That is what I would call topping now. Make sure and bring him in now for we'll not be able for all this lemonade ourselves!"

"Don't you worry," laughed The Canon as he nudged the Morris forward, "I'm not going to go home without a drop of it myself!" He rapped on the side of the Morris and drove off out the road.

Malachy hadn't realised that he was there himself all along

but sure enough there he was over by the gable end of the house, standing beside Cissie and Packie. They were chatting away to beat the band. She was holding on to his father's arm. They were talking about something that happened a long time ago, before he was born. Malachy didn't realise the cowman had been standing beside him at all until he heard him say "Ssh" and felt the cold coin being pressed into his hand. He looked down. It was a half crown. The cowman beamed. "For the best lad that ever lived in this town," he said.

The Canon stood at the edge of the lake and cupped his hands over his mouth. He shouted "Will you get up to hell out of that, Dummy! I have confessions at seven and then Benediction after that, so come on now—no more of this codding!" The Dummy had more sense than to argue with The Canon and the next thing you know there's this great splash and right up out of the middle of the blue water erupts an umbrella shower of diamonds and over to the shore with him as quick as he could for he had more sense than to keep The Canon waiting. The clergyman gave him a playful belt with his gloves. "Will you get in to hell out of that of that or they'll have all the lemonade drunk!" he said. Then The Canon grinned and put his arm around The Dummy and off they chugged towards town and the party that belonged to Thomas Little Chubbies McAdoo.

Which is all very well until you wake up of course and boy when you do are you in some shape. That old Malachy, his ribs were just about fucked and right down the side of his face there's a big talon of dried blood. He was a right-looking sketch and no mistake, clambering to his feet and shouting "Mr Bell, Mr Bell— I've got to talk to you!" Some fucking Night Stalker all right, wanting to talk to the big lug who had just gone and battered him senseless.

The Dead School

But Raphael was far too busy to talk to anybody. By now he was nearly hoarse cheering his daddy who had long since left each and every one of them far behind as he cut through the swaying field of corn like a clockwork machine, the blade of his sickle hook glinting in the sun. Evelyn was going mental, jumping up and down, shouting "Come on, our Daddy! Come on, our Daddy!" Uncle Joe puffed on his pipe and tapped it against his knee. "I think he's going to take it!" he said. And yes indeed it was looking good all right as his arms shot into the air and he cried to the open skies "Evelyn!" and she ran to him before they hoisted him aloft and bore him through the village, shouting their hearts out "He won the race! He won the reaping race!" As indeed he did and such a singsong there was in the pub, with Uncle Joe getting up to do his party piece and them all starting into Raphael: "You needn't think you'll get away without giving us 'Wee Hughie,' young Raphael! Come on now—get up on the table out of that and give us a couple of verses!" And whatever shyness there might have been in him, what could he do only take the floor and, with his chest out, proudly recite "He's gone to school, Wee Hughie, and him not four," as he had been doing for his boys for the past forty-three years, before they spoiled it, before she spoiled it, before they took his school and burnt it to the ground. Oh you can deny it, you can deny it all you like, my friends. You needn't think it'll worry me. I'm past worrying about things like that I'm afraid. I have more important things to do with my time I can tell you, for a start I'm going back to our house with mammy and daddy and all our neighbours and we're going to have a singsong because my daddy won the reaping race which is more than your daddy ever did and I'll tell you something else, my smart friends, it will be a long time before you spoil this, it will be a long time before you spoil anything again. Your spoiling days are over.

And so off through the village once more they trooped, Evelyn and Mattie Bell at the head of the throng, everyone with a soda cake or a bottle of whiskey or just a few rashers to throw on the pan, as Uncle Joe slapped the kitchen table and rose to his feet, calling "Order! Order here!" and cleared his throat as he raised his glass and proposed a toast to "The best family in the whole world!" The cheers lifted the roof and then Pony Brennan took the floor to sing "God Save Ireland" and it was sad because it made Raphael think of a man all alone in an open field with the blood pouring out of his mouth and the words he was trying to utter with his last breath weren't "God Save Ireland" or anything to do with Ireland but "Where is Raphael? Where is my little Raphael? Where is Evelyn? Where is my Evelyn?" and it nearly broke Raphael's heart as he looked down upon his father kneeling there all alone because it made him think of someone else too, it made him think of Nessa, his Macushla whose white arms would reach out one last time to touch him but they wouldn't would they, they wouldn't you see because that was when it happened, that was when he saw her sitting there. Not Nessa, not his one and only true love, but Evans. Evans with that sneer on her face, her eyes saying "Touch me go on touch me you know you can't, you can do nothing. Ask Father Stokes. Go on ask him. He's sitting over there or can't you see him? Are you blind as well? Don't tell me you're blind as well, you silly old man." And when Raphael saw Father Stokes sitting there fiddling with his fingers and looking at him with eyes that said "I'm sorry, Raphael," it was more than he could bear and that was why his fingers closed about her throat and why, for every unborn baby ripped from her and thousands like her, he squeezed her flesh and shook her like a broken doll, shook and shook and shook, crying *"You destroyed me!"* And such was his rage that he would have followed her to that pitch-black pit but for a soft voice that came to whisper "I'm down here, Raphael." And he looked far down into the valley, across the field of stubbled corn to where she was standing, a speck waving to him, his one and only Nessa, calling to him as she came towards him up the mountainside that they would be together again. Then her white arms reached out and he left Evans far behind, felt them touch him as once they had touched him in a Dublin boardinghouse in the long ago, her soft, perfumed skin close to his as she whispered his name over and over and at last he was free.

Which was more than could be said for Malachy Dudgeon as he came bursting through the door with a big bright hopeful face on him like he'd just won the sweepstakes. "I have to talk to you! I have to talk to you!" he gasped, as to his amazement he found his former headmaster half-naked swinging from the ceiling with his baldy lad up like Jemmy Brady's on a Sunday morning and a neat pile of excrement steaming on the floor behind him. Now whatever approach Jack Nicholson aka J. J. Gittes might have taken to the situation, vomiting all over himself and falling about the place going oh no and oh no oh Jesus Christ is hardly likely to have been one of them. None of this bothered Count John in the slightest of course and off he went again, full steam ahead, as the needle found its mark once more.

So there you are. That's Madeira Gardens for you, on the night of the fifteenth of September 1979. Whatever might have been said about it in the past, what with its stupid bin liners and its garden of nettles and its daft muttering old principal who was half-sodden with whiskey and should have been put away long ago, now, with the stench so unbearable as to almost make you faint and the sight of what had once been Raphael Bell swinging away from side to side with its fat tongue sticking out, not to mention the boxes of books and pencils and ink bottles and papers and charts and chalk and letters and ledgers and sums copies and all the other junk and rubbish from St Anthony's thrown around the place, it looked like The Dead School was, at long last, beginning to live up to its name. Creak creak and sob sob. That was all you could hear. It was a sad state of affairs. A sad state of affairs now and no mistake.

Small wonder the cop who came to investigate the report of a break-in nearly shit himself when he saw what he'd landed into.

Love

Across from him the old tramp gave him a mouthful of broken teeth and handed him the bottle. "Have a drink, pal," he said. "It takes the pain away." Malachy took it and put it to his lips. "What happened to you, pal?" asked the tramp. "You're in a bad fuckin' way. You're worse than me. Have the lot, pal. I don't need it no more." Malachy swigged and slipped away.

Standing in the doorway of the bungalow, Marion still looked as beautiful as ever. "Can you come in and look after this lot for just a second, Malachy?" she called to him. He smiled and nodded as she went inside. He wiped the sweat off his forehead and left the lawn mower back in the shed. Seamus, the guy next door, leaned over the garden fence and said "Well—there you are. The holidays over now another year. I suppose you can't wait to get back to the little terriers?"

Malachy laughed. "Oh now," he said, "they're not the worst. I have a great class coming into me this year by all accounts."

Seamus nodded. "I hear very good reports about this young fellow Pat Hourican. I hear you've been doing powerful things with him altogether."

Malachy ran his fingers through his hair. "Oh I wouldn't say that now," he said. "The way it is with Pat he needs no help from me. I'll tell you this—if they were all like him I'd be the lucky man."

"Do you know what it is," Seamus went on. "Between yourself and myself I wouldn't have that job of yours for a pension. I'm telling you it would drive me astray in the head. As for the old post office now—its not so bad at all. But teaching? Not on your life, Malachy, and that's not a word of a lie!"

Malachy smiled and went inside. Sorcha, Jason and Emer were sitting cross-legged on the carpet. When they saw him coming in they smiled. "Well—what's going on here, you little bunch of gangsters—what's on?" he said.

"Daddy, daddy—it's Bugs Bunny!" The three of them pulled eagerly at his trouser leg.

He sat down and got stuck into Bugs along with them. On the wall there was a framed portrait of Marion and himself on their wedding day. On the mantelpiece a souvenir of Torremolinos where they had spent their first holiday after Marion had Sorcha. A pile of copybooks rested on the table, waiting to be corrected. Marion came in from the bathroom wearing a white towelling dressing gown. She unwrapped the turban around her head and her hair fell free. Behind the rapt children she caught his eye and her lips moved silently. "I love you," she said and such was the depth of his happiness he almost wept.

Slán Leat

Everyone had expected a good attendance but this surpassed all expectations. It looked like just about every single child in Ireland had turned up. Hundreds and hundreds of kids of all shapes and sizes. There were kiddies from Cork and Kerry, kiddies from the slums of Dublin and kiddies from the mountains of Donegal. And did they look fantastic! Absolutely fantastic! As one woman said, with a tear in her eye, "They're a picture, God love them!"

All the convent girls wore white dresses and flowing veils and the boys starched white shirts and red ties. They carried Papal bannerettes. Each boy had his own set of rosary beads because, as they all knew, that was one of Mr Bell's special rules —St Anthony's boys must have them with them at all times, no matter where it was they might find themselves. In their lace veils and white socks, with their hands joined and eyes closed, the little girls seemed as angels come down from heaven. It was indeed a sight to behold.

What worried the organisers of the funeral was where on earth they were going to put them all. The big question of the day was—were there enough hotels in Dublin city to hold all these kiddies? Not to mention their teachers and their mammies and daddies and all the nuns and priests and past pupils and all the rest of them. As one old priest said to another in the foyer of the North Star Hotel when they were all getting ready for the big trip to Glasnevin where Raphael was to be buried "Do you know what I'm going to tell you—I haven't seen a crowd as big as this since the day of The Eucharistic Congress and that's a fact!"

Yes indeed, the City Of Dublin was on the march and by the holy, if Raphael Bell was going into the ground then, as Paschal O'Dowd observed, walking along behind the hearse, there was one sure thing and that was that all his old buddies and pals from years gone by were going to give him one father and mother of a sendoff. As the cortege made its way to the cemetery there was no end to the amount of stories that were to be told about the headmaster who was, as one man put it, "A legend." Everyone agreed. "That's what he was," they said, "A bloody legend." There was the story about the time he had to chase the goat out of the playground. "Didn't one of the tinkers bring a bloody goat to school!" they laughed. Then there was the time Nelligan got locked in the school over the weekend! It was priceless. The stories went on and on. Then of course there were the more serious stories. About how his class had got the highest marks in the Diocesan Catechetical inspections for twenty years running and the day the All-Ireland Football Trophy was brought into the school by the victorious captain, a past pupil. Not to mention of course the number of times the choir had been on Radio Eireann. "Oh now," they said, "you would travel the length and breadth of Ireland a fair while before you would come across a man the like of Mr Bell now, eh?" That was for sure.

There was a lovely little school band standing by the graveside, near a white-haired priest on crutches who had to have his prayerbook held for him because he could no longer hold it himself. The nuns had assembled the band especially for the day. They were all dressed up in their neat little uniforms and had been practising all morning. They were going to play Mr Bell's favourite song—"Macushla." Which the nun had told them earlier was the Gaelic word for "My Darling" or "My Beloved." So now they knew. Which in all honesty was about as much as they wanted to know, for as far as they could see, the words of it were just a jumble of old rubbish that made no sense at all, something to do with an old fellow who had nothing better to do than ask his wife to get up out of that and not be lying in the grave! Whatever that was supposed to mean!

Not that they exactly made it any more comprehensible with their rendition which began shortly after the mourners arrived. Just about the most magnanimous thing you can say about their performance is that it wasn't exactly going to win them the Band of The Year Prize. Between that and the wind whipping away half the words as they were playing, you would have been hard pressed to know what the hell was going on. All you could see were people holding their hats as the prayerbook pages flapped and Mario Lanza, Jr., put the crows out of business as he sang:

Macushla! Macushla! Your sweet voice is calling,
Calling me softly again and again,
Macushla! Macushla! I hear its dear pleading,
My blue-eyed Macushla, I hear it in vain.

Macushla! Macushla! Your white arms are reaching,
I feel them enfolding, caressing me still,
Fling them out from the darkness, my lost love, Macushla,
Let them find me and bind me again, if they will.

Macushla! Macushla! Your red lips are saying
That death is a dream, and love is for aye.
Then awaken, Macushla, awake from your dreaming,
My blue-eyed Macushla, awaken to stay.

What they were raving about, nobody had the foggiest notion. In fact, if you didn't know better, between the little fellow banging the bass drum and the cymbals crashing and the flutes and tin whistles playing different melodies at the same time, you might well have thought that they were some sort of comedy or circus band that had drifted into the graveyard by accident. Be that as it may, the scene was still too much for some people as they looked at the bright hopeful happy faces of the children and then stared at the yawning open hole into which Mr Bell was about to go very shortly. Especially when one of the little innocents gave a shy little wave and said *"Slán Leat A Mhaistir"*—Goodbye, Master.

It was hard to know how many people were there. If our old friend Nobby Caslin the funeral expert had happened along, it would have done his heart good. "This is more like it, boys," he'd say. "This is more like the real thing. How many now would you say is here? Five thousand? Ten? I'd go for the ten now. By Christ you won't get better than this!"

And you wouldn't have either—if it had happened like that which of course it didn't for there were no more multitudes and school bands there than Raphael Bell was going to jump up and call out to the gravediggers "Hold on there, lads! It's a mistake! I'm not dead at all!"

In fact, if poor old Nobby had indeed turned up, a more likely class of a speech from him would have been: "I seen the time when a schoolmaster the like of him would have pulled in over the six hundred mark and well above it. I mind Master Seamus that used to teach in the wee school out by the mountain, died of a heart attack one sunny day and him driving the car up the street. I remember it as well as if it was yesterday. Into a pole and the pair of them killed outright, himself and Reavy the contractor. As God is my judge, the day that man was crated, you wouldn't have got moving in the streets, that many turned out to pay their respects. It's a sad state of affairs when this is all that can be dragged out for a Master, a scatter of old biddies, a dying-looking hippy in a tramp's coat and an auld whinging bollocks of a priest, would you look at him, slobbering away there like a half-wit or what in the hell is wrong with him? Don't you think now you'd expect a bit more from a clergyman, taking into account the number he'd have put into the ground in his time, if you get my meaning."

The holy water sparkled in the air as the priest cleared his throat, beginning to read:

"Hearken O Lord, to our prayers, wherein we humbly beseech your mercy, that you will establish the soul of your servant Raphael, which you have bidden to depart from this world, in the abode of peace and light, and may you command him to be joined to the fellowship of the saints. Through Christ Our Lord Amen." He then closed the prayerbook and raised his head as he said "Eternal rest grant unto them O Lord," and then, responding for the throng that could not answer with one voice because it was not there, said softly to himself "May they rest in peace. Amen."

Malachy, with a big fat shiner on him and looking like he'd been dragged through a ditch backways, turned and walked toward the gate, and it has to be said that his spontaneous impression of Mrs McAdoo's walk after Thomas's funeral was not bad at all.

As the pine box was lowered on canvas straps, the white-haired priest was inconsolable and had to be led away. The officiating priest closed his prayerbook and averted his eyes as Father Desmond Stokes was helped into a car outside the cemetery gates.

A light rain swept towards the city.

You Don't Really Like
"Chirpy Chirpy Cheep Cheep," Do You?

So there you are now, that's the end of my story and what a sad end it turned out to be, what with brambles and briars growing all over poor Raphael, and nobody ever bothering their backsides to come near him, never mind remark on their Sunday strolls past Madeira Gardens "Do you remember old Mr Bell who used to live there?" or even "That house belonged to the headmaster of St Anthony's once upon a time." Even the young couple who lived in the house now hadn't the foggiest notion that it had once been The Dead School, which of course was perfectly understandable, for with its lovely garden full of geraniums and begonias and its beautiful whitewashed walls, you just wouldn't have believed it possible. But then of course, there's lots of things you wouldn't believe, such as the way things have been going in the town lately, for example. Maybe it's just as well poor old Raphael kicked the bucket when he did, for I doubt if his heart would have been able to stand up to all the carry-on. It's got so bad now that if you didn't know better, you'd think half the country was on drugs.

It all started in earnest when they sold the hotel where the bold Packie once upon a time loved to have his couple of bottles and the new owner decided that what was needed was a bit of exotic dancing to cheer the locals up. Then came the wet T-shirt competitions, mud wrestling four nights a week, and foxy boxing on Sunday mornings. The priest tried giving out about it at Mass saying that things had gone too far and he wanted it back the way it was when he was a young boy, when Sunday mornings were a time of togetherness, a special time, a holy time, when you would walk up the street with your mammy and daddy, then get the papers on the way home from Mass before you had your Sunday dinner and settled in to listen to Michael O'Hehir as the ball went high into the clouds and the cheers of the crowd brought joy to your heart. The priest got so excited when he was making the speech that he closed his eyes and went all red in the face as he pounded the pulpit, pleading with them to remember. "Do you remember!" he cried, half-choked. "Do you remember those days, my dear people!"

Of course they remembered them, I mean it wasn't all *that* long ago. Not that it mattered when it was, for as far as they were concerned, he could stick those days up his arse for they had been listening to him blathering about them long enough and if he didn't shut up, soon he might be counting himself lucky to find anyone in his stupid fucking church at all. Meanwhile, down went the fish factory with one whack of the wrecker's ball and up went The Copacabana, the disco to end all discos with its three neon waitresses ferrying cocktails across the roof and high-kicking over the town. Next door is Hollywood Nites video shop and through the open windows Robert Ginty The Exterminator takes on all comers as yet another asshole comes running right into his custom built flamethrower and he goes "Come on, motherfucker! Come on and die, you slimeball fuck! Fry, fuckhead—if that's what you wanna do!"

If Malachy had been twenty years younger, he might have got stuck into all this but he wasn't of course, not anymore, as a few of the young lads down the harbour reminded him in the time-honoured tradition one day when he was out with Cissie.

"Hey Baldy!" they shouted. "Why don't you go away and grow some hair, you wee fat cunt!"

Anyway, whatever about twenty years ago, getting stuck in now was pretty much out of the question, for by the time Cissie's looked after, most of the day is gone anyway. But at least it's not like in the beginning, when he was sure she was going to stage some sort of miraculous recovery, sitting there with her night noon and morning playing tapes and blathering shite into her ear and getting nothing only the goo goo treatment back. No, that's all history now. These days he just plays it by ear and waits to see what sort of humour she's in. If she's in a bad one, you've had it. She'll just take a swing with her one good hand and send bowl and spoon and the whole lot flying. That can be a right fuckup. Usually, however, one day is pretty much the same as the next. She wakes in the morning and looks at him with empty eyes as he eases her gently out of bed. He'll wash her first, then dress her and carry her downstairs. She likes to sit by the fire where he feeds her, and after that she'll sleep. Then maybe he'll read, or listen to Terry Krash. But most of the time he doesn't bother. He prefers just to sit there, waiting for them to come again, as he knows they will: a night in a Parnell Square dancehall when he searched the floor and saw that she was there, then held her close as her strawberry blonde hair brushed his cheek and he whispered "You don't really like 'Chirpy Chirpy Cheep Cheep,' do you?", that day in the park when a white unbroken blanket of snow stretched as far as the eye could see and she stood by a frozen river, staring at something far away, then slowly turned and looked into his eyes, her lips about to part to form three words.

About the Author

Patrick McCabe was born in 1955 in County Monaghan, Ireland. In addition to his work as a novelist, he is also a playwright. McCabe lives in London with his wife and two daughters.